The

by

He was goi...

Releasing her wrist, he put one finger beneath her chin and lifted her face to his. "Relax and let me…"

He couldn't wait any longer and dropped his head to fasten his mouth on hers, kissing her hard and deep, pouring all the longing and frustration of the past two years into the embrace. He felt her hands clench on his shoulders, but she wasn't pushing him away. Oh, no. He felt the way she melted against him, the way her fingers dug into his flesh and he knew she was going to be his again.

But this time, Wade promised himself, he wouldn't leave her without a word.

Betrothed for the Baby
by Kathie DeNosky

ᘒᔆᔆᘒ

From the desk of Emerald Larson, owner and CEO of Emerald, Inc.

To: My personal assistant, Luther Freemont

Re: My grandson, Hunter O'Banyon

My grandson, Hunter, has arrived in Devil's Fork, Texas, to take over running the Life Med Evac Helicopter Service. I'm sure he'll be less than pleased when he learns that his flight nurse is a single mother-to-be, who has no intention of grounding herself until just before she gives birth. However if our sources are reliable – and I have no doubt they are – he should not only come to terms with his past, but he'll find his future, as well. That said, I expect you to assist him in whatever way he deems necessary to bring about a complete and satisfactory conclusion to his current dilemma.

As always, I am relying on your complete discretion in this matter.

Emerald Larson

The Soldier's Seduction
ANNE MARIE WINSTON

Betrothed for the Baby
KATHIE DeNOSKY

MILLS & BOON®

Desire™

*First published in Great Britain 2007
Harlequin Mills & Boon Limited,
Eton House, 18-24 Paradise Road, Richmond, Surrey TW9 1SR*

The publisher acknowledges the copyright holders of the
individual works as follows:

The Soldier's Seduction © Anne Marie Rodgers 2006
Betrothed for the Baby © Kathie DeNosky 2006

ISBN: 978 0 263 85019 2

51-0607

*Printed and bound in Spain
by Litografía Rosés S.A., Barcelona*

THE SOLDIER'S SEDUCTION

by
Anne Marie Winston

ANNE MARIE WINSTON

RITA® Award finalist and bestselling author Anne Marie Winston loves babies she can give back when they cry, animals in all shapes and sizes and just about anything that blooms. When she's not writing, she's managing a house full of animals and teenagers, reading anything she can find and trying not to eat chocolate. She will dance at the slightest provocation and weeds her garden when she can't see the sun for the weeds any more. You can learn more about Anne Marie's novels by visiting her website at www.annemariewinston.com.

Dedicated to the memory of those animals who perished when they were left behind during Hurricane Katrina and with warmest thanks to every rescuer and animal lover who responded and saved so many others

One

It wasn't what he'd expected.

Wade brought the rental car to a halt along the curb and simply absorbed the sight of the modest, cozy home nestled in the small-town neighborhood. Phoebe's home. Phoebe's neighborhood.

He cut the ignition and eased himself from the car, taking in the pretty autumn wreath on the front door, the carved pumpkin on the second of the brick steps leading to the porch, the fall flowers in bright shades of rust, burgundy and gold that brightened up the bare spaces in front of the small bushes along the foundation.

He'd assumed she would live in an apartment. He didn't really know why he'd thought that, but every time he'd pictured Phoebe since he'd learned she had moved away, he'd imagined her living in an apartment or a small condo. Nothing so...permanent, as this house appeared to be.

He'd gotten quite a shock when he'd finally returned home, eagerly anticipating his first sight of her—only to learn that she'd left California months earlier. He didn't even want to think about the bleak misery that had swept through him, the letdown that had been so overwhelming that he'd just wanted to sit down and cry.

Not that he ever would. Soldiers didn't cry. Especially soldiers who had been decorated all to hell and back.

Living at home had been difficult. Only two short months before he'd been injured, he'd gone home on leave for his mother's funeral. While he was recuperating, his father made valiant attempts to keep things as normal around the house as possible. But without his mother, there was a big hole nothing could disguise.

He made casual inquiries about where Phoebe had gone, but no one seemed to know. By the time he was home for a month, he was desperate enough to start digging. The secretary of her high school graduating class had no forwarding address. A light Internet search turned up nothing. He finally thought to call Berkeley, the university she'd attended, but they wouldn't, or couldn't, give him any information.

He was about ready to consider hiring a private investigator when he thought of calling June, the only girl other than Phoebe's twin sister Melanie who he could really remember Phoebe hanging around with in high school. Geeky little June with her thick glasses and straight *A*s. Someone Melanie wouldn't have been caught dead hanging out with, but as he recalled, a genuinely sweet kid.

They really had seemed like kids to his four-years-older eyes back then. But by the time the twins had graduated from high school, those years had no longer seemed to be of much consequence.

Getting in touch with Phoebe's old friend was a stroke of luck. June had gotten a Christmas card from Phoebe four months after she'd moved. And God bless her, she'd kept the address.

That address had been quite a shock. She'd gone from California clear across the country to a small town in rural New York state.

Ironically, it was a familiar area. Phoebe's new home was less than an hour from West Point, where he'd spent four long years in a gray uniform chafing for graduation day, when he could finally become a real soldier.

He wouldn't have been so impatient for those days to end if he'd known what lay ahead of him.

He climbed the small set of steps carefully. His doctors were sure he'd make a full recovery—full enough for civilian life, anyway. But the long flight from San Diego to JFK had been more taxing than he'd anticipated. He probably should have gotten a room for the night, looked up Phoebe tomorrow when he was rested.

But he hadn't been able to make himself wait a moment longer.

He knocked on the wooden front door, eyeing the wavy glass diamond pane in the door's upper portion. Although it was designed to obscure a good view of the home's occupants, he might be able to see someone coming toward the door. But after a few moments and two more knocks, nobody showed. Phoebe wasn't home.

Disappointment swamped him. He leaned his head against the door frame, completely spent. He'd counted on seeing her so badly. But…he glanced at his watch. He hadn't even considered the time. It was barely four o'clock.

The last time he'd seen her, she was a year out of college with a degree in elementary education, and she'd been teaching first grade. If she still was a teacher, she might soon be getting home. She probably worked, he decided as relief seeped through him.

If she wasn't married, he thought, trying to encourage himself, it stood to reason she'd need income. And June hadn't heard anything about a husband. If she had married, she hadn't taken his name, which didn't really fit with the quiet, traditional girl he'd known so well. And he knew she hadn't taken anyone's name because he'd checked the local phone book and found her there: P. Merriman.

Fine. He'd wait. He turned and started for his car, but a porch swing piled with pillows caught his attention. He'd just sit there and wait for her.

If she'd been married, he wouldn't be here, he assured himself. If she'd been married, he would have left her alone, wouldn't have attempted to contact her again in this lifetime.

But he was pretty sure she wasn't.

And despite the good reasons he had for staying away from Phoebe Merriman, despite the fact that he'd behaved like a jerk the last time they'd been together, he'd never been able to forget her. Never been able to convince himself that being with her had been a mistake. He'd thought of little else during his long months of recuperation and therapy. He'd nearly reached out to her then, but some part of him had shied away from a phone call or an e-mail.

He wanted to see her in person when he asked her if there was any chance she'd let him into her life again. Sighing, he dragged one of the pillows up and leaned his head against it. If only things hadn't gotten so screwed up at the end.

It had been bad enough that Phoebe's twin Melanie had died because of him. Indirectly, maybe, but it still had been his fault.

He'd compounded it in the biggest damn way possible when he'd made love to Phoebe after the funeral. And then he'd run.

Phoebe Merriman jumped when the mobile phone in her minivan began to play the jazzy tune she'd programmed into it. That phone hardly ever rang. The only reason she had it, really, was so that Bridget's babysitter could always reach her in case of an emergency.

Alarmed, she punched the button to take the call. A quick glance at the display had the dread in her stomach lurching uncomfortably. Phoebe had good reason to fear unexpected phone calls. And just as she'd feared, it was her home number. "Hello?"

"Phoebe?" The babysitter, Angie, sounded breathless.

"Angie. What's wrong?"

"There's a man sitting on the front porch. In the swing."

The news was almost anticlimactic, considering that she'd been fearing a high fever, blood or broken bones.

"Sitting? And what else?"

"Nothing else." Phoebe realized Angie wasn't breathless; she was whispering. "He came to the door but I didn't answer, so he sat down on the swing and I thought I'd better call you." Her voice quavered a little.

Phoebe remembered how young her sitter was, newly graduated from high school and still living with her parents on the next street over, taking evening classes at a local community college. Phoebe had met Angie's mother in her Sunday-school class and had felt lucky to find Angie.

"You did exactly right," she assured the younger woman. "If all he's doing is sitting there, just stay inside with the doors closed. I'm only a few blocks from home."

She pulled into her driveway a few minutes later, the cell phone's line still open. There was a gray sedan with a rental tag parked in front of her house. Maybe it belonged to whoever was waiting on her front porch.

"Okay, Angie," she said. "I'm home. You stay right where you are until I come inside."

She took a deep breath. Should she call the police? Common sense told her whoever was waiting on her porch probably wasn't a criminal. Otherwise, he wouldn't be here in the middle of the day, unconcerned about the neighbors taking down his license plate or identifying him. She positioned her keys between her fingers with one key thrust outward, as she'd learned in the self-defense class she'd taken when she'd first started college. Then she pivoted on her heel and headed up her front walk.

She started up the porch steps, unable to see the swing because of the trellis of roses blooming across the front of the porch. She knew from experience that a person sitting there on the swing could see out much more easily than anyone could see in.

As she reached the porch, a very large man came into view. Adrenaline rushed through her as he began to rise from the swing. She angled her body to confront him.

"What are—*Wade!*"

As the man's identity registered, a wave of shock slammed into her. It couldn't be.

Wade was dead.

Her knees felt as if they might buckle and she groped for the railing behind her. The keys fell to the floor with a loud jangle. "You—you're Wade." An inane statement. Of course it was Wade.

He was smiling but his eyes were watchful as he took a step forward. "Yeah. Hi, Phoebe."

"B-b-but…"

His smile faded as she took a step backward. One eyebrow rose in a quirk as familiar to her as her own smile in the mirror. That quizzical expression had been only one of the things she'd loved about Wade Donnelly. "But what?" he asked quietly.

"I thought you were dead!" She blurted out the words as her legs gave way and she sank to the top step, dropping her head onto her knees as incredulity warred with a strong desire to cry hysterically.

Footsteps rang out as Wade crossed the porch and then the boards of the top step depressed as he sat down beside her. One large hand touched her back. "My God," she said, the words muffled. "You really are here, aren't you?"

"I'm really here." It was definitely Wade, his distinctly masculine tone one she would recognize anywhere. He touched her back again, just one small uncertain touch, and she had to fight the urge to throw herself into his arms.

He never really belonged to me, she reminded herself.

"I'm sorry it's such a shock." His voice was quiet and deep and rang with sincerity. "I *was* presumed to be dead for a couple of days until I could get back to my unit. But that was months ago."

"How long have you been home?" He'd been deployed right after Melanie's funeral. The memory brought back others she'd tried to forget, as well, and she focused on his answer, trying to ignore the past.

"About five weeks. I've been trying to find you." He hesitated for a moment. "June gave me your address and she knew I survived. I assumed she— or someone back home—had told you."

"No." She shook her head without lifting it. She'd stopped reading the news from home the day she'd read his obituary. And though she'd sent June a Christmas card this year, they hadn't exchanged more than signatures since she'd moved.

Silence fell. She sensed that he didn't know what to say any more than she did—

Bridget! Shocked that she could have forgotten her own child for a moment—particularly this moment—Phoebe leaped to her feet, ignoring Wade's startled exclamation. "Just—ah, just let me put my things inside," she said. "Then we can talk."

Her hands trembled as she turned away from the man she'd loved throughout her adolescent years and into young womanhood. The keys were slippery in her sweaty grasp and she dropped them again. Before she could react, Wade came to her side and stretched down for the keys.

"Here."

"Thank you." She took the keys carefully, without touching his hand, fumbled the correct one into the lock and opened her front door.

Reality hit her in the face again. Wade Donnelly was alive and waiting to talk to her. And she had to tell him she'd borne his child.

Angie rushed forward as Phoebe came through the door and closed it firmly behind herself. Before the sitter could speak, Phoebe put her finger to her lips to indicate silence. She walked through the front rooms toward the back of the little house and dropped her things onto the kitchen table. "Listen," she said to Angie in a quiet tone, "there's nothing to worry about. He's an old friend I haven't seen in a long time. Can you stay a little longer in case Bridget wakes up?"

Angie nodded, her eyes wide. "Sure."

"We're going to talk outside. "I don't—I'm not inviting him in and I don't particularly want him to know about Bridget, so please don't come out."

Angie nodded, an uncharacteristically knowing smile crossing her face. "No problem. I wouldn't want to cause trouble for you."

Phoebe paused in the act of walking back through the living room. "Cause trouble for me?"

"With people back where you came from." Angie gestured vaguely. "I mean, I know everybody has babies without getting married these days, but if you don't want anyone back home to know, that's your business."

Phoebe felt her eyebrows rising practically to her hairline. She opened her mouth, then closed it abruptly before hysterical laughter could bubble out. Dear innocent Angie thought she was hiding Bridget because she was ashamed of having an illegitimate child. If only it were that simple!

She swallowed as she slipped through the front door again, closing it securely behind her. Wade was standing now, leaning against one of the porch posts, dwarfing the small space. Lord, she'd forgotten how big he really was.

She drank in his appearance, trying to reconcile the grief she'd carried for the past six months with the reality of seeing him alive and apparently well. His dark, wavy hair was conservatively short compared to the out-of-control locks he'd sported in high school, but quite a bit longer than the last time she'd seen him, when he'd had a high and tight military cut that had stripped every bit of curl away. If he weighed an ounce more than he had then, it wasn't noticeable; his shoulders were still wide and heavily muscled, his hips narrow and his belly flat, his legs still as powerful looking as they'd been when he'd been a running back for the high school football team. That had been almost a dozen years ago, and she'd been a silly middle-school teen at the time, already pathetically infatuated with her older, totally hot neighbor.

Then she realized he was watching her stare at him, his gray eyes as clear and piercing as always beneath the black slashes of his eyebrows. She felt her cheeks heat and she crossed her arms over her chest.

Taking a deep breath, she voiced the question burning in her mind. "Why were you reported dead if they weren't sure?" Her voice shook with the remembered agony of learning that Wade was gone forever. "I read about your funeral…" The sentence died unfinished as she realized she'd read about the *plans* for his funeral. In his obituary.

Wade blinked, but before his gaze slid away from hers, she caught a glimpse of a haunting pain. "Battlefield mistake," he said. "They found my dog tags but not my body. By the time the mistake was corrected, word had already gone out that I'd been KIA."

She put a hand to her mouth, fighting the tears that desperately wanted to escape. All these months she'd thought he was dead….

"I was injured," he said. "In the chaos that followed the explosion, a friendly Afghani hid me. It took the guy three days to make contact with American troops, and it wasn't until then that the mistake was caught. The fellow who died whom they'd assumed was me had already been shipped to Germany for autopsy. They'd have caught the mistake eventually, but I sure gave a lot of people a shock. And just for the record," he added, "Mom and Dad didn't actually have a funeral. It was planned, then canceled. I guess you didn't attend or you'd have found out."

She opened her mouth, then closed it again and simply shook her head. She still wanted to cry. Badly. *I was having your baby at the time* was so not the thing to say.

She risked a glance at him and was almost undone by the pain in his eyes.

Unable to bear being the cause of that pain, she said, "I couldn't come back for the funeral." She turned away and settled on the porch swing. "It took every penny I had to move here." *Well, that wasn't a lie.* She'd been lucky to find this place, luckier still that, although she had few assets, her credit history was good and with the teachers' credit union behind her, she'd been able to qualify for a mortgage. It hadn't hurt that the cost of living in California was so much higher than it was here. She'd never have been able to afford even this modest little home if she'd stayed on the West Coast.

"Why did you move?" he asked suddenly. "All the way across the country? I know you don't have any family to keep you in California, but that's where you grew up, where your roots are. Don't you miss it?"

She swallowed. "Of course I miss it." *Terribly. I miss the cobblestones on the beaches and the freezing cold water, the balmy days and cooler nights that rarely vary. I miss driving down to Point Loma, or over to Cardiff, and watching whale migrations in the fall. I even miss the insanity of driving on the freeway and the fire danger. Most of all, I miss you.* "But my life is here now."

"Why?"

She raised her eyebrows. "Why what?"

"What makes rural New York state so special that you have to live here?"

She shrugged. "I'm a teacher. I'll have tenure in two more years and I don't want to start over again somewhere else. The pay is good here and the cost of living is more manageable than in Southern California."

He nodded. "I see." He joined her on the swing, sitting close but not touching. He placed an arm along the back of the swing and turned slightly toward her. "It's good to see you." His voice was warm, his eyes even more so.

She could barely breathe. He was looking at her the way she'd dreamed of for years. Years when he'd been too old for her to do more than dream of, years when he'd been her sister's boyfriend, more recently when she'd thought he was dead and she was raising his child alone.

"Wade…" She reached out a hand and placed her palm gently against his cheek. "I'm so glad you're alive. It's good to see you, too, but—"

"Have dinner with me tonight."

"I can't." Fear infused her voice with a touch of panic. She started to withdraw her hand but he covered it with his, turning his face into her palm, and she felt the warmth of his lips whispering against the tender skin.

"Tomorrow night, then."

"I—"

"Phoeber, I'm not taking no for an answer." The silly childhood nickname gave the moment an even deeper intimacy. "I'm not leaving here until you say yes."

She stepped back a full pace as he finally released her hand. Dinner was a bad idea, given the way her heart still pounded at the mere sight of him.

She'd grown up in the months since she'd become a parent. She no longer believed in the kind of love she read about in romance novels. At least, not mutual love that was returned. And she'd stopped allowing herself to believe that what had happened between Wade and her that day at the cabin had been anything but his reaction to the shock of her sister's death.

Now Wade was here, back from the dead, untying every neatly packed-away detail in her memories. Confusing her, rousing feelings she hadn't let herself feel in more than a year, the warmth of possibilities in his eyes scaring her to death.

She wanted to go back an hour, to come home as always to an empty porch and no tough conversations.

But she had to tell him about Bridget.

It was the last thing she wanted to do, but she had to. A few weeks before she thought he had died, she'd realized she couldn't keep Wade's child from him. Telling him in an e-mail or on the phone was unthinkable, however. She'd been planning to visit him, wherever he was stationed, as soon as she could travel again, and a promise was a promise. Even if it was only to herself.

But not yet. She could hardly just invite him in, not with the bassinet and high chair, the board books and infant toys, unmistakable signs of a baby in residence. And anyway, Angie had class tonight so she wouldn't be able to stay much longer. Phoebe needed to get rid of him, plan the best way to tell him of his fatherhood.

"All right," she finally said. "Dinner tomorrow night because I have something to tell you." The words nearly choked her.

Wade raised an eyebrow in question, but when she didn't elaborate he made no comment. All he said was "Shall I pick you up at seven?"

"I'll meet you," she said quickly. "Are you staying in town?"

As it turned out, he was staying at a hotel on the other side of town. Attached to it was a restaurant that she knew had somewhat secluded booths along the walls, so she suggested they meet there. Then she stood on the porch and watched as he walked to the gray sedan.

He smiled at her over the roof of the car before he climbed in. "See you tomorrow night."

She nodded, her heart stuttering at the warmth

in his eyes, even though she reminded herself it wasn't anything more than friendship she saw there. "See you then."

But as she watched him drive away, she wondered if it wouldn't just be easier to vanish, the way people in the witness protection program did. Anything had to be easier than telling Wade he was the father of a child. Her child.

Memories bombarded her....

She was twelve. Her twin sister Melanie perched beside her on a pink bike exactly like Phoebe's purple one, and they both watched the neighborhood boys playing baseball on the local park's grassy ball field.

"I'm gonna marry Wade when I grow up," Melanie announced.

Phoebe frowned. "He's going to be grown up before we are. What if he marries somebody else?" The thought of Wade Donnelly marrying anybody made her feel all twisted up inside. Wade lived across the street from them, and he was four years older than they were. Phoebe had had a crush on him since before she could remember.

"He won't marry anybody else," Melanie said confidently. "I'm going to make him love me."

And she had.

When they were seniors in high school,

Melanie had initiated her move. Phoebe went to the prom with Tim DeGrange, a friend from her Latin class. Melanie had asked Wade, even though he had just graduated from West Point that year, and to Phoebe's shock he had said yes. Prom night had been long and miserable. Melanie had clung to Wade all evening. He'd looked so handsome in his brand-new dress uniform that he'd made Phoebe's heart hurt, and she'd been suddenly so shy she could barely force herself to talk to him.

That had been the beginning. Melanie and Wade had dated through the early summer until his leave had ended and he'd headed off for his first assignment at a training school. It had been hell for Phoebe, seeing them together. But it had grown much, much worse when Melanie had begun seeing other guys while Wade was away....

"We're not exclusive, Phoebe." Melanie's voice was sharp as she responded to the censure in her twin's eyes.

"Wade thinks you are." Phoebe was certain of that. She'd been all too aware of Wade's devotion to her sister throughout the early weeks of the summer.

"I'm sure he doesn't expect me to just sit at home while he's gone," Melanie said. "It's not like he's on a short vacation. He's in the army."

"If you're going to date other people, you should tell him."

But Melanie hadn't listened. Which was nothing new. Melanie had never listened to Phoebe's words of warning since they'd been very small girls.

It hadn't taken Wade long to realize that Melanie's affections for him were…something less than he clearly wanted. And it had wrung Phoebe's heart when he'd come home on leave to find that Melanie wasn't waiting for him. The two had had fight after fight. They'd finally broken up for good a year and a half later, after Christmas of the girls' sophomore year in college. Phoebe only knew the details from a distance, since she'd gone to school at Berkeley, hours north of their home in Carlsbad, California. Melanie had stayed closer to home and, although the sisters had stayed in touch largely through e-mail and instant messaging, Melanie hadn't volunteered much about Wade. Phoebe, always terrified her attraction to him would be noticed, had never asked.

After Wade and Melanie had broken up, Phoebe had noticed Wade came home less and less often over the next few years. His parents, who lived two doors down the street, had occasionally mentioned his travels to her mother, but they never shared enough information to satisfy Phoebe's hungry heart. And after her mother had passed away at the end of her junior year at Berkeley, she'd heard even less.

Then came her high-school class's five-year reunion. Melanie had invited Wade...and everything had changed forever.

Two

The following evening, Wade was ready a full fifteen minutes early. He went down to the bar in the restaurant and took a seat facing the door. And barely ten minutes later, Phoebe arrived. Also early.

He took the fact that she was early as a good sign. Did she still want to be with him the way he wanted her? Yesterday's conversation on her porch had been confusing. One moment he'd have sworn she was about to fall into his arms; the next, she seemed as distant as the moon, and only slightly more talkative.

How had he missed seeing how beautiful

Phoebe was all those years they'd been living on the same damned street?

Wade knew the answer as he watched her come across the room toward him.

Both Merriman sisters had been pretty, but Melanie's dramatic coloring had always drawn more attention. Melanie had been a strawberry redhead with fair, porcelain skin, and eyes so blue they looked like a piece of the sky. Phoebe's darker, coppery curls and deeper blue eyes were equally lovely but her quiet, reserved personality kept her from joining her exuberant, vivacious sister in the limelight. Which wasn't a bad thing, he decided. Melanie had been volatile, her moods extreme, her desire for attention exhausting sometimes. Hell, most of the time, if he were honest.

She had had a sunny, sweet side and, when she was in a good mood, she was irresistible. But she'd always been excited about something, always looking for something to do.

Phoebe was calm and restful. And capable. She had always seemed very self-sufficient to him. If Melanie had had a problem, Phoebe had been the one to whom she'd turned.

Melanie. He'd successfully avoided thinking about her for a very long time. It seemed inconceivable that she wasn't leading some man in a merry dance somewhere in Southern California. Instead, she was locked forever in his memory at the age of twenty-three.

The same age Phoebe had been when he'd realized he had been chasing the wrong twin for several years.

As she drew near, he drank in every detail of her appearance. Her hair was longer than it had once been, and she wore it up in a practical twist. She had on a khaki-colored pencil-slim skirt with a sweater set in some shade of a pretty green-blue that he didn't even have a name for. Although she probably thought it was a modest outfit, the skirt ended just above her knees, showing off her slender, shapely calves and ankles, and the sleeveless top beneath the outer sweater clung enticingly to her curves. Tendrils of curls had escaped from the twist and danced around her face in the light breeze.

She was looking down at the floor rather than at him and he had a sudden moment of doubt. She'd been all he'd thought about since the last day he'd seen her. Even when he'd been in combat, or leading troops, he'd carried the memory of her deep in the recesses of his mind, where everything he couldn't afford to think about in the heat of battle lived.

Guilt—and being deployed halfway around the world—had kept him away from her in those months after the funeral, but nearly losing his life in the mountains of Afghanistan had made him realize how sorry he would be if he walked away from the possibility of a life with Phoebe.

Had he waited too long? It had been fifteen months since the fateful class reunion that had changed their lives forever, since Melanie's death and their unexpected intimacy after the funeral.

Did Phoebe regret that? Or even worse, did she blame him for Melanie's death? That niggling little fear had lodged in his brain months ago and, despite the memories of Phoebe's shining eyes at the reunion and the sweet way she'd kissed him a few days later, he couldn't shake his worry. It didn't help that deep down, he knew he *was* to blame. He'd been Melanie's date that night, he'd known how possessive she could be and yet, when he'd taken Phoebe in his arms on that dance floor, he'd forgotten everything but the wonder of what had suddenly flared between them.

After her initial shock had faded yesterday, she'd been a little too distant for comfort. She'd always been reserved, but never with him. He'd enjoyed drawing her out and making her laugh, even when they'd been young, but he'd never realized just how much he took it for granted that she relaxed around him.

On her porch last afternoon, she hadn't been relaxed.

Maybe she had a serious relationship, even though she wasn't married or engaged. He knew because one of the first things he'd done was check out her ring finger. And besides, her name hadn't changed. She had been listed as Merriman in that phone book. *I have something to tell you,* she'd said. It had sounded ominous and he'd had to struggle not to react. He sure as hell hoped she wasn't going to try to brush him off for some other guy. He'd been a clueless idiot when they were younger, had failed to realize what a treasure she was. But he knew now, and any man who thought he had a claim to Phoebe could think again.

She was going to be his.

"Hello," she said. "Is my lipstick smeared or something?"

He jolted and smiled wryly. She'd caught him staring. "No," he said honestly. "I just couldn't take my eyes off you."

Phoebe blushed as he rose and came around the table to seat her. To his astonishment, her entire pretty face turned pink.

Returning to his seat, he said, "You look beautiful. That sweater makes your eyes even bluer."

Her face was still chair. "You don't have to say

that," she said. "Melanie was the beautiful one in our family."

"One of the beautiful ones," he corrected, studying her expressionless face. "Melanie drew attention to herself and people noticed her. You did the exact opposite and managed to make yourself practically invisible most of the time. Quite a feat for a woman as beautiful as you are."

Her gaze flew to his. Finally. "Thank you," she whispered. And when their eyes met, he felt again that sudden shiver of knowledge, a "we are meant to be" moment unlike anything he'd ever felt with any other woman. He'd felt it yesterday when she'd first noticed him; if he hadn't, he wouldn't have been here now.

He could remember the first time he'd experienced it as clearly as if it *had* been yesterday. Funny that he and Phoebe had grown up in the same neighborhood, had known each other all their lives, but suddenly one night, everything had clicked into place, and he'd recognized the woman he wanted to spend forever with....

He stood by the bar and finished his soda, watching his date. Melanie sat at a table across the room on some guy's lap. She was shrieking with laughter and as Wade watched, she tilted a glass to her lips and drank. She listed to one side and nearly fell off the man's lap, and Wade suddenly realized how drunk she was. Why had he ever thought she was what he wanted?

Because you were listening to the brain in your pants, dope.

He'd been stupid to say yes when Melanie had asked him to accompany her to her first class reunion. He knew her well by then, well enough to know that Melanie didn't really want him so much as she wanted the effect she had on people when she walked in with a man in uniform. It didn't bother him anymore the way it once had, but he wasn't going to stick around here and wait for her for the rest of the evening. Phoebe had driven Melanie to meet him here, so he wasn't obligated to get her home.

He raised his glass and finished the drink, then straightened and headed for the exit.

"Wade! Wait!"

He turned at the sound of the husky female voice, his irritation fading. "Hey, Phoeber," he said. "I'm heading out. Melanie's going to catch a ride with someone else."

"You're leaving?" Her dismay was plain.

He nodded. Over the beat of the music, he said, "Yeah. I'll see you before I leave again. Promise."

"But…" Phoebe's eyes were fastened to his and he thought for a moment that she was fighting tears. Had someone hurt her feelings?

Behind her, the band segued into a familiar slow song and couples began flocking to the dance floor.

Phoebe swallowed and licked her lips. "I was hoping you'd dance with me tonight."

Because it was Phoebe, and because he sensed she wasn't very happy, he turned away from the exit. "All right." He took her hand and began to draw her after him to the dance floor. Whatever had upset her, he could worm it out of her while they danced.

He pulled her into the middle of the crowded area and turned to draw her into his arms. There were so many people they were literally pushed together.

Phoebe's slender body slid against his and settled as if she'd been made just for him. He realized suddenly that he'd never danced with her before. Never.

Would it have been like this between them before now if he'd been smart enough to dance with her? His heart began to pound and arousal began to stir. Automatically, he began to move to the beat of the music, and she moved with him, her soft curves a shocking temptation beneath his hands.

It was heaven. He turned his head slightly and breathed in her scent, and his entire body tightened.

What the hell… This was Phoebe. His little neighbor.

Not so little anymore. She was the same age Melanie was, though he'd bet his paycheck she was far less experienced. Stunned, confused, he actually stopped dancing right there in the middle of the crowd.

"Phoebe?" He pulled back far enough to see her face, wondering if she was feeling as overwhelmed as he was.

She tilted her head back and her entire face was shining as if someone had lit a lantern inside her. "Yes?"

When she met his eyes, something clicked into place. Something precious and irreplaceable, something that filled a spot inside him that he hadn't even realized was empty. He forgot everything he'd been going to say, everything in his head, everything in the world. Nothing else mattered because everything he needed was right here in his arms, her eyes telling him that she felt the magic they were making together as well as he.

"Never mind," he said at last. He pulled her close again, then grasped her hands, which had been resting on his shoulders, and slid them up behind his neck. The movement increased the intimacy of their position and he had to fight the urge to shift his hips against the soft body plastered to his. This was crazy. *He* was crazy. Crazy about a woman he'd known most of his life without really knowing her at all.

Phoebe made a small sound and turned her head toward him, nestling against his chest. He bent his head to hers and set his lips against her ear. "The rest of the evening."

A shiver rippled down her spine and he delighted in the knowledge that she was as aroused as he was. Her head came up and their lips were a whisper apart. "What?"

He smiled and dropped his head farther, then brushed his nose lightly across hers. He wanted to kiss her worse than he'd ever wanted anything, including his first brand new bike and his ranger tab. But when he kissed Phoebe for the first time, he didn't want an audience, and he didn't want to have to stop. "You're dancing with me for the rest of the evening."

She shot him a glowing smile, and he swore there were stars twinkling and sparkling in the depths of those blue eyes. "All right."

* * *

Dinner was the most nerve-racking experience Phoebe had ever had in her life. In the back of her head a steady cadence hammered: *I have to tell him I have to tell him I have to tell him.*

It was so insistent that she couldn't relax and enjoy these moments she'd thought were gone forever. But she couldn't tell him here, not in a restaurant.

Fortunately, Wade didn't seem to want to discuss serious topics, either. He asked about her teaching job and seemed honestly interested. He asked questions about the little house in which she lived and how she'd found it. He asked about New York and how it was different from California, but he didn't ask her why she'd moved. Thank heavens. Maybe he simply assumed that she'd wanted to get away from all the memories.

He told her a little bit about where he'd been and what he'd done. A lot of it was classified, but he could share generalities.

They didn't talk about anything important. Neither of them mentioned the reunion, or the magical moments they'd shared, or what had occurred between them after the funeral.

And they didn't talk about Melanie.

Melanie, for whom Wade had cared deeply for years before one evening of dancing...

"Phoebe, you'll never guess who's coming to the reunion with me."

"I give." She smiled as Melanie breezed into the living room of her small apartment on the weekend of their first class reunion. It had been nice to move away from home and get away from her sister, but it also was nice to see her from time to time. Melanie was lovable; she was just...too much sometimes. "Who?"

"Wade!"

Phoebe froze. She'd been expecting her sister to name a classmate, probably a male one, knowing Melanie. "Wade didn't graduate with us," she said carefully.

"I know, silly." Melanie shook her head in exasperation. "I invited him."

"But..."

"He's going to wear his uniform." Melanie waved a hand as if she was fanning herself. "I can't resist a man in uniform."

Neither could Phoebe, if that man was Wade. But she couldn't say that to Mel.

The doorbell rang then, saving her from making

a response. Melanie said, "That must be Wade. Let him in, will you? I've got to finish getting ready!"

Phoebe resisted the temptation to salute as she reluctantly moved toward the door and opened it.

"Wade." It wasn't hard to smile as she lifted her arms. It was much harder not to appear too thrilled. "It's great to see you."

"You, too." Wade's arms came around her and he kissed her lightly on the cheek before she backed away. "How've you been, Phoeber? You look terrific."

He released her and stepped back a pace. "Seriously terrific," he added, as he scanned the simple navy-blue dress she'd chosen.

"Thank you." She knew she was blushing, and not just because of the admiration in his eyes. The feel of his hard arms around her had been overwhelming to senses that had been starved for even the sight of him. To suddenly be in her version of heaven was too much. She took a deep breath. "You look good, too. The army's agreeing with you?"

He nodded. "And you're enjoying teaching." It wasn't a question; they had stayed in loose touch by e-mail once or twice a month since she'd graduated from high school and headed off to Berkeley. As badly as she longed to hear from him, Phoebe always forced herself to wait at least a week before e-mailing him back. The last thing she wanted was for Wade to realize how she felt about him.

She nodded. "I think I told you I'm switching from first grade to fourth next year. It'll be an interesting change."

He grinned. "Yeah, the boys will have gone from being mildly annoying to thoroughly bratty."

She laughed. "Hmm. Sounds like personal experience speaking."

"Fourth grade was the year I got sent to the principal's office for putting a tadpole in Miss Ladly's Thermos of iced tea."

"I've heard that story before. Guess I'll be checking before I take a sip of anything."

They smiled at each other and a companionable silence fell for a moment. But then she broke the mood. "How long are you home for, and where do you go after that?" He probably had no idea that she could recite every move he'd made in the nine years since he'd graduated from high school.

Wade's face suddenly seemed guarded, his gray eyes darkening. "I have a few more days left of my two weeks' leave and then I'm being deployed to Afghanistan."

Afghanistan. The fear she'd always lived with rose, almost choking her. "Oh, God, Wade."

"I'll be back," he said. "Who would come around to bug you once in a while if I didn't?"

She forced herself to smile. "Just be careful."

He nodded, reaching out a hand and rubbing her arm. "Thanks. I will."

"Hey there!" Her sister's voice singsonged a flirtatious greeting Phoebe had heard her employ dozens of times before. And just like many of those other times, Wade's head swiveled around and Phoebe was instantly forgotten.

Lowering her eyes, she stepped away and busied herself gathering a few items for her evening bag while Melanie threw herself into Wade's arms and gave him a loud kiss.

For the rest of the evening, she avoided looking at Wade and her sister as much as she could. It was just too painful.

Not long after they arrived at the reunion, she lost herself on the other side of the crowd. Her best friend from high school, June Nash, had come. June still lived in town. She'd married a former classmate and was expecting her first child. Phoebe felt conspicuously alone as she looked around. Everyone seemed either to be married by now or to have brought a date.

But June was genuinely delighted to see her, and they spent the mealtime catching up on the years since high school. Although they faithfully exchanged Christmas cards, their e-mails and phone calls had gradually slowed as their lives took different paths.

"So you're teaching." June smiled. "I bet you're fantastic with children. I still remember how great you were when the student council helped with Special Olympics."

Phoebe shrugged. "I enjoy it." And the school district in which she taught was far enough from where she'd grown up that few people knew her as "the quiet twin."

"That's good." June nodded her head in the direction of another group. "I see Melanie and Wade are an item again. I thought that ended a couple of years ago."

Phoebe winced. "It did. But we've all stayed friends and Melanie invited him as her date tonight."

Thankfully, the band began to play at that moment and she was spared any more discussion. June wasn't dancing since her first child was due in less than two weeks and she said she felt like a hippo in a mud hole. But a group of girls Phoebe had known when they were all in the marching band dragged her up to the dance floor with them, and Phoebe decided she was going to enjoy what was left of the evening. She danced with a group of her classmates until the first slow song and then moved to another table to visit, forbidding herself to look around the room for Wade.

An hour later, she'd had enough. She'd seen the people she'd wanted to see, had danced and laughed and done her best to give the impression that life was treating Phoebe Merriman well. Melanie, as always, was the life of the party. She had abandoned Wade for a guy Phoebe barely remembered, and the two of them were knocking back drinks with a like-minded group.

This time Phoebe did look for Wade. He was standing alone by the bar and, as she watched, he set down his drink and approached Melanie. After a brief exchange, Melanie laughed and Wade turned and walked away.

When she realized he was heading for the door, she panicked. Plain and simple, she couldn't bear the thought of Wade leaving without at least speaking to him one more time.

"Wade!" she called out. "Wait!"

Two little words. She could still remember them. Two little words that had altered her life. And not just hers. Three lives had been altered by that evening, four if you counted Bridget. If Wade had left the dance when he'd intended to, Melanie might still be alive. If Melanie were still alive,

Phoebe and Wade would never have walked up to that cabin, would never have…and Bridget would never have been conceived.

Try as she might, Phoebe couldn't regret those stolen moments of heaven she'd experienced with him. Nor could she imagine her world without her beautiful baby daughter in it.

"Would you like to go to a movie when we're finished eating?" Wade smiled at her across the table. A movie. With Wade.

There was a time when she would have given an arm for that invitation. But things were different now. What she wanted and what was reality were two very separate things.

"Thank you, but no," she said. "I have to get home pretty soon."

He looked taken aback and, as she watched, the warmth in his eyes drained away. "All right."

"Wade." She leaned forward and took an irrevocable step. "I'd like you to come with me. There's something I have to tell you."

"You mentioned that yesterday," he said, but she noticed he seemed to unbend a little. "Sounds scary."

She couldn't even smile. "I hope not."

They left the restaurant and he followed her minivan directly back to her house. She'd offer him a glass of wine first, she decided, and then…

then she'd have to decide how to tell him. But none of her opening lines sounded good. And now she had a new worry.

What if Wade didn't want to be a father? What if he rejected Bridget and didn't want to be part of her life?

Since yesterday, Phoebe had been trying to brace herself for sharing Bridget with her father when he came East. Which could be quite infrequently. After all, the man was probably going to be out of the country most of the time. If Wade didn't want anything to do with them, their lives wouldn't change appreciably.

But it would break her heart if he didn't find Bridget as miraculous and irresistible as she did.

He followed her into the house at her invitation.

And it was then that she realized the flaw in her plan. Duh. How could she possibly explain the presence of a nanny?

Angie rose from the couch and gathered up her schoolwork. "Hi, Phoebe. Give me a minute to get organized and call my brother. I have an econ test tomorrow."

Phoebe managed a smile. "Do you think you're ready?"

Angie shrugged. "As ready as I'll ever be."

She glanced at the ceiling. "Everything went fine this evening."

Phoebe was having trouble getting out words. Her chest felt like there was an enormous weight bearing down, preventing her from taking one good, deep breath. "Good."

Angie nodded and went to the phone. A moment later, she said, "He's on his way."

"I'll walk out with you." One more minute. Just one more minute to plan what she was going to say. Her hands were shaking as she followed the sitter to the end of her driveway. Angie's brother was already rounding the corner and walking toward them, and Phoebe returned his wave as Angie moved away.

Then she took one last stab at a deep breath and turned toward her home again.

Wade stood framed in the doorway. His face was in the shadow, and golden light from her cozy little home streamed around him, illuminating the tall, unmoving figure. It looked right, she thought. Then she immediately censored the notion. There was no point in wishing for the moon.

Phoebe mounted the steps and he moved aside to let her enter. His brow furrowed as he watched her close the door behind herself. "You have a housekeeper?"

"No." She took a deep breath. "No, I don't. Angela is my nanny." It wasn't, perhaps, a perfect opening line, but she might as well jump in. She had to get this over with.

She watched the expressions move swiftly across his face: simple acceptance of an answer, then shock, and a growing incredulity as he took in what she had said. "Why do you have a nanny?" He looked around as if to confirm the obvious conclusion, but the books and toys had been put away in the large basket beneath the window, so there was no obvious evidence of a child in residence in the living room.

"I have a daughter."

"I see." His expression had gone so noncommittal she wondered what in the world he was thinking. Of all the reactions, calm acceptance wasn't the one she'd anticipated.

"Wade?"

To her shock, he had started for the door. "This was a mistake," he said. "Goodbye, Phoebe."

"Wade!"

He stopped halfway to the door without turning around. "Yeah?"

"Don't you even want to know about her?"

There was a long moment in which she held her breath. Then he turned around and in his eyes she saw a sadness so deep she couldn't fathom what was wrong. Surely the existence of a child couldn't be that terrible, could it? Maybe it reminded him of what he would never have with Melanie—

"No," he finally said. "I don't."

"But—"

"What we did—after the funeral—meant something to me."

And she had known it would. He'd had a sense of honor a mile wide as long as she'd known him. It was one of the reasons she had been so loath to tell him she was pregnant. Even after she'd gotten past the hurt and the anger that he'd never contacted her after what they'd shared, she'd feared his reaction. She knew Wade well. He would have felt obligated to ask her to marry him.

The last thing she wanted was a man who felt forced into a loveless marriage with his child's mother. But dear Lord, if he'd asked her to marry him then…she wasn't sure she'd have had the strength to turn him down.

"I assumed it meant something to you," he added.

"It did!" He was the first and only man she'd ever been with. He couldn't possibly know what that meant to her.

"But you've moved on." He laughed, but it wasn't a sound of humor. "You've moved on in a big way."

She couldn't follow…. "I didn't have a choice," she said.

"Is the father still in the picture? I presume you're not married or you wouldn't have gone out with me tonight. I hope," he said coolly.

She blinked, completely thrown off stride. He thought she'd—he thought Bridget was—"No," she said. "You don't understand. There is no other man."

"Maybe not now, but—"

"She's yours."

Three

Wade froze, his face a classic mask of disbelief. Finally, as if he were sure he hadn't understood what language she was speaking, he said, "What?"

"She's your child," Phoebe said. She probably should have been angry at his initial assumption that there'd been another man, but he looked so totally poleaxed now that she couldn't summon much outrage.

"Are you kidding me?" He sounded as shocked as he looked. "We only—that one time—"

She nodded sympathetically, understanding his shock. "That's how I felt when I found out, too."

"When you found out." He pounced on that like a cat waiting for the mouse to come out just far enough, shock morphing into anger right before her eyes. "Just when in the hell *did* you find out? And why didn't you bother to tell me?"

She forced herself not to stammer apologetically. Instead, she indicated the couch. "Would you like to sit down? I'll explain it all."

"Hell, no, I don't want to sit down!" The words exploded with fury. "I just want to know why you didn't tell me you were going to have a baby!"

She wanted to shrink into a little ball and hide beneath the furniture, exactly like a frightened mouse. The guilt she had lived with since his death flared to life. "I don't know," she said in a quiet voice. "At the time, it seemed like the thing to do. Now— for some time now—I've known it was wrong."

"So why didn't you look me up and tell me?"

"You were dead! At least, I thought you were."

He fell silent, clearly taken aback. "I keep forgetting that," he said in a slightly milder tone. Then his eyes narrowed. "But I wasn't dead when you found out you were pregnant."

She had to look away. "No," she said, "you weren't."

Silence fell. She wrapped her arms around

herself and turned away, feeling the rage crackling in the room behind her.

"I want to see her," he said.

"All right." She swallowed. "Tomorrow after school—"

"Now." The word was a whip and she jumped as it lashed her ears.

"She's asleep," she said protectively. But Wade's face was stony and unmoved when she looked back at him. "All right." She blew out a breath of nerves and exasperation, realizing she'd been stupid to imagine she could tell Wade about his child without letting him see her for himself immediately. "I'll take you up to see her if you promise not to wake her."

There was another tense silence. Finally, Wade said, "So let's go."

She turned on her heel and walked to the stairs on shaking legs, leaving him to follow.

She was extremely aware of his large presence at her back as she went up the steps and down the hall. At the door of her daughter's room, she paused. Her chest felt as if someone were sitting on it and she couldn't get enough air. She'd swear she could feel Wade's breath on the back of her neck and she didn't have the courage to turn around. Over her shoulder, she whispered, "Her name is Bridget. She's six months old."

The door was open just a shred, and she grasped the knob and carefully pulled it wide, then stepped aside and gestured. "Go ahead."

Wade nodded once, a sharp jerk of his head, and she watched from the doorway as he took slow, almost hesitant steps toward the crib against the far wall.

He stood there for a long, long time, looking down at the sleeping baby in the low light she'd switched on. He didn't move to touch her, didn't glance around the room at the charming wallpaper border with the red-and-blue alphabet-blocks motif she'd found, the gingham curtains or the shelves filled with board books, stuffed animals and toys to stimulate a growing baby. He just... stood.

Finally, she entered the room and went to his side.

"Is she really mine?" His low voice was wondering and she understood he wasn't trying to offend her.

"She's really yours," she assured him softly. "You can touch her." His big hands were still, grasping the rail of the crib. He made no move but Phoebe could practically feel the longing radiating from him. Finally, she couldn't stand it. She took his hand, and when he didn't resist, she lifted it and tugged him forward so his palm rested flat against Bridget's small back.

Phoebe found she had a lump in her throat. Her daughter's body looked so tiny and fragile with Wade's hand covering her whole back.

Her own hand tingled where she'd touched his skin. It wasn't fair. Even an innocent touch like that set her pulse racing. In the years before and after Wade, she'd never met another man who could affect her so effortlessly. She doubted he even knew he'd done it.

But she knew. For the rest of her life, she'd always be comparing any man she met to Wade. She hoped to marry someday, but she was realistic enough to know that she wasn't going to be able to offer a man the kind of all-consuming love she felt for Wade. She also knew she could never pretend to care for someone just to get a ring on her finger, and she feared that there might be many lonely years in her future, broken up by the joys of motherhood.

She was distracted from her morose thoughts by movement. Bridget had squirmed and twitched in her sleep, and Wade had automatically soothed her with gentle circles on her back. The baby gave a sigh and stopped moving, but he didn't. He extended his index finger and very, very lightly brushed it over the smooth petal softness of his daughter's cheek. He stroked it back and forth over the wild red curls that sprang from her tiny head. Then his hand moved to touch her much smaller one.

And Phoebe thought her heart might break when Bridget grasped one big finger and held on for dear life, still sound asleep. A lump rose in her throat and she fought not to sob aloud at the tenderness of the moment.

She swallowed hard several times until she felt she had enough control not to cry. Then she opened her mouth to whisper an apology, but when her gaze landed on his face, the words dried up in her throat.

Wade had tears on his cheeks. Silvery in the moonlight, they made gleaming trails where they fell from his eyes and rolled down his face. He didn't even seem to notice them, not even when one fat tear dripped from his jaw onto the back of the hand that still clutched the side of the crib.

His sorrow hit her harder than anything in the world had since the news of his death. And guilt was right on its heels. *She* was the cause of this agony. *She* was the source of the sadness that gripped him. She hadn't told him about her pregnancy when she'd had the chance, and then she'd lost the chance, she'd thought, forever.

Wade turned away from the crib and made his way from the room slowly. She followed him equally slowly, her own battle with tears completely lost. As they moved down the hallway, she swallowed the sob that wanted to surge up and said, "Wade, I—"

"Don't." He held up one large hand in a gesture of denial without even turning around. "I can't talk to you right now," he said as he started down the steps.

Shaken by both his tears and the controlled ferocity in the low tone, Phoebe stopped talking.

And watched, stunned, as Wade walked out the front door of her home without another word.

Wade knew she went to work the next day because he was sitting in his parked car down the street, waiting for her to come home. When she emerged from her little minivan, she walked around to the passenger-side sliding door and unloaded what looked like a fifty-pound satchel, presumably full of work to be graded.

The sight of Phoebe lugging that obviously heavy load up her front steps aroused two emotions in him. The first was an instinctive protective urge. She shouldn't be lifting things like that. The second was another blast of the anger that had consumed him since last night, when it had fully begun to sink in that he had a child—and had missed more than half a year of her life because Phoebe had chosen to deny him the knowledge of his fatherhood. He didn't even know his child's birthday but he could guess approximately when she had been born.

God, if only Phoebe had told him when she'd learned she was pregnant…it might have made all the difference in the world.

He'd have married her. Hell, he'd known he wanted to marry her since they'd danced together at her class reunion and he'd realized what had been right under his nose for years. But then Mel was killed and things had gotten more and more out of control after that.

She'd been extremely drunk and upset that night and it had been his fault. The thought would haunt him forever, and he knew it had to have occurred to Phoebe. He could have stopped her from drinking so much. He could have gone after her faster. God, was it any wonder Phoebe hadn't wanted to contact him when she'd found out she was pregnant? If she blamed him for Melanie's death, how must she feel about having slept with him the very day of her twin's funeral?

He took deep, calming breaths as he got out of his

rental car and strode along the sidewalk to her house. A twinge in his hip reminded him that he wasn't quite as healthy as he wanted to be just yet. He had to get a grip. Yes, she'd been wrong, but shouting at her wasn't going to help the situation any.

Even if it would make him feel one hell of a lot better.

The door had barely closed behind her when he turned into her walk and bounded up the steps. He rapped briskly on the door.

Phoebe pulled it open a moment later. "Yes? Wade!" She clearly hadn't expected it to be him. Maybe she'd thought he'd gone back to California. *Think again.*

He stepped across the threshold, forcing her to step back. Her babysitter was just getting ready to slip out the door but she paused, brown eyes alight with interest.

"Bye, Angie." Phoebe held the door open and waved a hand, ushering the younger woman out. "See you Monday. Have a good weekend." The nanny was barely through the door when Phoebe closed it behind her. Then she turned to face him. "Hello. Would you like to come in?"

He snorted at her sarcasm, but he'd been thinking all night and he wanted to get things straight right from the get-go. "Okay. The way I see it, we have two choices. We go back to California, or we stay here."

Her blue eyes widened to the size of saucers. "*We? You* can do whatever you like but—"

"I'd like to take my daughter back to California to meet her only surviving grandparent," he said harshly.

Her lovely face registered horrified shock. "You can't just take off with my child."

"No, but I can take off with my child," he said.

He could see the moment that his earlier words registered. Phoebe's forehead wrinkled and her eyes widened as she said, "One grandparent? Wade, has one of your parents passed away?"

"My mother." Anger was preferable by far to the grief that still gripped him at unexpected times. "She died seven months ago."

"Oh, my God." Phoebe looked stunned. Her eyes filled with tears. "I need to sit down." Her voice was faint and she stepped backward until the couch hit the backs of her knees. Then she collapsed onto the cushion, her hands clasped together so tightly he could see her knuckles whiten. "Oh, Wade, I'm so sorry. What happened?"

"She had a stroke," he said flatly. "Ten months ago. It was terribly debilitating and she didn't want to live. Three months after the first one, she had another." *But if she'd known she'd had a grand-child, things might have been different.* He could see in Phoebe's horrified eyes that the thought had occurred to her as well.

She pressed the heels of her hands hard against her eyes, elbows resting on her thighs. "I am so sorry," she said in a muffled voice.

He knew she wasn't offering condolences. No, she was apologizing—again—for not telling him he had a child. "I want Dad to meet Bridget," he said, "before much more time passes."

"But…I can't just quit my job and go off to California."

"I didn't ask you to," he said evenly.

Phoebe's face lost what little color it still had. "Are you…are you going to fight me for custody?"

He took his time answering, finding himself a seat in the comfortable armchair angled close to the sofa. "Are you going to force me to?" He waited until she met his gaze. "I want to get to know my daughter. I want to be with her every day—I can't get back all the time I missed but I sure as hell don't want to miss any more." He closed his eyes against the surge of anger that shook him and waited for her to argue.

"Okay." Her voice was small.

He was startled. "Okay?" The Phoebe he knew

might be quiet and calm, but underneath she was a fighter when she believed in something.

But she nodded. "Okay." She swallowed. "I was wrong not to tell you as soon as I found out, Wade. I'm sorrier than you'll ever know."

He didn't know what to say to that. She was right—she had been wrong. Because she'd chosen not to tell him, his mother had died without ever knowing she had a grandchild.

He simply couldn't utter the words to accept her apology yet. He liked to think he was a big enough man that he'd soon be able to forgive her… but he didn't feel that magnanimous right now. Instead of answering, he stood and went out the front door to his car.

When he returned, Phoebe was still sitting on the couch with her hands clasped. She jumped up when he walked back in without knocking and dumped his duffel on the floor inside the door. There were tears on her face, which she hastily wiped away, and then she did a double take.

"What are you doing?" She already knew, and she was aghast.

"Moving in." He shrugged. "It's the only way to really get to know Bridget without taking her away from you."

She nodded as if she saw the logic, but a

moment later, she shook her head vigorously. "Wait! You can't just move in here!"

"Why not? You and I have always gotten along well. We probably know each other better than a lot of couples do. And you have an extra bedroom. I saw it last night. I'll pay rent."

She opened her mouth, then closed it again and shook her head helplessly. Finally, she said, "This is outrageous. So how did you just make it sound so utterly logical?"

He grinned, feeling a lot more relaxed now that she hadn't kicked him out first thing. "I'm gifted that way." He'd hoped her obvious guilt would help sway her to his point of view and, apparently, it had worked.

Suddenly, he realized she hadn't spoken. She was staring at him as if he'd grown a second head. "What?"

She shrugged. "That's the first time I've seen you smile since you got off that swing yesterday."

"I haven't had much to smile about," he pointed out.

Instantly, the angry tension was back in the room, humming between them like a downed electrical wire. He was about to speak again, to get more answers to the questions she'd never given him a chance to ask, when an odd whispering sound filled the air.

It was barely audible, but Phoebe reacted instantly, a blinding smile lighting her. face. "Bridget is awake."

His body reacted to that smile. But—

"A-ba-bah-bah-ba," It was a little louder now. Wade glanced around the room and spotted a baby monitor on one end table. Aha.

Phoebe started for the stairs. "If I don't get her fast, they'll hear her down at the end of the street. I'll be back in a minute."

Wade smiled to himself as she took the steps two at a time. Bridget was six months old. That had to be a bit of an exaggeration—

"A-bah-bah-BAH-BAH!"

Whoa. His kid had a set of lungs on her like Pavarotti.

"Bridget." Phoebe's voice was a gentle singsong. "How's my girl? Did you have a good nap?"

The baby gave a delighted squeal that just about split his eardrums. Did Phoebe have that monitor turned up too high?

"Hello, my sweet baby girl." No, the monitor wasn't too loud, because Phoebe's voice sounded normal. "How was your nap? I've got somebody downstairs who wants to meet you." He heard her chuckle. "But first we'd better change your diaper or he's liable to keel over."

He listened to the rustle of the plastic diaper and the baby cooing, to Phoebe talking and singing little nonsense verses. It sounded surprisingly *right*. But he shouldn't be surprised. Phoebe had always had a sensible, motherly streak. Years ago, if someone had asked him if he could envision her as a mother, he wouldn't have hesitated for an instant before saying yes.

A wave of intense sadness swamped him. And now she was the mother of his child. If he hadn't been determined to find Phoebe, he'd never even have known he had a daughter.

Footsteps on the stairs alerted him that they were coming, and he shook off the moment of melancholy and braced himself for his first clear sight of his daughter. He knew from what he'd seen last night that her hair was some shade of red, but the low light of the nursery hadn't yielded much more.

Phoebe's legs came into view, and then the rest of her appeared. She was carrying a baby girl with the wildest red hair he'd ever seen in his life. Quirking in ringlets all over her head. Even at this young age, Phoebe had pulled the front of it atop her head with an elastic hair tie. Bridget's hair was much lighter than Phoebe's, and far more vibrant than Melanie's pale strawberry had ever been. His kid's hair looked like a live flame.

Her face was a pretty little oval with a slightly more determined chin than was probably good, her eyes blue and sparkling as they found him. His heart skipped a beat. He actually *felt* it trip and miss, and he took a deep breath. God, she looked a lot like Phoebe.

His throat closed up and he just stood there as they approached. Phoebe was talking to the baby as if she could understand every word she said, telling her about a friend of Mama's from far away who was coming to stay with them for a little while.

A little while? Ha. She might not choose to accept it, but he was here for good.

He swallowed the thick knot clogging his voice. "Hi, Bridget," he said. He was at a loss. What did you say to somebody this size?

The child grinned, a wide smile that sent a cascade of drool down her chin and showed him two tiny pearly white teeth on the bottom. Then she turned her head abruptly into her mother's shoulder.

Before he could figure out what to say, Phoebe saved him. "Daddy," she told his child. "Bridget, this is your daddy."

The baby peeked out at him with one blue eye, then grinned before hiding her face again.

"Flirt," said Phoebe. She walked across the room and expertly unfurled a large baby blanket while still holding the child on her hip with the other hand. Then she set the baby in the middle of the blanket.

Bridget wobbled for a moment, then seemed to find her balance and sit straighter. "She just started sitting up by herself two weeks ago," she told Wade over her shoulder. "Why don't you come sit down and play with us? She's not usually shy and she should get used to you quickly."

"All right." He strove for a normal tone although his heart felt as if it were going to fly right out of his chest.

He joined them on the brightly colored blanket. Phoebe was building a tower of blocks. Every time she'd get three or four stacked up, Bridget swiped her hand and knocked them over, squealing and chortling. Once, when Phoebe stopped for a moment, the baby smacked her little hands together and yelled, "Ack!" in a tone that left no doubt what she wanted.

Wade hastily reached for another block. "Way to get what you want, kid."

Phoebe chuckled. "She has a mind of her own. And if she doesn't get her way, she lets me know about it."

"Reminds me of Melanie." He'd said it without thinking. The moment the words hit the air, he knew they'd been a mistake.

The happiness drained out of Phoebe's eyes, leaving them guarded and sorrowful. "Yes," she said quietly. "Bridget does seem to have a stronger personality than I ever had."

He wanted to protest. There was nothing wrong with Phoebe's personality. Just because Mel had been more vocal about everything under the sun didn't mean Phoebe's personality was any less pleasing. She just wasn't loud and attention-grabbing, that was all. But he didn't know how to say that in a way that made much sense, and he could almost feel the resistance in the air. She didn't want to talk about Melanie, that much was clear.

A pang of guilt shot through him, tempering the anger that still simmered. He was blaming Phoebe for not telling him about the baby...but he'd been responsible for her sister's death. No wonder she hadn't told him.

The baby had grabbed a board book and was busily manhandling the sturdy pages. As he watched, she put it in her mouth.

"Here, honey." Phoebe extended a brightly colored set of rings and confiscated the book. "We don't chew on books."

Wade looked at the frayed corners of the one she held. "Apparently, some of us do."

She smiled, and abruptly it felt right between them again. "I'm working on it," she said wryly. Then she glanced at her watch. "It'll soon be dinnertime. Would you like to stay and eat with us?"

He raised one eyebrow.

"Are you planning to stay here *tonight?*"

"That's the plan." He stood and folded his arms. "If you spend the weekend teaching me how to take care of Bridget, then I could keep her while you work."

"Don't you have to work or something?" she asked in an exasperated tone.

"Or something," he agreed.

"So you have to go back to California." It wasn't a question.

"No. I'm pretty sure I'm retiring from the service."

She looked shocked. "But that's what you've always wanted to do. To be. A soldier."

"I'm not physically able to perform on the battlefield to the army's satisfaction anymore," he said quietly. "And I'm not interested in a desk job staring at a computer monitor all day. So I'm taking early retirement."

"But what will you do?"

He shrugged. "I'm checking out a number of options. One of them is with a freelance security firm out of Virginia. I'd be establishing a West Coast office."

"So you'd be going home?"

He noted with satisfaction that she still referred to California as home. But all he did was nod. "That would be the plan." He shrugged. "But now, everything has changed." He looked down at his daughter, who had rolled onto her stomach and was making swimming motions as she tried valiantly to get to another toy just out of reach. "Everything."

Four

Phoebe still sat on the blanket at Wade's feet and he reached down, putting his hands beneath her elbows and lifting her to her feet.

Her eyes were fastened on his face; her hands fell to rest against his chest for a moment before she moved away. She cleared her throat. "I understand it's going to take some time to get used to being a father," she told him, indicating the baby playing at their feet. Her voice was huskier than normal.

His body was having no trouble understanding that the woman he'd dreamed of for months—hell, years—was standing practically in his arms. *The mother of his child.* The anger he'd been hiding couldn't be summoned. Instead, he found the thought surprisingly arousing. Here, right before them, was something they'd made together during those wild, impossibly wonderful moments they'd shared in the cabin.

He exerted a little pressure until she stopped resisting and let him draw her forward. "It's amazing that we created that."

She nodded, looking straight ahead at his throat rather than tilting her head back. "It's a miracle."

He pressed a feather light kiss against her temple and felt her body shudder. "I'm still pissed at you. But thank you."

"I, ah—I don't think—"

"Don't think," he urged. "I won't if you won't."

He wanted to kiss her. He'd dreamed of it for so long that he could hardly believe this was real. Releasing her wrist, he put one finger beneath her chin and lifted her face to his. "Kiss me," he said. "Relax and let me—ahhh." In unison, they made an involuntary sound of pure pleasure as his thighs pressed into the cradle of her hips and his hardening body nudged the tender flesh between her legs.

He couldn't wait anymore. He dropped his head and fastened his mouth on hers, kissing her hard and deep, pouring all the longing and frustration of the past two years into the embrace. He felt her hands clench on his shoulders, but she wasn't pushing him away. Oh, no. He felt the way she melted against him, the way her fingers dug into his flesh and he knew she was going to be his again. But this time, he promised himself, he wasn't going to be a cad, wasn't going to leave her without a word.

This was a dream, Phoebe thought. It had to be. She'd imagined Wade kissing her so many times in the past year that it felt unreal to have him here, holding her against him. His tongue demanded her response, his big arms molded her close to the lean strength of his body. His state of arousal was impossible to miss, plastered against him as she was.

And memory rushed in, recalling the other time they'd been in this kind of embrace….

She was in heaven.

Phoebe nestled her face into Wade's throat and felt him shudder as they danced. This was a dream. It had to be. But oh, what a dream. She never wanted to wake up.

"Hey, you." She felt Wade's lips move against her forehead.

She lifted her head and smiled up into his gray eyes. Even in the low light on the dance floor, they seemed to blaze with heat and desire. For her? She was definitely dreaming.

"I want to take you home tonight." His voice was rough. "But I can't. You've got the car."

"You can drive," she offered. "Since we're practically going to the same place."

"I wish we were going home together," he said. "I'd like to hold you all night long."

His frank words were shocking, in a knot-in-the-belly exciting kind of way, and she knew her eyes widened.

"I don't want to rush you," he said quickly. "I realize this is new—"

"It's not new for me," she broke in. She reached up and placed a soft palm against his cheek. "Wade, don't you know I've—" loved you "—wanted this for a long time?"

He placed his hand over hers, holding it in place as he turned his head and pressed a hot kiss into her palm. He closed his eyes briefly. "I'm a dope. I never realized—"

"Shh. It's okay." She didn't want him to feel bad, or awkward, about anything. "Let's just start from this night."

"That sounds like a solid plan to me." He

smiled. Then his hand slid down, freeing hers as he cupped her chin and lifted her face to his.

She caught her breath, sure he was about to kiss her. Oh, God, she would melt right into the floor if he did—

"What's going on here?" The voice was strident, female, furious—and familiar.

Phoebe jolted, tearing herself free from Wade's arms.

Melanie stood in front of them, hands fisted on her hips. "Thanks for taking such good care of *my date,* sister dear," she said in a taut, sarcastic voice.

"Back off, Mel." Wade's voice was cool and commanding. "You didn't even notice I was leaving. Why the scene now?"

"Wade." Melanie turned luminous blue eyes on him and, instantly, the anger vanished and tears welled. "You—you brought me to the reunion. Why would you treat me this way?"

Wade shook his head. "Save the act for somebody who buys it. You couldn't have cared less what Phoebe and I were doing—"

"Phoebe and you." Anger distorted Melanie's pretty features and she tossed her long, shining hair back. Her eyes narrowed as she focused on Phoebe. "Sneaking around behind my back. My own sister. My twin. You've always wanted him, haven't you?

You've been in love with him the whole time, but he was mine."

"That's enough." Wade took Melanie's elbow, but she shook him off. Around them, people had stopped dancing and were staring openly, watching the drama unfold.

And Melanie loved it, Phoebe knew. She was the quintessential drama queen. This act was perfect for her.

"No," Melanie said, and her voice grew shrill. "That's not nearly enough. I will never forgive you for this, Wade. And you." She stabbed an angry finger in Phoebe's direction. "I wish I never had to see you again!"

And with one final toss of her bright tresses, Melanie whirled and stomped away, fury radiating from every move. The only thing that spoiled it was that she'd had far too much to drink and she staggered as she headed for the door, jostling a gaping group of classmates. "Get out of my way," she shrieked. She had worked herself into a sobbing fit of tears by that time.

Wade turned back to Phoebe. "We'd better go after her. She's had way too much to drink."

"Yes." She nodded. "It's a good thing she doesn't have a car."

"Come with me." He held out a hand.

She shook her head, her throat clogged with sobs. "No. She'll be impossible if she sees me. You know she'll calm down if she doesn't see us together."

Wade nodded, letting his hand drop to his side as he acknowledged the truth of her statement.

She turned and walked to the table where her small evening bag lay. "Here." She extended her car keys. "You take her home. I'll catch a ride later."

Wade took the keys. Then he caught her hand with his free one, bringing it to his lips for a moment. "I'll call you," he said.

Her heart leaped at the tender gesture. Could he really mean it? Could this evening, the moments between them on the dance floor, really be the day she'd dreamed of since she was old enough to feel her heart beating faster in his presence?

She offered him a shaky smile. "I'll look forward to it," she said, clutching the promise to her heart as he started away.

Just then, they heard tires shrieking in the parking lot.

"What the hell…?" Wade began to run full-out.

Phoebe rushed after him. She reached the door just in time to see her car flying out of the parking lot and down the road, and she knew immediately what had happened. Melanie knew Phoebe kept a spare key in a magnetic box in the wheel well. She'd taken the car.

Phoebe tore her mouth from Wade's. "This isn't— we can't do this." She was embarrassed that she was practically panting. And then she realized that she had a death grip on his wide shoulders. And worse, she'd made no move to separate their bodies, which were stuck like two slices of the peanut butter bread she often slapped together for lunch.

Wade's eyebrows rose. There was a glint in his eye that looked almost dangerous. "We just did."

"Anymore," she tacked on belatedly, removing her hands and stepping back, forcing him to release her.

"Ever?"

"Ever."

"Because…"

"Because your life is in California—" she spread her hands "—or wherever, and mine is here in New York now."

"Mine won't be wherever anymore," he informed her. "I'm going to live here if that's where you two will be. It's not half-bad."

"It gets really cold in the winter."

"I lived at West Point for four years, remember? Believe me, I know how cold it gets here."

"You always said you wanted to live somewhere warm," she reminded him.

"Being around for my daughter is a lot more important than worrying about the temperature. So your reasoning doesn't hold. What else is bothering you?"

"Well… It isn't fair of you to spring this on me without giving me a chance to think about it." *I can't get involved with him.*

Why? He wanted you after the funeral. And before, at the dance.

Wanting isn't love.

It's a start.

No false hope, she lectured herself. *He wanted to teach Mel a lesson at the reunion. It wasn't his fault she'd flown off the handle and everything had gone so horribly wrong. And the other… What guy's going to say no when a woman pretty much tears his clothes off and has her way with him?*

"Take your time. I'm listening."

But he wasn't. His eyes were on Bridget, watching her every move with an intensity that was painful to see. It was obvious he'd forgotten all about the kiss.

Bridget was happily oblivious. She was still lying on the floor with the toy she'd finally managed to snag. She rolled over on her back and was vigorously shaking it so that a musical chime sounded inside.

"She entertains herself well for her age." Phoebe glanced at her watch, trying to keep her voice from quavering. It tore at her heart to see Wade so desperately interested in his child. "But any minute now she's going to realize that it's snack time."

Friendly. Neighborly. That was the ticket. She could ignore her temporary lapse in judgment if she just concentrated on remembering Wade several years earlier as he'd been before—before anything had happened. They'd been friends. No reason they couldn't continue to be friends.

Wade still wasn't looking at her although she had a feeling he knew exactly why she'd changed the subject. But he didn't object, merely followed her cue. "Won't a snack spoil her dinner?"

"Not if it's a small snack like a cracker. And we don't usually eat until close to six." And then they'd sit down to dinner together, just like a real family.

A real family? What was she thinking? They were *not* a family. They were two people who had known each other for a long time and who now shared a child. But they hadn't shared most of the other basic details that members of a real family would have.

And they might not be a real family, but they certainly were going to be doing many of the things that families did. Her best bet, she decided, was to treat him as a tenant. Or no, maybe a boarder... he'd already announced he was moving in, so they were going to have to handle all the dumb little details, like meals and who bought toilet paper.

And there was the fact that they hadn't really talked about custody or visitation or any of the much bigger issues that had been haunting her all day. "I have to get dinner organized," she said, knowing she sounded less than gracious. "Nothing fancy, just a roast I put in the Crock-Pot this morning."

"I love red meat. It doesn't have to be fancy." He said it with a straight face and perfectly innocent eyes. Was she only imagining the double entendre?

She felt her face slowly heating and she turned away before he could see her blushing. "I'll make dinner if you'd like to play with Bridget."

"What do you do with her when you're alone?"

"She comes into the kitchen with me. I used to put her in an infant seat and sing to her but recently I've been able to lay a blanket down and let her roll around on it."

"She looks like you." He was watching Bridget again.

"Until she decides she wants something. When she's determined, she sets her jaw the same way you do, and her eyes get that intense look."

"I do not set my jaw."

Phoebe smiled. "Okay. I must have imagined it about a million times in the last twenty years."

He had to chuckle at that. "You know me well." The amusement faded from his eyes. "And that's another reason I need to be in Bridget's life. She deserves to know how her parents met, that we grew up together."

How her parents met? He made it sound as if they were an old married couple. That thought hurt. Hurt enough that she couldn't face him anymore, and she walked away without looking back. But when she reached the kitchen door and she did glance his way again, Wade was still standing there eyeing her with a speculative expression that made her very, very wary. She knew what he'd said about not fighting over Bridget... but could she trust him?

She watched him walk over and lower himself to the floor, tailor-fashion. He was incredibly limber for such a big man. Any man, really.

Bridget turned toward him with a delighted smile as he picked her up and set her in his lap. She promptly grabbed his finger and dragged it into her mouth.

Wade looked at Phoebe over his shoulder with a pained expression. A chuckle bubbled up and nearly escaped, and she couldn't help smiling as she moved into the kitchen. He was the one who'd wanted to get to know his daughter.

But she sobered rapidly as she checked the roast. Dear heaven, what was she doing? She couldn't just give in and let Wade live in her house!

But she didn't have a choice. If she didn't let him have free access to Bridget, he'd go to a lawyer.

In her heart, she knew she could never fight him on the issue, anyway. She felt terrible for keeping her pregnancy from him, worse that she'd never told him about his child. Guilt would kill her if she denied him one moment of time with his child.

And she'd never forgive herself for not telling him—or his family, when she'd thought he was gone forever—and letting his mother die without ever knowing she had a granddaughter.

Even if he'd been dead, as she'd assumed, she should have gone to his parents. She knew it, and she knew it was part of the anger that leaped in his eyes each time he dropped the carefully friendly facade.

She shivered as she assembled ingredients for biscuit dough and got out broccoli. He would never forgive her for that. Never.

The kid was a ball of fire. He sat on the floor of his daughter's bedroom later that evening, listening to the sounds of her bath progressing. He wondered who was wetter, Phoebe or the kid. Bridget made noise nonstop, giggling, squealing and occasionally shouting. In the background, intermittent splashing indicated that the bath wasn't quite over yet.

A few moments later, he heard Phoebe's footsteps in the hallway. She stopped in the doorway to the bedroom, the baby in her arms.

Bridget was wrapped in some kind of white towel with a hood, and she sent him a cheery smile that showed her two front teeth. Phoebe set her down beside him, and her diaper made a funny plastic hiss when she plopped down on the carpet. She immediately began waving her little arms, opening and closing her fingers, her babbling beginning to escalate in pitch until Phoebe snatched up a book and thrust it into her hands. Bridget squealed, a sound so high-pitched that it made him wince.

Yep, definitely a ball of fire.

And he meant that almost literally, Wade decided, eyeing the brilliant curls, still damp from her bath, that peeped out from beneath the edges of the white terry cloth on her head.

"Time to get you into your pajamas, little miss." Phoebe came over and sank down beside them holding a set of pink pajamas. "Here," she said to

Wade. "If you want to keep her next week, you'd better start practicing how to get baby clothes on and off. Sometimes I think the manufacturers sit around and brainstorm ways to confuse parents. Hey, c'mere, you." She deftly snagged the baby, who had begun to roll out of reach. "Oh, no you don't. It's bedtime."

Bedtime.

If someone had told him he'd be sleeping under the same roof with Phoebe two days after he'd flown east, he'd have figured they were nuts.

Bedtime. Phoebe.

How the hell was he going to sleep knowing she was right in the next room?

His daughter screeched as Phoebe set her in front of him again. "Go for it," she said, smiling.

"You're going to enjoy this, aren't you?"

"Oh, yeah." She chuckled. "I had to learn by doing, so it's only fair that you have the same experience."

"Thanks." He picked up the pajamas. There were snaps in places he didn't even know snaps could be sewn. And his hands were about twice the size of the little piece of clothing. This was going to be interesting. To his relief, Phoebe returned to the dresser from which the pajamas had come and began putting away items from a clothes basket set atop it.

Twenty minutes later, he breathed a sigh of relief. "There. I think that's it."

She came over and knelt beside him to look, then raised her gaze to his and nodded. "You got it. You pass Clothing the Baby 101."

He snorted. "What's 102?"

"Well, 102," she said, "is the class where you learn the Murphy's Laws of Childrearing. Like, 'a child does not have to go to the potty until after you have completely zipped, buttoned and snapped every loose fastener on a snowsuit.'"

"Sounds like you already know them."

"Teaching," she said, "has taught me at least as much as I've taught my students. Which reminds me, no school tomorrow. It's Saturday," Phoebe said. "Bridget's not much for sleeping in so we'll be up anytime after six or so."

"Six! You're kidding. I'm on leave."

She shook her head. "No such thing when you're a parent."

"I'll get up with her if you'd like to sleep in."

Phoebe looked at him as if he'd spoken another language. "You'd do that?"

"Well, sure. It must be tough being the one on call every minute of every day."

"It's not so bad." Her tone was stiff, as if he'd offended her. "You're welcome to get up with us," she said, "but until you learn your way around the kitchen and our morning routine, it's probably best if I get up."

"Phoebe." He rose and stopped her with a hand on her arm as she moved by him. "I am not trying to take your role in her life away, and I wasn't trying to slam you again for—I just want to learn everything there is to know about her."

She nodded, although she wouldn't look at him. "I'm sorry for getting prickly." The air of tension left and her shoulders sagged. "This is going to take some getting used to."

That it was. He watched as she bent over and picked up a discarded shoe and sock. She'd changed from the neat skirt and blouse she'd worn to school that day into a pair of faded jeans and a T-shirt, although she'd neatly tucked the shirt in and added a belt. Probably her version of hanging-around slob clothes.

Her backside was slim and rounded beneath the jeans. Damn, but he was annoyed with himself. He had a lot more important things than sex to think about tonight, and yet every time he looked at Phoebe all rational thought fled and he became one big walking male hormone.

Bridget let out a squeal and he came back to earth abruptly. Phoebe scooped the baby into her arms. "What are you fussing about, you silly girl?" she asked. "Would you like your daddy to read you a story?"

The kid couldn't exactly answer yes, but Phoebe motioned him over to the big maple rocker and set Bridget in his lap anyway. She came to him as if she'd known him all her short life, settling easily into his lap, then popping her thumb in her mouth. He read the story but after just a few minutes, her little head nodded against his chest and the thumb fell from her slack lips. Glancing down, he realized she'd fallen asleep.

His throat was tight and his chest ached; she was so precious! It was almost too much to believe, that this beautiful child was his.

He wanted to snuggle her against him but he was afraid if he moved she'd wake up. And so he sat with Bridget in his lap until Phoebe stuck her head around the corner of the door frame. "Is she asleep?" she asked in a hushed tone.

He nodded.

She came into the room and knelt at his side, lifting the baby into her arms. As she transferred Bridget's weight, the underside of her breast pressed against his arm for a moment, and her warm, intoxicating, feminine fragrance teased his senses. Instantly, awareness rose, and with it arousal. He wanted to kiss her again. Hell, he wanted to do a lot more than that. He watched silently as she rose to her feet with his child in her arms, and the knowledge that they had made this precious little person together was, oddly, a whole new kind of aphrodisiac. Their daughter had been conceived that day in the hunting cabin, and it didn't take much effort at all to recall the sweet, sizzling passion that had bound them together in far more than just a physical way.

Then Bridget's tiny arms hung limp and her head fell onto Phoebe's shoulder as Phoebe lifted her into her crib. She brushed a kiss across the fiery red curls as she laid the child down, and he swallowed hard, another emotion joining the riot of sensations rushing through him.

How was it possible to go from not even knowing his child existed to loving her more than he loved his own life in less than a day? He didn't even know her, really. And yet…he did. And he would. Another shock jolted him as he realized he could imagine her five years from now—because he'd known her mother at that age as well.

Phoebe turned and left the room on nearly silent feet, and he slowly pushed himself upright. He walked to the crib and gazed down at his daughter for a long moment. *I promise to be the best daddy I can be,* he vowed silently.

Then he followed his child's mother out of the room. They needed to talk about the changes that were about to occur in their lives.

Five

Phoebe was already at the table in her small dining room when he came down the stairs after unpacking his duffel, removing papers from her satchel and making neat piles carefully spaced on the table. She glanced up and sent him an impersonal smile. "Time to grade math tests."

He walked through the living room to her side, looking down at the work she was spreading out before her. "You do this often?"

"Just about every night." She smiled wryly. "The kids complain when I give them assignments, but I really should be the one whining. Every assignment they hand in multiplies my work by twenty-four students." She shrugged her shoulders as she pulled out her chair and took a seat. "It's going to get even more interesting when I start my next class. I'm taking a children's lit class that begins in January."

"I thought you already had a degree."

"Yes." She pulled out an ink pad and a stamp with a smiley face on it. "But in order to keep my teaching certificate I have to do continuing education every so often or work toward my master's degree. The specifics vary from state to state, but the general concept is the same. You probably have to do the same thing—keep your skills current, I mean."

"Yeah. Except now, if I were to stay in the Army, I'd be stuck behind a desk. My ability to hit a target dead center fifty times in a row isn't quite so critical anymore."

She bit her lip and he could see the moment when she realized that she'd reminded him of his forced change of career. Still, she continued to stare up at him, concern in her face. "Will you tell me what happened to you?"

He felt the muscles of his face tightening with the effort to keep a casual expression in place. "I have a piece of shrapnel in my leg. It's too risky to remove." He tried to smile. "Plays hell with airport security."

She didn't return the smile. "I meant how it happened."

He turned away, heading for the living room where he'd laid his book and reading glasses down. "One of my buddies stepped on a mine."

Out of the corner of his eye, he saw her flinch. "Did you see it?"

He nodded. A lump rose into his throat and refused to ease.

"I'm sorry," she said softly.

He managed a nod. "Yeah, me, too."

"You always wanted to be a soldier, didn't you?" A fleeting smile crossed her face. "I remember when Mel and I were about eight, you and the Paylen boys from down the street recruited us to be the enemy."

The lump in his throat dissolved as memory came flooding back, and with it came an irresistible urge to laugh. "Only that didn't last very long once my dad found out we were launching rocks at you out of that homemade catapult." He shook his head ruefully. "He always did have eyes in the back of his head."

Phoebe snorted. "He did not. Melanie ran and told on you."

"That twerp." His tone was fond. "I should have known. She ran and left you there alone. You were picking up the rocks and throwing them back. I never knew a girl could throw that hard, especially one your size."

She smiled smugly. "That's what the other softball players used to say when I was in high school."

Memories of Phoebe as a child, of himself during those same carefree years before the world had demanded its pound of flesh, came flooding back and he returned her grin. "We're lucky, aren't we, to have such good memories? I'd love to go back and be that age again."

To his surprise, her smile vanished. "I don't. You could not offer me anything to live my childhood over again." There was a grim, flat note that he'd never heard before in her voice that told him he'd struck some nerve.

His interest sharpened immediately. "That surprises me," he said.

"Growing up without a father in the picture wasn't always easy."

Now that he thought about it, he could recall occasional unkind comments about the twins' illegitimate birth. But… "You and Mel seemed pretty happy to me."

Her face softened, the line of her mouth relaxing

as her lips curved up the tiniest bit. "We were," she said softly.

He chuckled, determined to get her to relax her guard again. "Happiest when you were tormenting the poor boys in the neighborhood who were all fighting over you."

"You're confusing me with my sister now. I never tormented anybody. All the boys I knew had the hots for Melanie."

"Not all." He said it quietly, but the instant he spoke, the atmosphere changed. Electric awareness sparked and crackled as her gaze flew to his.

But she looked away again immediately. "You, too," she said, and in her face he saw her determination to keep things light between them. "When she and I were seniors, she chased you until you caught her, remember?"

He smiled wryly. "I remember. Are you going to hold it against me forever? I was a teenage boy. And God knows boys that age are helpless against an attractive female who's as determined as Melanie was."

To his surprise, she chuckled. "She *was* determined, too. All she talked about that summer was you. What to wear so that you noticed her, where to stand so that she just happened to be where you were headed. You told her once that she looked good in pink so we shopped for pink for the next three months. Have you ever tried to find a good shade of pink for a redhead to wear?" She shook her head, still smiling. "You didn't stand a chance."

He didn't stand a chance now, either. Did she know how desirable she looked? Her eyes were soft and faraway, her body relaxed where she'd angled herself toward him. Her lips looked so soft and inviting as they curved with happy memories....

They *were* soft and inviting. His entire body revved for action as the memory of the afternoon's kiss leaped into the forefront of his mind again. All he'd wanted to do was sink into her sweetness, live the dream he'd kept in his head during terrifying moments of hiding when he'd been sure he would be discovered any minute. Make love to her for real, not just in his imagination while he lay in an American military hospital in Germany. He'd wanted her so badly he'd nearly forgotten the child playing on the floor mere feet away.

And when he'd remembered, it had taken every ounce of self-control he possessed to look away and focus his attention on his daughter.

"Is it really that bad an idea?"

Her unusually timid tone dragged him out of his introspection. "What?"

She was regarding him with thinly veiled curiosity. "A penny for *those* thoughts. I said you're welcome to invite your father to visit for a few weeks if you like. He might enjoy the chance to get to know Bridget."

"What?" he asked again.

"I said—"

"I know what you said! I guess I'm just…surprised at the offer. Are you sure you want my father underfoot?"

She smiled. "I always liked your father. Unless he becomes a werewolf at the full moon, or has some really weird habits I don't know about, it would be fine with me."

"Or we could take Bridget to California to visit him. He's not a young man anymore, and he's never been on a plane in his life."

A fleeting expression crossed her face so quickly he wasn't even sure if he'd seen it or imagined it. Had it been panic? Dismay? "You could fly home and then come back with him," she said. "You know, so he wouldn't have to fly alone."

"I could." He spoke slowly, watching as she twisted her slender fingers together in a sure sign of nerves. But what the hell was it that was making her so uptight? "Don't you want to come home? See the old neighborhood? You could manage one long weekend, couldn't you?"

Her fingers were practically tied in knots. "I…I guess so." Although, she sounded so reluctant he nearly let it drop. But his curiosity was aroused. She didn't seem to care if she ever went back. Why not? She'd grown up there; her family was buried there. "We can visit Melanie's and your mom's graves, and I can show you where my mother's buried."

"All right." Her voice was quiet. "Let me check the calendar and see when we could go."

Had she really agreed to go back to California with Wade? Phoebe wanted to slap herself silly. He'd been in her life again for just two days and already he was turning her world upside down. She should boot him out.

But she knew she never would. Keeping Bridget's existence a secret had been more than a mistake, it had practically been criminal. And she deserved his anger. She'd really been like that overused cliché—an ostrich with its head in the sand. But at the time, it had been so much easier simply to cut her ties with her old life.

If only she had told his parents about Bridget when she first realized she was pregnant. Or… even after she'd thought he was dead.

But other people would have found out eventually. She could hear them now.

Just like her mother.

At least she knows who the father is. She and her poor sister didn't even have that.

Oh, yes. She knew how small towns could be. At least, the small town where she had grown up. Vicious gossips. Not everyone, of course. She'd known many sweet, wonderful people in her hometown. But she'd known more than she liked of the kind who didn't want to let their daughters come over to play with Phoebe and Melanie.

As if illegitimacy was catching.

If she was thankful for anything, it was for the fact that the world had changed since her own childhood. There were families of every kind out there today, and a child without a father wasn't treated any different than a child with two mothers, or a child who shuttled back and forth between her mother's and father's homes in the middle of the week.

She sighed as she looked at her calendar. She had two days off in October, and if she took off another day, they could go to California for a long weekend and make it back without being so pressed for time that it wasn't even worth the flight. She wasn't sure her courage was up to the task of introducing Wade's father to a grandchild he didn't even know existed, but she could tell that Wade wasn't taking no for an answer.

* * *

"Are you sure you'll be okay? Angie is just one street over if you need her," Phoebe told him for at least the tenth time on Monday morning.

"We'll be fine," Wade said. Again. "I'll call Angie if I need anything. And if anything happens, I'll call you immediately."

"All right. I guess I'll see you this afternoon."

"Bye." He held the door open for her. "Don't worry."

She stopped on the verge of descending the porch steps and looked back at him, a wry expression on her face. "I'm a mother. It's in the job description." Then she heaved a sigh and headed for the car as he closed the front door.

It had taken some fast talking on his part, but yesterday she'd agreed to let him keep Bridget this week without anyone stopping by to check on him. And even better, she'd informed him that she'd worked out her schedule so that they could go to see his dad in just a few weeks. She had to clear it with the principal of her building, but she hadn't anticipated any trouble. So he'd make the plane reservations as soon as she came home and gave him a green light tonight.

His dad. How in hell was he going to explain this to his father? From the time he'd entered adolescence and his dad had sat him down for their first big "talk," the watchwords of the day had been *responsible behavior* and *protection*. Not to mention *morality*.

He'd never mentioned his feelings for Phoebe to his parents, never really had the chance, given what had happened with Melanie's death. And then, after the funeral, after things had gotten so wildly out of control, he hadn't had the chance. He'd had to leave the next morning. And Phoebe hadn't answered her phone, although he'd tried half the night to contact her.

He could have simply walked down the street and banged on her door. Should have, he amended. But he'd known she was grieving, and he'd felt he had to respect that. And he'd felt guilty, taking advantage of her trust when she'd been so vulnerable. He should have stopped her.

In the end, he'd given up, promising himself that he'd get in touch with her in a day or two. But he'd been deployed to Afghanistan earlier than expected, with barely twenty-four hours to prepare and he hadn't had time or opportunity to do anything more than think about her.

A month or two later, he'd learned from his mother that she'd left town, that no one seemed to know where she'd gone. The East Coast, someone thought, so he'd made up his mind to visit her the next time he came home. He'd e-mailed her at the same address he'd used for years now—and to his shock, it was returned as undeliverable. And then his mother had had the stroke and all Wade's phone calls and e-mails with his dad had been filled with medical concerns. He'd only been home twice during that hectic time, once not long after his mom's first stroke, the second after her funeral.

He'd come home for that on a three-day leave and gone right back again afterward. He wouldn't have had time to look up Phoebe if she'd just moved to the next town, much less across the continent. Just days after that, he'd watched one of his buddies die when he'd stepped on an unexpected land mine. Others had been dragged away by insurgents operating out of the Afghanistan mountains. He'd barely been able to conceal himself, but he'd managed it. And then unexpected help in the form of an Afghan villager had saved his life and gotten him back to his own troops. On a stretcher, but alive.

He'd had plenty of time to think about her then, while he'd been recuperating. He'd needed her, had finally admitted to himself that he wanted to see if there was any chance that they might have a future together. He'd considered trying to find her, but he didn't really want to call her and tell her he was lying in a hospital bed. So he'd waited until he was well enough to look for her in person.

But he'd never stopped thinking about her, about any of the all-too-brief time they'd spent together. The revelation of his feelings—and hers, he was pretty sure—at the dance. Which had promptly been put on indefinite hold when Melanie had been killed.

And then Melanie's funeral. Or more specifically, what had occurred right afterward. God, if he'd relived that once he'd been through it a thousand times. And that was probably a conservative estimate. He would never forget making love to Phoebe for the first time, no matter the circumstances....

"Are you okay?"

Phoebe looked up, clearly surprised. She'd been sitting on the swing under the rose trellis at one side of her uncle's home. Just sitting and staring.

Her eyes were red and puffy as she looked at him, and Wade realized what an inane question it was.

"I mean, I know you're not okay, but I didn't want to… I couldn't leave without talking to you."

Her nod seemed to take enormous effort. Slowly, she said, "I just needed a break from it." Her voice trembled. "I can't go back in there and talk about her anymore."

The graveside service was complete; Melanie's family and friends had gathered at her mother's stepbrother's home to console each other, to share memories and simply to visit. It was a terrible thing that it took a funeral to bring everyone in a family together again. Phoebe's father had never been in the family picture, as far as Wade knew. And her mother had passed away the second year the girls were in college. Mrs. Merriman's two stepbrothers lived in the same area, although Wade had never heard either Phoebe or Melanie talk much about their extended family; he'd gotten the distinct impression at the funeral that the family hadn't really approved of Phoebe's mother.

He looked down at Phoebe and a fierce wave of protectiveness swamped him. God, what he wouldn't give to go back to the night of the reunion. He'd almost said no to Mel when she'd asked him to go. If he had, they might not be sitting here today.

But if he hadn't, he might never have realized or appreciated his feelings for Phoebe.

Wade cautiously sat beside her, waiting for her to tell him to get away from her. When he'd first gotten the news about the accident, he'd waited for his doorbell to ring. Waited for Phoebe to come scream at him for sending her twin sister off in such a rage that she'd wrapped her car and herself around a tree as she'd sped away from the reunion.

But Phoebe hadn't come. She hadn't called. And he hadn't dared to contact her. He could hardly move beneath the weight of the guilt he felt; if Phoebe piled more on him, he might just sink right into the ground.

His mother had heard about the funeral arrangements before he had. And it never occurred to her that he might not be welcome. Wade didn't have the heart to explain it all, so he'd gone with his family to the service and tried to stay as far away from Phoebe as he could. God, she must hate him now.

Still, when he'd seen her alone, he'd known he had to talk to her, no matter how she felt about him.

But she didn't seem to hate him. Instead, she leaned her head against his shoulder. "I wish it was last week again." Her tone was forlorn.

"Me, too." She felt as fragile as she sounded. He put an arm around her.

Phoebe sighed and he felt her warm breath through the thin fabric of his dress shirt and t-shirt. "Could we take a walk?"

He nodded. "Sure."

He rose and held out a hand. When she curled her small fingers around his much larger ones, he

felt like bursting into song. Entirely inappropriate—
and insensitive—under the circumstances.

He led her through the apple orchard and into the
forest above the house, following a well-worn path
that both wildlife and human had helped to create.
They simply walked for a long time. When the path
narrowed, he helped her over roots, up steep rises
and around boulders, and across a small creek.

They came to a small cabin, a tiny rustic struc-
ture. "What's this?" he asked.

"My uncles occasionally use it when they
hunt up here."

Along one side was a large pile of wood that
looked to him like a grand place for snakes to be
hanging out. When Phoebe started forward, he
stepped ahead of her, scanning the ground. Most
Californians went their entire lives without seeing
a rattlesnake; he'd just as soon be one of them.

He pushed open the door of the cabin and
stepped inside. When Phoebe followed him, there
was barely room for two people to stand in the
small space. It held a woodstove, an ax in surprisingly good shape, two wooden chairs and a table-
top that folded flat against the wall, a bunk bed
with a mattress nibbled to shreds by squirrels or
mice, and two shelves above the table. One shelf
was crammed with an assortment of canned goods

and a couple packs of matches. The other held a kettle, a large pot and a scant, mismatched pile of dishes with a few spoons and forks thrown in. There was no electricity, no light. An oil lantern and a bucket hung from pegs on the bunks.

"Wow," he said. "I guess this is just for emergencies. But it's got everything you'd need." Indeed, he'd seen much worse in some of the homes in the Afghan villages he'd been through.

"They come up here and clean it out before hunting season each year. They stock it and add a couple of towels and blankets." She rubbed an absent circle in the dust on the table. "We used to play up here. Thought it was the best playhouse in the world."

We, he knew, meant she and Melanie. He imagined to two little girls it had seemed pretty grand. But he didn't know what to say now that she was talking about her twin again, so he didn't say anything.

"One time Mel got her finger pinched pretty badly by a big crawfish we found in the stream," she said, pointing through the open door down the hill to where the pretty little brook wound its way through the dappled shade and rushed over the rough rocks. "And I saw a snake on that rock another day." She smiled a little. "I don't know who scared who more. I screamed. He couldn't move out fast enough."

She stepped back a pace, forcing Wade to move back against the bunks. Even so, her body brushed lightly against his and he was annoyed with his instant reaction. *Relax,* he told himself. *This is not the time to be thinking of sex.*

Phoebe didn't seem to notice that he was getting hard just being close to her. She was looking at the back of the door. When she went still, he put his hands on her hips and moved her a shade to one side so he could see what she'd been looking at.

There, cut into the scarred wood on the old door, were initials. PEM. MAM. Phoebe Elizabeth and Melanie Adeline. He almost smiled thinking about how much Mel had hated that middle name. She'd always complained that Phoebe got the pretty one.

"We did that," she said softly, "when we were about ten. I remember how daring we felt. It was Melanie's idea, of course." She reached out and traced a finger over the rough-hewn initials. "I never told anybody, and I don't think she did, either. It was our big secret." Her voice wavered. "We said we would bring our daughters up here someday and show them."

Her breath began to hitch, and his desire died instantly, submerged beneath concern. He turned her around, and she immediately wrapped her arms around his waist, pressing herself against him like a little animal burrowing into a safe place as she started to sob.

"Hey," he said softly. "Phoebe. Honey." Finally he gave up and just stroked her hair as she cried. His own eyes were a little damp. He'd known and loved Melanie, too. Even though she'd been a brat occasionally, she'd been a part of his life since he was just a kid. She'd been more important than anything else in his life for a short while, until he'd realized that they had very little in common, that he'd never be happy with her. So he'd cut the strings.

He never should have agreed to go to the reunion, but he'd thought it might be fun. Instead, it had been…a revelation. He hadn't anticipated what had happened with Phoebe that night.

How the hell could he have missed it? For so many years, she'd been right next door…and he hadn't seen that the woman of his dreams was right under his nose. No, he'd even dated her sister and still he hadn't realized that Phoebe was the right one for him.

He'd figured it out that night at the dance. Unfortunately, so had Melanie.

Mel hadn't been unkind, he reflected. Just self-absorbed most of the time. She would never have reacted so badly to the sight of Phoebe and him if she hadn't been drunk. He should have realized how out of control she was. But he'd been too wrapped up in Phoebe to care.

And her death was his fault.

Phoebe stirred then, lifting her head. She pressed her mouth to the base of his throat and he felt the moist heat of her breath sear him.

"Hey," he said. A guy could only take so much and he had just reached his limit. He doubted if she even realized how erotic the action had been. He took her arms in a light grasp and tried to step back. "Maybe we should head back."

"I'm in no rush." She spoke against his skin and, this time, she pressed a very deliberate open-mouthed kiss in the same spot. And holy sweet hell, her arms were still around his waist, holding him tight against every soft inch of her.

"Phoebe?" His voice was hushed. "Ah, this isn't such a good idea—"

She kissed the underside of his jaw and then his chin. As she strained upward on her tiptoes, her full weight slid against him. He exhaled sharply. He wasn't going to look down at her. If he did, there was no way he'd be able to keep from kissing her. And if he kissed her, he wasn't going to be able to stop with just a few kisses. Not the way he felt.

He stared straight ahead and set his jaw—

And then she sucked his earlobe into her mouth and her tongue played lightly around it. He dragged in a rough breath of raw desire.

And looked down.

Six

Holy hell.

Wade realized he was still standing at the front door. Which, thankfully, he had already closed, since no one passing by could possibly miss his body's reaction to that memory in the clinging sweatpants he wore. He shook his head ruefully. His system had been at full alert ever since he'd seen Phoebe standing in front of him on her porch Wesnesday afternoon.

It had only been five days ago that he'd found her, he realized with a jolt, and only two since he'd moved in. And yet in some ways it felt very familiar, very comfortable, as if they'd been together a long, long time. Pretty weird considering that they'd never really even dated, much less lived together.

But that was going to change.

He didn't do such a bad job for a novice on his first day alone with Bridget. Phoebe had shown him the whole diapering deal, and had prepared bottles and baby food for lunch. She'd told him that Bridget did well as long as she was kept to a reliable schedule, so he made sure he followed the instructions she'd left for him.

He'd gotten up early with Phoebe and they'd eaten breakfast while she went over the directions she was leaving for him. And then she'd left.

He knew it had been hard for her to walk out the door and leave them alone. If she'd said, "Call me at school if you have any problems," once, she must have said it ten times.

He took Bridget to a park at the end of the street in the morning, then brought her home and gave her a bottle. He didn't even have to rock her, just laid her down in her crib, since her little eyes were practically shut already. Then, while she was sleeping, he opened and dealt with a large envelope of mail that he'd brought with him in case he had time to kill sitting in a hotel room.

Bridget woke up again about two hours later, so he laid a blanket on the living-room floor and played with her there until time for lunch. Phoebe had told him he needed to feed Bridget promptly if he didn't want her to get cranky.

God forbid the kid should get cranky. He'd hate to have to call Phoebe for help. So he heated the mushy-looking stuff Phoebe had left in a small dish and opened up some pureed apricots to mix in with the cereal Phoebe had left out, all of which Bridget devoured as if she hadn't had a square meal in a month. Which he knew was a crock because he'd watched her tuck away a similar mushy mess for breakfast. Not to mention the bottle he'd given her before her nap.

After lunch, he walked around the yard with her in his arms, and they played a little more before she went down for her afternoon nap. When she awakened, he brought her out to the backyard to play until Phoebe got home.

"Hello there!"

Wade glanced away from the sandbox. An elderly woman in a faded brown dress covered by a stained gardening smock stood at the fence between the two yards. She resembled a tiny elf, with white hair twisted up in a messy bun and twinkling eyes that crinkled as she smiled at him.

"Hello." He got to his feet, lifted Bridget from the sandbox and covered the few steps to the fence with his hand outstretched. Before he could elaborate, the elf clasped his hand in a surprisingly firm grip and pumped his arm up and down in vigorous welcome.

"It's so nice to meet you, Mr. Merriman. I'm Velva Bridley, Phoebe's neighbor. She's a dear, dear girl and that little one is too sweet for words." She poked a gnarled finger into Bridget's tummy, eliciting the now-familiar squeal. "Phoebe's never talked much about you. Are you back for good now?"

"Ah, yes. I was in the army in Afghanistan. But yes, I'm here to stay." He figured he'd better get a word in edgewise while he had the chance. Later he could decide whether or not it had been the right word.

"That's wonderful! Just wonderful. Bridget's really at that age now where she needs to have her daddy around. I bet it about killed you to be overseas when she was born. I know it would have done me in for sure, if my Ira had missed an important event like that. Here." She reached into the basket hooked over her arm without even taking a breath and came up with a handful of some kind of pink flowers. "Last snaps of the season. I was

going to bring them over after Phoebe got home
but you can take 'em in and set 'em in water. Might
earn you some points, you know?"

"Snaps?" She'd lost him a few sentences back.

"Snapdragons. I always start mine indoors.
Never bring 'em out until the twentieth of May on
account of late frosts, my daddy always said, so I
start 'em in the house and set 'em out bright and
early on the twentieth. Got the first ones in the
neighborhood, and the last ones, too," she added
proudly. "Mine are hardy."

"That's, ah, that's nice." He cleared his throat.
"So you've known Phoebe since she moved in?"

She nodded. "Sweet, sweet girl. I brought her
my raisin cake that I always take to new neighbors,
and we hit it off right away. I was a teacher a long
time ago, before I married my Ira, and my good-
ness, it's amazing how things have changed in fifty
years."

He smiled. "You sound just like my father. He'd
happily go back fifty years to what he calls 'the
good old days.'"

"Not me!" Velva shook her head. "Give me the
age of technology any day. I love being able to
instant message my grandchildren and find out
what they're up to right that minute."

He almost laughed aloud. As it was, he couldn't

hide his grin. "Computers sure have made communication easier."

"My great nephew is in Iraq," Velva told him, "and getting e-mails a couple times a week really helps his wife to stay strong. I guess you and Phoebe know all about that, though."

"Hello there!"

Wade spun around. Phoebe stood on the back porch of her little house. "Hey," he called back. To Velva, he said, "It was nice to meet you, ma'am. I hope to see you again."

She looked amused. "Well, I expect if you're living next door, you're gonna see me from time to time. Now go greet your wife the way you want to."

Oh, boy. The lady had no idea what she was suggesting. He strode through the yard with Bridget and stepped up onto the back porch. Phoebe stood there in the navy skirt and the matching sweater with crayons on it that she'd worn to work.

"Hi," she said. "How did it—mmph!"

The sentence stopped abruptly as Wade hooked an arm around her waist and brought her up against his free side, setting his mouth on hers at the same moment.

He sought her tongue, sucking lightly and then probing deeply as he felt her body yield to his, her tension evaporating. She had put her hands up and clutched his shoulders when he'd grabbed her, and after a moment she flattened her palms, smoothing them over his back and up to his neck. Kissing Phoebe was like a drug, he decided, juggling the baby so that he could pull her closer. Addictive. Very, very addictive.

When he finally gentled the kiss and released her mouth, he blew out a breath. "Wow."

"What was that for?" She rested her forehead against his shoulder. Her hands slid down his chest and grasped his forearms.

"Ack!" Bridget threw herself forward and Phoebe put up her arms just in time to catch her.

"Hi, sweetie," she said. "We didn't mean to ignore you." Her face was red and she didn't meet Wade's eyes as she jiggled the baby and blew kisses against her neck, making Bridget giggle.

"For Mrs. Bridley," he said.

"Hmm?" She raised her gaze to his, but the connection to her earlier question seemed forgotten.

"The kiss," he said patiently. "Your neighbor is delighted that I'm home from Afghanistan. I didn't think we should disappoint her."

Phoebe's forehead wrinkled. "Oh." It was slightly gratifying to see that his kiss had scrambled her circuits so thoroughly. It was nice to know he wasn't the only one who felt that way.

He reached around her and held the screen door open, ushering her into the kitchen. "Interesting that she thinks you have a husband."

"I never told her that." Phoebe sounded startled.

"I guess she assumed. She's an interesting woman." He gave the adjective special emphasis, and Phoebe finally smiled.

"She's unique."

"Good word for it. How was your day?"

"My—? Oh, fine. How did you two get along?"

"Famously," he assured her. "I managed to change a couple of diapers and get more food into her than on her, and she took both her naps. So I'd say we were successful."

"Good." She looked genuinely pleased. "No emergency calls to Angie, hmm?"

"Nope. Not a one." He took the baby as she got down two glasses and filled them with ice and sweet tea. She cut a slice of lemon, which she squeezed into his, then stirred with a long spoon. As she slid one across the table to where he'd taken a seat, he said, "You remembered."

She stopped with her own glass halfway to her mouth. "Remembered what?"

He lifted his glass as if he were toasting her. "My tea. With lemon."

Her color had almost returned to normal from

their kiss on the porch, but it was back in an instant. "Just a lucky guess," she said.

Right. A warm feeling stole through him. She'd remembered.

She made spaghetti for dinner while he set the table and changed Bridget. It was just bizarre, Wade decided. To go from not even knowing how to find her to living with her in less than a week.

He had anticipated—hoped—that she would still be free and still have feelings for him when he finally tracked her down. And he'd thought about the rest of his life and he'd known he wanted it to include Phoebe. But he'd expected to court her, to date until she felt comfortable with him. So much for expectations, he thought, eyeing the cozy table, the baby in the high chair at one end, and the easy way Phoebe moved around him as if he'd always been there to get in the way.

He'd take this any day, although it certainly hadn't been anything he'd imagined in his wildest dreams.

While they ate, he told her about the other dad with the eight-month-old son he'd met at the park earlier, and she recounted her day. He set Bridget in her infant seat while he helped Phoebe clear the table, and then he said, "I'd like to invite my father to visit at Thanksgiving or Christmas. Do you have a preference?"

She was still looking at him and her eyes went wide. "Thanksgiving or Christmas?" she said faintly. "The holiday season is more than a month away."

He was puzzled. "Yeah. And...?"

"Exactly how long are you planning to stay in my house?" There was a note of what sounded like panic in her voice.

He looked at her closely, unsure he'd heard her right. "I don't have any plans to leave," he said evenly.

"But...but you can't just live with us forever! What if I wanted to—to get married or something?"

"To who?" He couldn't have kept the note of naked aggression out of his voice if he'd tried. He hadn't seen any signs of a man in Phoebe's life, but that didn't mean there wasn't one. "Is there somebody I should be worrying about?"

"No." As soon as the word popped out, she closed her mouth abruptly, as if she was aware that she'd just given him a major tactical advantage.

"Good." He stepped closer and she backed away, but the table was behind her and she couldn't go any farther. And he stepped forward again, until they were almost nose to nose. He reached for her wrists and captured them with his hands, then very slowly leaned forward until their bodies were pressed together from neck to knee. And just like the first time on the dance floor, he felt that little frisson of awareness, that feeling that this was right, click into place. "If you want to get married, that's fine. But the only man who's going to be putting a ring on your finger is me."

She gaped at him. Literally stood there with her mouth hanging open. "Marry...you?" Her voice was faint.

"Yeah." Dammit, she didn't have to act so repelled by the idea.

"No way."

Her instant refusal rattled him, but he wasn't about to let it show. "Why not? We share a child."

"That's not a reason to get married!"

"It is in my book," he said, struggling to keep his voice even. "You and I grew up in the same community, we have a lot of memories in common. We owe it to Bridget to give her a solid foundation." His eyes narrowed. "Don't you ever wish your childhood had been a little different?"

"I—no." She shook her head, avoiding his gaze, and he wished he knew what was going on behind those blue eyes.

"Why not?" he asked again. "Give me three good reasons why you won't marry me."

She was silent, looking aside with her head tilted down.

"You can't, can you?" He still held her hands and he slowly raised them, pulling them around his neck. She didn't embrace him but she didn't drop them when he released her hands and slid his arms around her, settling her more tightly against him. "We are good together, Phoeber," he said in a lower tone, "and you know it as well as I do. We know each other so well. We could make this work."

He put one hand beneath her chin and lifted her face to his, slowly setting his lips on hers. Her mouth was warm, her lips pliant as he kissed her, but slowly she began to respond, kissing him back with an ever-growing fervor that he remembered from the single time he'd made love to her. The response awakened the need for her that always lurked just beneath the surface, and he growled deep in his throat as he gathered her even more closely against him, pressing her head back against his shoulder as he sought the depths of her mouth.

She clung to him, giving him everything he demanded. Sliding one hand up her hip, he slipped it beneath the bottom of her sweater. The skin above the waistband of her skirt was warm and silky, and an even stronger surge of desire shook him.

"Marry me," he muttered against her mouth.

"This isn't fair," she said, pulling her mouth back far enough to get the words out.

He kissed the line of her jaw. "I don't care about fair. All I care about is making us a family."

Was it his imagination or did her body tense the slightest bit?

It was definitely not his imagination that she withdrew from the kiss slowly but surely, stepping back and straightening her sweater. "Give me time to think about it. This is the rest of my life we're talking about here." Her voice was quiet but he recognized that tone. When Phoebe dug in her heels about something, there was no budging her short of using dynamite. And he had the sneaking suspicion that might not even do it.

"It's the rest of all of our lives," he reminded her.

"I know." She sounded weary. "Let me think about it."

"When can I expect an answer?"

She spread her hands. "I don't know. We can talk again…when we come back from California. All right?"

He nodded grudgingly, not happy about it but unwilling to push further in case he really annoyed her and she decided she couldn't stand him for the rest of her life. "All right."

The following weekend, Wade made the travel arrangements for their California trip. The weekend after that, they left right after Phoebe took leave from school at lunch on Friday.

Bridget fussed for a bit early in the flight but, after a bottle and some cuddling, she settled down and went to sleep for a while. As Phoebe looked down at the beautiful baby girl in her arms, she was amused again by the determined little chin…oh, that was Wade all over.

Wade. Amusement faded as she thought of his marriage proposal, if it could even have been called that, and the fist squeezing her heart tightened painfully. He wanted to marry her to make a home for their child, and because they knew each other well enough to make it work. But he hadn't said anything about love.

Could she marry him, knowing that he didn't love her the way she wanted? Oh, he cared for her, she didn't doubt that. And he clearly desired her. But he'd *loved* and desired Melanie once, and she knew that her sister would always hold his heart. She, Phoebe, had never expected that she'd have any part of him, much less marry him and bear his children, so how could she complain?

As the jet began its landing descent, Phoebe hungrily gazed out the window. There was Mission Bay, the water sparkling in the sunlight, and the golf course of La Jolla. The university, the naval base, the zoo. The lighthouse, high atop a cliff.

The freeway heading north was packed with traffic all rushing to exit the city, all driving at typical breakneck speed California-style. She could hardly wait to be in the middle of it.

And before she knew it, they were. Wade had rented a car for the long weekend since he didn't have a car of his own. He'd never seen the need before, he'd told her. When he'd come home, he'd just driven one of his parents' vehicles.

As they entered the outskirts of their old neighborhood, Phoebe realized she was holding her breath.

It still looked much the same. Small yards shaded by flowering trees; tricycles, bikes and skateboards littering yards and driveways; brilliantly colored flowers fronting many of the carefully kept small homes.

You could see the ocean from the end of their block, she knew. And as Wade drove to the end of the dead-end street and turned around so that he could stop the car along the curb in front of his father's house, she craned her neck to look out over the steep cliff just beyond the barrier the city had placed there.

She couldn't see the beach, which had to be

reached by going down a steep, winding road from the top of the hill, but the vast expanse of the ocean lay before her. Today it was a deep, dark blue, with bouncing whitecaps tossing spray into the air in all directions. A wave of nostalgia hit her like a rough breaker, smashing over her, swamping her.

She'd missed that view so much. Who was she kidding? She wasn't an East Coast girl. She loved the wild, untamed Pacific. She wanted Bridget to grow up with memories of smooth, rounded cobblestones littering the beach, of water so cold it made your teeth chatter. She wanted to take her daughter to the pretty beach in Laguna Niguel where they had spent a day each year on a sort of family mini-vacation, to tell her stories about her grandmother and her Aunt Melanie….

But it was harder here, Phoebe thought, swallowing. Here where all the memories of her sister and her mother lurked, it was harder to ignore her grief and go on. That had been one of the main attractions about the job in New York. But now the past she'd run from had caught up with her, and because of her own stupidity, she owed it to Wade to stop running and let him get to know his daughter.

Phoebe turned her gaze to her old home, four doors down the street, wondering about the family who lived there now. Did they have a pet? Her mother's poodle, Boo-Boo, had dug holes all over their backyard until he'd gotten too old to do more than lie on the porch and yap at the neighborhood kids on their bikes.

Were there children? She couldn't tell from the outside. The garage door was down and there were no bikes or kid equipment littering the yard. And a tall hedge made it impossible to see into the backyard. Was the lemon tree her mother had planted still there?

"Hey." Wade's voice was quiet. "You okay?" He touched her back lightly.

"I'm okay." She squared her shoulders. "It's odd to come back here and not be able to go home, if you know what I mean."

He nodded. "I can imagine, even though I've never experienced it."

But in a way, he had. "How different is it without your mom?"

He shrugged. "Not so. Dad always did give her a hand with the housework and cooking, so it's not like he was helpless."

"But the dynamics change." Oh, did they ever. Some of the most miserable times of her life had been the weekends and college breaks she'd spent at home in the first year after her mother had passed away. It wasn't like it had once been before between Melanie and her. They'd each been grieving, but instead of drawing closer, their grief had isolated them and she'd found herself reluctant to visit as much. It was easier to stay on campus and immerse herself in her life there than it was to go home and enter the silent world of grief that she and Melanie had shared. Mel had stayed in their house, gone to a community college. She'd never really gotten away from the memories and Phoebe had sometimes wondered if Mel resented her for that. It had been Melanie's choice to keep living there, but had it kept her grief from lightening?

Phoebe grieved, too, but life had gone on and, somewhere along the way, she'd made the decision to do the same thing.

"I guess you know all about the way a family changes," he said quietly.

She nodded.

"When your mom died, things changed. But after Melanie died, your whole world was different, wasn't it?" The quiet sympathy in his voice was nearly her undoing.

She swallowed. "Yes. Losing Mom was hard. But losing Mel… Logically, I know that her death wasn't the catalyst for my life taking such an unexpected turn, but sometimes it seems as if one thing just led to the next."

A muscle jumped in his jaw and she realized he had clamped his teeth tightly together. "I guess it must." He sounded as if his words were being dragged from him and she glanced at him, wondering what on earth was wrong.

"Are you feeling well?" she asked as she unbuckled Bridget's car seat.

That appeared to startle him. "Yeah." He indicated the child still sleeping on her mother's shoulder. "Let's go in and introduce Sleeping Beauty here to her grandpa."

Phoebe's stomach was in knots as Wade guided her to the side porch door that the family always used. He opened the door and gestured for her to precede him. As he entered behind her, he called, "Hey, Dad. Where are you?"

"Hello." A deep rumbling voice much like Wade's came from the direction of the kitchen.

Wade stepped around her and headed down the hallway leading to the kitchen, and a moment later his father appeared. "Well, this is a surprise! I thought you were going to be on the East Coast for at least a month." The two men grabbed each other in a typically male, back-pounding hug.

Phoebe stood, rooted to the spot in horror. A *surprise?* Hadn't Wade told his father about Bridget yet?

"...someone here I want you to meet," Wade was saying as the men walked toward her.

Reston, Wade's father, did a double take when he saw her standing there. "Phoebe Merriman. I didn't know you were back in town, honey! It's great to see you—and who's this?" His tone was filled with delight. "I didn't even know you'd gotten married and here you're a mama."

An immediate silence fell, awkwardness hanging in the air like thick smoke.

"Aw, hell." Reston scrubbed a hand over his face. "Forget I just said that. Mothers don't have to be married these days, I know." He stumped on toward Phoebe, and she remembered that his uneven gait was the result of arthritis that forced him to favor one hip. When he reached her, he peered down at the sleeping child she had shifted to hold in the cradle of her arm. "Aren't you a beauty?" he asked, his tone tender as he brushed a finger along Bridget's cheek, catching one fiery curl on his fingertip. He chuckled. "Got that Merriman red hair, didn't she?"

Phoebe nodded, forced herself to smile. "When she was born, all the nurses laughed because it was sticking straight out all over her head."

Wade cleared his throat. "Ah, Dad? Can we sit down?"

Reston straightened and shot his son a wary look. "Okay. You bringing bad news?"

Wade shook his head. "No, I think you're going to like this news." He ushered Phoebe ahead of him into the living room and took a seat beside her on the couch. "There's no easy way to tell you this, so I might as well just say it. Phoebe and I…well, the baby's name is Bridget and I'm her father."

Seven

I'm her father.

Phoebe wondered if Wade's words sounded as shocking to his parent as they did to her. How long was it going to take before she accepted that Wade was really alive—and in her life for good, if he had his way?

Reston Donnelly's eyes widened and his mouth fell open. "Get out!"

"It's true." Wade smiled at his father's obvious astonishment. "You're a grandfather."

Reston's gaze flew back to Bridget. "That's—you're—she's my granddaughter?"

Wade nodded.

"Why…?" Reston cleared his throat. "Why didn't you tell me?"

"He didn't know," Phoebe said hastily. She couldn't bear the look of hurt on Reston's face. "I'm sorry I didn't tell you—"

"Phoebe thought I was dead." Wade cut off her attempt at apology. "She heard the first news after my unit got cut off, but she never got the correction when I was found."

Reston's head snapped up from his inspection of Bridget, his expression changing from hurt to horrified. "Oh, honey. If I'd known where to find you, I'd have let you know. No one knew where you'd gone after…"

"I know. I needed a fresh start."

Reston nodded. He looked back down at the child in Phoebe's arms. "I imagine you did." His gaze landed on his son. "How'd you find her?"

Wade uttered a short bark of laughter. "Hounded every person she'd ever known, hoping someone could tell me where she was. I finally got lucky with one of her high-school friends."

"Must have been the shock of your life when he showed up alive." Reston transferred his gaze back to Phoebe.

"You could say that." No way was she getting into that minefield. "Would you like to hold her?"

Reston nodded. "You bet." Phoebe's heart melted at the look in Wade's father's eyes. Dazed. Delighted. Tender.

Reston nodded. "Please." He settled back in his chair as Phoebe rose and approached, laying Bridget in his arms. He cradled her in one gnarled hand, gently brushing her cheek with the other. "Oh, you're a little beauty," he whispered. "Bridget. Bridget Donnelly. That's a good Irish name." He shook his head and the light reflected the sheen of tears in his eyes. "Your grandma surely would have loved you."

Phoebe's chest hurt as she fought not to sob. She didn't dare glance at Wade. She could imagine the wintry expression on his face without having to see it. But she didn't try to correct Reston's assumption about Bridget's last name. There would be time for that.

Bridget started to fuss and Wade said, "Here. Let me see if I can settle her." Phoebe did glance at him then, but he wasn't looking at her. He lifted the baby and held her against his shoulder; it was amazing how natural the gesture looked after such a short time. Bridget quieted immediately and Wade grinned. "She's turning into a daddy's girl."

Phoebe relaxed, one of those silly maternal things that happened when one's child was well-behaved. Before Bridget, she'd never understood how parents could be so uptight. A screaming session in the middle of Wal-Mart could change your perspective pretty quickly. She dug in her bag and handed Reston a photo album into which she had slid pictures of Bridget right after her birth and at various ages since. "I brought you some pictures."

Reston moved to the sofa and patted the seat beside him. His face was soft. "Sit down here and tell me about her."

"I'll join you." Wade's voice was quiet.

She glanced up at him, but he was looking at the album and wouldn't meet her gaze. She knew he'd looked through the photo albums she'd kept since Bridget's birth…but she'd never told him much about his daughter's early days, she realized.

Remorse shot through her for about the zillionth time, and she mimicked his father's motion, patting the cushion on the other side of her. "That would be nice. I haven't told you that Bridget was almost born in the middle of a wedding."

Wade froze. "What?"

She tugged on his arm and he sank down beside her, patting Bridget's back in a distracted manner.

Smiling, she opened the photo album. On the first page, she'd placed the only picture she had of herself during her pregnancy.

"This picture was taken the day Bridget was born. I went to the wedding of a coworker and the photographer snapped this shot before the service while I was standing at the guest book." She chuckled. "It's a good thing he got a picture of me then!"

"You went into labor at the wedding?" Wade was looking a little green around the edges.

"I was already in labor," she corrected. "But I was too dumb to realize it until about halfway through the ceremony. I just thought my back hurt from being on my feet so much the day before."

Reston guffawed. "Bet you'll never be that dumb again."

A silence followed his hoot of laughter. A *pregnant* silence, she thought, as she cast around for a response. Would she ever be pregnant again?

Wade wanted her to marry him…but she hadn't really let herself dwell on exactly what that would mean. Would he want other children?

An involuntary quiver deep in her belly made her shiver suddenly as her thoughts immediately turned to how those children would be created. Every nerve cell in her body homed in on Wade's large, warm body sitting so close to hers. Hastily, she shoved the photo album into Wade's hands and leaped to her feet. "I'd like to freshen up."

Sometimes it seems as if one thing just led to the next.

Wade could still hear the grief in Phoebe's voice as he lay in the single bed in his childhood room that night. That phrase had been haunting him.

God, but he felt like the lowest of the low. She hadn't said it, and he was pretty sure she hadn't even thought about how it had sounded. But he knew that her life would never have turned out the way it had if it wasn't for him.

If it wasn't for you getting her pregnant, you mean.

Well, yeah, that was what he'd meant. If he'd kept his hands off her, if he'd given her the comfort that she'd really needed instead of the sex she'd thought would make her forget the pain, if he'd been less of a self-absorbed jerk afterward…. If, if, if.

No point in going any farther down that road. It was what it was. He and Phoebe had a daughter together. And they owed it to Bridget to work out their issues and give her the happy, stable home she deserved.

Which was why he had to figure out a way to get Phoebe to marry him. She had seemed so resistant to the idea. Why?

He was sure it wasn't physical. God knew, they had enough chemistry between them to start a brush fire.

Unable to sleep, he rose and padded down the stairs in his bare feet. The little photo album Phoebe had given his father lay on the coffee table in the living room. The streetlight outside cast a few bars of light across the room and he idly picked up the scrapbook and flipped through it. Phoebe had spent more time earlier taking them through Bridget's young life. Rolling over, sitting up, first teeth. Stuff he would have laughed at if the married guys in his unit had talked about it.

"Wade?"

Startled, he nearly dropped the album and he juggled it for a moment until he had it in his hands again. Phoebe stood on the lowest step.

"What are you doing?"

Her hair was down. Even in the darkened room, he could tell it was long. Longer than it had been a year and a half ago. He hadn't realized it because, until now, she'd worn it scrambled up in a messy knot atop her head. It should have looked ridiculous but it was oddly charming. And even more so since he was pretty sure she hadn't tried for that effect. For Phoebe, it was expedient to shove her hair up out of the way.

If it had been Melanie, she'd probably have worked on it for an hour in front of a mirror to achieve a like effect. *Melanie.* Were they ever going to talk about her? Her memory hovered between them like a helium balloon tied to a kid's hand.

"Are you all right?" She was standing there with a concerned look on her face, clad in what resembled a men's-style button-down shirt, although from the way it caught her at mid-thigh and fit her curves, he was pretty sure it hadn't been designed for a man.

"I'm not sure," he said slowly.

Before he knew what she intended, she was down the steps and across the room, placing one small, cool hand on his brow. "Do you feel sick?"

He looked at her, standing so close to him in the shadows of the small living room, her eyes wide and worried. "No," he said. "I'm not sick."

Immediately she began to withdraw her hand but he caught it before she could move away. "Don't go."

She stilled, but didn't speak. Her gaze flew to his face again as he tugged on her hand, drawing her closer. He threaded one hand through her hair, cupping her cheek, and rubbed his thumb lightly over her lips. She swallowed. "Wade, I..." She stopped and shook her head. "I'm glad we came to visit your father."

He smiled, letting his hand drift from her face to play with the cool, silky strands of hair. "Me, too. Bridget's already got him wrapped around one of those little fingers. Thanks for letting him give her a bottle tonight."

"He never stopped talking to her the entire time. Did you notice that?"

He nodded. "He sounded pretty ridiculous."

"Like someone else I know."

"Hey! I do not sound ridiculous."

"You're right," she agreed. "Just infatuated. Totally, ridiculously infatuated."

"It would be impossible not to be," he agreed. "She's perfect."

"Well, almost, maybe," she conceded.

"She's a lot like her mother," he said. "Wrapping men around her little finger."

She snorted beneath her breath. "You know darn well I never wrapped a man around any part of me."

Silence fell between them as her retort registered.

Immediately, his thoughts turned to the cabin in the woods where he'd made love to her. She'd been wrapped around him then, her long, slim legs gripping his hips as he'd plunged into her with so little restraint he winced at the memory even as his body responded to it. "I'd have to disagree with that," he said, aware that his voice had roughened.

Phoebe moaned softly, dropping her head so that her hair fell forward to hide her expression. "Bad choice of words."

He put a finger beneath her chin. She might not be willing to talk about Melanie, but he'd be damned if he was going to let her ignore what was between them, too. "Not so bad. It reminds me of making love with you." He caressed her bottom lip with his thumb again. "Do you remember what it was like between us?"

She drew her breath in sharply and her body tensed. For a moment, he thought she wasn't going to answer him at all. But finally, she whispered, "I remember."

He was more pleased than the two small words warranted that she'd admitted it. Sliding his arms around her, he drew her close. "Let's make a new memory."

She didn't resist as he found her mouth with his. His pulse doubled its rate when he felt her small hands creep around his back. Her mouth was soft and yielding beneath his, her body equally so. Touching the closed line of her lips with his tongue, he gently traced the tender seam until she opened for him, then deepened the kiss as he gathered her closer.

He took her arms and pulled them up around his neck as he feasted on her mouth. She was so much shorter than he was that she had to stand practically on her toes, throwing her off balance and bringing her body to rest against his. Her soft belly pressed against him and his hardening shaft nestled into the cleft at her thighs, sending a surge of pleasure dancing up his spine.

Tearing his mouth from hers, he kissed a trail along the silken column of her neck, then nuzzled the collar of the nightshirt out of the way. She had only buttoned it as high as the one between her breasts, and he exposed a generous expanse of her pale flesh until the shirt drooped off one shoulder.

"Beautiful," he breathed against her skin. He brought up a hand and cupped one breast in his palm, lightly brushing his thumb across the nipple through the thin fabric of the shirt.

She made a small sound and her head fell back.

"The baby was fussing so I—" Reston stopped halfway down the stairs with Bridget in his arms. Even in the dim light, Wade could see his father's eyebrows rising.

Phoebe jerked upright with a startled sound, but when she tried to pull away, Wade refused to let her go. She buried her face in the front of his shirt as Wade met his father's speculative gaze over her head.

"You do know this is how you got the first one, right?"

Wade couldn't prevent the snort of laughter that escaped. "No, Dad," he said. "This is absolutely, positively *not* it."

It was Reston's turn to grin while Phoebe made a quiet moan of mortification. "So," he said. "You gettin' married?"

"Yes," said Wade.

"No," said Phoebe.

If his father's eyebrows had moved any higher they'd have merged with his hairline. "I see." He turned and started back up the stairs with the baby, who appeared to have gone back to sleep. But just before he disappeared, he stopped and looked back, and his shadowed eyes held a sober expression that contrasted sharply with the grin of a moment ago. "That would please your mother," he said quietly to Wade. Then he looked at Phoebe, who still hadn't moved. He shook his head and his shoulders slumped. "Sometimes I still can't believe she's not here. She'd be tickled down to her toes with that baby girl."

"Old manipulator," Wade said quietly when he was sure his father was out of earshot.

Phoebe lifted her head from Wade's chest, although she couldn't bring herself to meet his eyes. His father's final words echoed in her ears, awakening all the guilt and remorse she felt for keeping the news of Wade's child to herself.

Looking down the path her life was about to follow, it didn't take a fortune-teller to predict heartbreak. Then again, if she didn't marry him, that was a given.

She knew she was going to say yes, even before she opened her mouth. She'd rather live with Wade, knowing he didn't love her the way she craved, than live without him. She'd thought he was dead and gone forever and it had felt as if half of her had died, too. She was going to take him any way she could get him, regardless of the pain she knew lay in wait.

"All right," she said quietly.

"What?" Wade looked puzzled. He was still staring at the doorway where his father had been a moment ago.

"All right, I'll marry you."

That got his attention. Wade's gaze shot to hers again and his gray eyes focused on her with a blazing intensity that made her cringe inwardly. "My father catching us kissing made you change your mind?"

She shrugged. "I just—I know Bridget deserves a family. An intact family," she amended. He'd been right. A child *was* a good reason to get married. Every child deserved a set of parents.

And grandparents. I will never forgive myself for depriving her of knowing her paternal grand-mother. If it was for a day, or a month, or even years and years, I should have thought about how they would feel.

Wade was looking down at her and his eyes still felt like two lasers examining her soul.

God, had she really just agreed to marry this man? This man whom she'd loved since she'd been a child on the playground? She had reasons, she reminded herself. Bridget needed a father; she deserved a stable childhood with two parents. Raising a family on a teacher's salary could be done, but it wouldn't be easy. With Wade's help, they'd be able to give their daughter the things Phoebe wanted for her: music or dance lessons, sports opportunities, all the myriad activities that children of the modern world pursued.

Phoebe, on the other hand, only needed one reason to marry Wade: love. She'd loved him for what seemed like forever. And then he'd died and she'd had to accept it, though it had felt as if her heart had been permanently shattered.

And then…then she'd found out he hadn't died at all.

Her stupid heart had bounced back a lot faster than her head. She was still having trouble believing that all this was real. But her heart was having no trouble at all loving Wade with even more intensity than she had when she was seventeen years old and he'd belonged to her sister.

"Good," Wade finally said, startling Phoebe out of whatever internal argument she was having with herself. The expressions fleeting across her face ranged from tenderness to the deepest sadness he'd ever seen. He wasn't sure he wanted to know what she was thinking about. "When?"

"I don't know!" She looked startled again. "Do we have to decide tonight?"

He nodded. "Yeah. Before you change your mind." He snapped his finger. "I know. We could stop in Vegas on the way home."

Phoebe's expression was horrified; he almost laughed out loud. "I am *not* getting married in a quickie wedding chapel in the gambling capital of the world! Besides, what would we do with Bridget?"

He shrugged. "Take her with us?"

"No," she said. "Absolutely, positively no way. We go back to New York and apply for a license like normal people, wait until we get it, and do this right. I have no intention of telling Bridget we got married in Las Vegas on the spur of the moment."

"Or our other children." He tried to make it sound innocent; he couldn't resist teasing her.

"Our other—" She stopped and narrowed her eyes. "You said that just to rattle me," she accused.

He grinned. "Did it work?"

A wry smile lifted the corners of her mouth. "I guess it did."

He was still embracing her, still deeply aware of the pounding of his pulse, of her soft curves and the way her hips cradled him. Holding her gaze, he put both hands on her hips and pulled her more firmly against him. Then he shifted his hips slightly, pressing himself so snugly against her that he nearly groaned aloud. "I want you," he said quietly.

She closed her eyes. "Not here." Her voice was so soft he could barely hear her.

"No." He pressed a short, hard kiss to her full pink lips. "Not here. But soon."

Eight

They were off the plane in New York and heading away from the airport. Bridget had just fallen asleep in her car seat when Wade said, "Thank you for letting me bring Bridget out to meet Dad. He adored her."

He glanced over to see Phoebe smiling a little uncertainly. "You don't have to thank me." The smile faded. "I should have gotten in touch with you as soon as I found out I was pregnant."

Unspoken between them was the knowledge that his mother had never known she had a grandchild on the way, or a granddaughter.

"You should have," he agreed.

Even from the driver's side, not looking right at her, he could tell that Phoebe's body went stiff. The temperature in the car dropped about ten degrees. If he'd been looking to pick a fight, he'd have been satisfied with the first volley. But…

"But I understand why you didn't. And maybe it wouldn't have mattered," he said, and with the words, the hard knot of anger that had hidden deep inside him finally uncoiled. "My mother's body was giving out. After she had the first stroke, I learned a lot more about strokes, what causes them, what kind of progress stroke patients make, what therapies are used…. It's probably a blessing for both her and my dad that she didn't live for years with minimal function."

"How can you say that? Don't you think your dad would rather have had her alive in any condition—"

"I'm sure he thinks he would have. But while I was recuperating I saw a lot of victims of head injury and soldiers who'd had strokes after other catastrophic injuries. And I know my mother never would have wanted to live like that." He paused. "There's no dignity in some kinds of living. I wouldn't have liked that for either of them."

She nodded and her silky hair slid over the back

of his hand. It felt like cool silk and his one-track mind instantly shot ahead to the night looming before them. The night when they would put Bridget to bed and then it would just be the two of them. Alone.

The next few hours crawled by. They arrived back at Phoebe's house and unpacked the car, then had a late dinner. They'd lost three hours on the trip east but it was still only eight o'clock when Bridget went down for the night.

Wade followed Phoebe into the room as she laid the baby in her crib, and they looked down at her together.

"She's incredible," he said softly.

Phoebe smiled. "She is, isn't she?"

He put his arm around her shoulders and led her from the room. Phoebe tugged the door nearly shut as they entered the hallway. When she turned back to him, she met his eyes with a wry smile and blew out a breath. "I'm nervous," she said with a laugh.

He smiled. "You don't have to be." He took her hand and led her into the bedroom and across to the big bed in which she slept. Setting his hands on her shoulders, he drew her to him and slid his arms around her, simply holding her, absorbing the amazing sensation of having Phoebe in his arms.

She slipped her arms around his waist and snuggled close.

It was a sweet, sweet moment. Wade felt his heart swell with emotion. *I love you.*

He nearly said it aloud. Might have, except that he was a coward. Plain and simple, a coward.

The night they'd danced, he thought Phoebe had indicated she could care for him. But was it long-term? Sure, she'd made love with him—after her sister's funeral when no one in their right mind could say her judgment was sound. And she'd clearly been overwhelmed to see him again after she'd thought he was dead. But he was the father of her child. And they'd been friends since their own childhood. She didn't have to love him to be thrilled that he was alive.

She got so quiet every time Melanie's name came up that he could barely stand it. Did she blame him? God knew, she wouldn't be wrong. He should never have let Mel leave alone that night.

So he didn't speak aloud. Her very silence suggested that her heart wasn't entirely in this relationship and that made him nervous as hell. She might never forgive him for Melanie's death but there was no way he was going to let her shove him out of her life. He loved her, even if he could never tell her.

Tonight, he would show her.

He stopped beside the bed and took her into his arms. After a moment, she lifted her face to him and his heart leaped as he lowered his mouth to hers. Whatever else was between them, there was no arguing with the chemistry they created together. He kissed her for a long, long time, using his lips and tongue to show her how he felt, simply made love to her mouth until they both were breathing hard and his blood was pounding through his veins.

When he lifted the hem of her T-shirt, she raised her arms and let him pull it over her head. She shook her head as he tossed the shirt aside and her hair fell around her shoulders, emphasizing the lacy white bra she wore.

"You're beautiful." He reached around her and dispensed with the bra, and wanted to howl at the moon when the full, firm mounds of her breasts, capped by rosy nipples, were revealed. He cupped them in his hands and smoothed his thumbs over the taut tips as she lifted her hands to the buttons of his shirt.

She managed to get about half the buttons undone before she threw her head back with a half laugh and said, "I can't concentrate."

He smiled, lowering his head to the slope of her breast and tasting the tender flesh. "Can I help?"

He quickly tore the shirt open and shrugged it off, then unfastened his pants as well and pushed them off along with his boxers. Turning his attention to her pants, he unzipped them and put his thumbs at the sides, pushing until she, too, had kicked the last of her clothing away.

Then he urged her onto the mattress.

As he followed her down, he said, "Do you have any idea how many times I dreamed about this?" He cupped her breast again, pulling her close with one arm beneath her head. "You kept me warm on a lot of damn cold nights halfway around the world."

To his shock, her eyes filled with tears. "I was so mad at you for leaving," she said. "For not coming to say goodbye. And then—and then—"

And then she'd thought he was dead. Gone forever. He read the anguish in her eyes.

"Shh," he said. "I'm here, and I'm never leaving again." He smoothed a hand down over the silky skin of her belly as he bent his head and took one nipple into his mouth. Suckling strongly, his own body pulsed in response as her back arched off the bed and her hands threaded through his hair to hold him to her.

He eased his weight over her, settling himself into the heated cove between her thighs, feeling the damp curls and the soft, soft flesh below. He couldn't wait.

Slowly, he pushed into her, groaning at the tight, slick feel of her body clasping his. Too tight, he realized belatedly.

"Relax, baby, you're okay." He stopped moving and held every muscle still, though his body was screaming at him to move. Guilt ate at him. He should have been thinking of her, and instead all he'd been able to do was think about how badly he wanted to be inside her. It wasn't even completely sexual, but something more, instinct urging him to stamp every inch of her with his scent and feel, to make her his again in the most basic way there was.

"I'm sorry," she whispered, squirming with discomfort. "I had a couple of stitches after Bridget was born and—"

"Shh," he said, kissing away a tear that trailed from the corner of her eye. "It'll be okay. We're in no hurry here."

She was taking deep, fast breaths, her breasts heaving as she fought to cooperate, and he knew he needed to help her. He didn't want her first time after Bridget's birth to be something she just wanted to forget.

He lifted himself a little away from her and stroked one hand between them, down her belly to the spot where they were joined. His fingers found the tiny, tender button hidden in her curls. Lightly, hoping that she would enjoy his touch, he rubbed a finger over her. And nearly had a heart attack when her body jolted involuntarily beneath his, driving him even deeper into her tight sheath.

She sucked in a sharp breath and he said, "Did you like that?"

He felt, more than saw, her nod in the darkness, so he did it again, starting a small circular pattern that massaged the little nubbin gently. Her hips began to move beneath his and he felt her muscles quiver. His own muscles were trembling with the effort it took to hold still when everything within him was urging him to thrust forward, but still he resisted. Her hips were moving steadily now, creating a delicious rhythm in time with his circling finger and he locked his jaw, holding on to his control by the slimmest of threads as her motions drew him in and out, in and out.

"Oh, yeah," he said through clenched teeth, "Oh, baby, I'm sorry—I can't—I can't—"

Wait was what he'd meant to say, but he never got the chance. Without warning, she arched beneath him and he felt an incredible sensation as she came in heavy waves of completion, her inner muscles squeezing his aching flesh over and over again. Control fell away and he shoved his hips forward, then withdrew and hammered into her again.

She was still shaking and jerking beneath him as he felt his body gather, gather, gather—and then release in a hot, drenching burst of pleasure that went on and on and on until both of them lay spent, gasping for breath.

His head was on the pillow beside hers and he smiled as she turned her head and pressed her lips briefly to his.

The sweetness of the gesture humbled him. How had he left this woman without telling her that he intended to return and make her his forever? He'd been so wrapped up worrying about what he'd done to her when she was grieving and vulnerable, so determined to give her space to think, that he'd nearly lost his opportunity forever.

What if she'd met and married someone after she'd thought he'd been killed? The idea didn't bear thinking about.

Instead, he focused on the one thing that had been nagging at him since their discussion over the weekend. "So when do you want to get married?" he asked.

He felt her smile against his throat. "Sounds like you already have a time in mind."

"Yeah." He snorted. "Yesterday. How long will it take to get a license here in New York, anyway?"

"I have no idea what the law is here," she said. "Since you'll be home this week, why don't you find out? I assume that once we have a license we can just go to the courthouse."

"All right. Is that what you want?" he asked. "A civil ceremony?"

She shrugged and the motion sent a pleasurable chain reaction rippling through his system. "I don't need a big church wedding, if that's what you're asking. It would seem sacrilegious, given that we already have a child." She stopped, then said, "Unless you think that would be important to your dad. Will you invite him?"

He was warmed by the concern she showed for his father's feelings. "I'll invite him, but I doubt Dad is about to get on a plane. Not even for that. He's not going to care if we get married here."

"All right." She nodded, as if that were settled. "You find out what we need to do and we'll set a date."

He nodded. "Leave it to me." Then he moved his hips experimentally and grinned when her body clenched around him. "Hmm, wonder what we can do until then?"

She laughed as she drew his head down to hers.

And as he began to kiss her again, he thought of an idea for a unique wedding gift that he knew would mean a great deal to her. It was time to lay some ghosts to rest.

But he could pursue that tomorrow. Right now, he had better things to do.

A week passed, then two. They decided to get married in the first week of December, a simple ceremony at the county courthouse, and Phoebe planned ahead to take a personal day.

One evening in the beginning of November, he said, "I applied for a job in the private sector today. The thought of being stuck behind a desk working for the Department of the Army, having to move every couple of years, doesn't appeal to me."

She looked up from the papers she was grading. "What kind of work is it?"

He lifted a glossy dark folder that he'd been reading and passed it to her. "Private security."

"As in being a bodyguard?" She tried not to let her dismay show. Wouldn't a bodyguard need to live with or near his employer? Possibly travel with the individual, as well?

"Not exactly." He smiled. "I heard about this company from a friend of mine who got out of the service and went to work for them. This firm

performs a number of different specialized services. They are called in when kidnappings occur,
they're quietly hired for operations that the gov-
ernment wants done without any fanfare, they set
up protective services for people and property.
Last year they provided security for a huge gem
exhibit at the Met."

"What's it called and where is it?"

"Protective Services, Inc." He hesitated. "The
main company is located in northern Virginia, but
they're planning on starting up at least one branch
operation. The first one will be in L.A."

"So we'd move back out there?"

He nodded. "If you wouldn't mind."

"No." She smiled. "I wouldn't mind." Then she
said, "Do you know what type of work they'd want
to hire you for?"

"Actually, I'm hoping to run the whole branch,"
he said. "That's the position they need and if
nothing else, being an army officer equipped me
for organization." Then he grinned again. "The
Long Gray Line is everywhere."

She stared at him. "What?"

"The Long Gray Line," he repeated. "The U.S.
Military Academy grads are called that because of
the uniforms we wore as cadets. Graduates of West
Point have networking contacts all over the world.

A retired soldier who works for PSI graduated a few years ahead of me. One of Walker's buddies talked to a friend of mine who knew I might be job hunting and word got back to them."

"That's amazing. You didn't even go looking for this job, did you?"

"Not exactly. But I had already decided to take medical retirement so it might work out well. And I think I'd enjoy the challenge." He made a wry face. "I'd be bored to death doing the same old thing over and over every day."

"That's one reason I enjoy teaching," she said. "There's always something to challenge me. A child with a special need, a new approach to try, even parent meetings are rarely boring."

"I bet you're a good teacher," he said.

"I try to be. Teaching the next generation is one of the most important jobs there is, I believe." Then she gestured at the piles of paperwork in front of her. "And speaking of jobs, I'd better get back to work on these spelling tests."

"Ahh. Teacher talk." His smile flashed. "It turns me on."

Phoebe's hand paused, as she lifted her gaze to his. "Teacher talk turns you on?"

He rose from the easy chair and began to walk toward her. "Yeah. Wanna see?"

"Wade!" She made a token effort to scoot away as he grabbed her and pulled her against his body. "I've got to finish grading these papers. It won't take me long."

He paused. "How long?"

"Not long!" She twisted her arm so that she could see the face of her watch. "Ten minutes or so."

"Ten minutes? Sorry, can't wait that long."

"You're impossible," she said as he lowered his head and set his mouth on hers, then pulled her up against his body.

"Impossible to deter," he muttered against her skin, kissing his way along her jaw and sucking her earlobe into his mouth, swirling his tongue around it.

She felt her knees buckle beneath the sheer delight that being in his arms always brought. Wrapping her arms around his neck, she let her head fall back as her muscles went lax. Wade took immediate advantage of the exposed slender length of her neck, sliding his mouth down the warm, silken column, nuzzling aside the scooped top of the knit shirt to nip at her collarbone. Phoebe murmured with pleasure, her body humming, response blooming inside her.

He bent and slid his arms beneath her knees, sweeping her into his arms and carrying her up the stairs. She clutched at his neck as he took the steps two at a time. "I'm too heavy for this. You'll hurt yourself. Put me down."

He laughed aloud. "Do you know how many pounds I used to carry up the side of a mountain? Trust me, honey, you're not too heavy." He paused at the top for a deep kiss, sweeping his tongue into her mouth and enticing her into exploring him as well. "Besides," he said when he lifted his head, "when I was packing a load up a mountain, I didn't have this kind of incentive waiting for me at the top."

It took him only a moment to cover the steps to her bedroom, only a moment more to cross the room and set her beside the bed. Although she had steadfastly refused to allow herself to think of him during waking hours, she had dreamed of Wade over and over, even after she'd believed he was dead. But none of the dreams had ever come close to the heady reality of being in his arms. Even now, she wasn't sure it was real sometimes.

He pulled her shirt over her head as she set her small hands to work unbuttoning his, then unhooked her bra. She paused so that he could slide it off her shoulder and toss it aside, and then, as he cupped her breasts and began to lightly rub his thumbs across the rosy nipples, her hands slowed and fell away.

He tore his gaze from the sight of the plump,

beautiful mounds in his hands to look into her eyes. Heat and passion filled his gaze, and to her delight, she felt his body shudder in anticipation against her. Reluctantly, he took his hands from her and stripped off his jeans and briefs, then tugged her slacks and panties down and off in one smooth, efficient motion. He reached around her and peeled the bedcovers back before urging her down onto the cool cotton sheets.

Taking her hand, he guided it down between them to his aching length. "Help me."

He jumped when her small hand closed around him. Savoring the silken feeling of his body, so taut and hard, she tightened her grip the way she knew he liked and stroked him once, twice and yet again. His hips lifted and thrust against her and he growled. "Tease."

She lightly bit his shoulder. "Tell me you don't like it and I'll stop."

He sounded as if he were having trouble dragging air into his lungs. "Like that's ever going to—oh, baby, yeah."

As she positioned him at the throbbing entrance to her body, she lifted her hips. He was hot and solid and she cried out as he surged forward, embedding himself deeply within her. Her hands clenched on his buttocks, urging him to move, and within moments they established a fast, frantic rhythm that built a blazing fire within her. His body hammered against her, creating an ever-rising tension that stretched tighter and tighter until finally it snapped. As her body bucked and writhed in his arms, and then he was hoarsely calling her name as his body stiffened and froze in a shattering climax that left him shaking and gasping for breath.

When she could breathe again, think again, she stretched up and pressed a kiss to his shoulder. "Wow."

He snorted and chuckled. "Yeah. Wow." He rolled to one side and pulled her into his arms and she relaxed against him, enjoying the cuddling. "I think we've mastered that."

"You do? As an educator, I can tell you that research shows that even when a skill has been mastered, a certain amount of practice is necessary to reinforce the concept."

"Is that so?" He stroked a hand gently down over her hip and lightly squeezed her bottom. "In that case, I suppose we'll just have to keep practicing until we're sure we've got it right."

Now it was her turn to laugh. "Could take a while."

"It could," he agreed.

Nine

Wade had a job interview on Friday with the company out of Virginia, the specialized security firm that was setting up a new branch. He'd met the personnel director already, and today's interview, he told Phoebe, was with the owner of the company.

"He's going to love you." She picked up her coffee cup as he rose to put his dishes in the dishwasher. They'd gotten into a pleasant weekday routine in which they had breakfast together before she left. He usually had some kind of start on dinner before she arrived home, which meant she got her work done faster if she'd brought any home to grade, which meant that right after Bridget went to bed, she and Wade could go to bed, also.

Or at least go to the bedroom, she amended.

Every night he made love to her, stoking the blaze between them into a raging inferno of need. She awoke in his arms in the morning to a wild sense of unreality.

She'd had more than a year to accustom herself to the idea that Wade would not be a part of her life, and during half of that time she'd believed that he was dead. Sometimes it was difficult to believe that she really could be so happy. Although *happy* was a pale imitation of the feelings that rioted through her when she came through the door in the evening to see him there waiting for her, holding their daughter in the crook of one muscular arm.

When he pulled her to him and kissed her sense-less, she was able to silence the one niggling voice in her head that reminded her that Wade might desire her...but he didn't love her.

"Don't worry about Bridget," she said. "Angie is watching her all day."

Wade nodded. "I could be back by lunch if this doesn't fly. If it does...it'll be late when I get home."

She rose on tiptoe to kiss him as he straightened his uniform, liking the way he'd said *home*. As if they truly were a family already. "Good luck."

She watched as he climbed into the rental car he still had, and waved as he drove off. "I love you," she murmured.

Would she ever be able to say it aloud? He seemed happy, and he clearly was thrilled with fatherhood. And when he touched her…well, they had no problems in that department. She smiled to herself as warmth radiated through her. But sometimes she caught him staring into space with a faraway expression on his face and she wondered what he was thinking about.

She was afraid she knew. And she was afraid to ask.

Melanie. Oh, she remembered everything that had happened the night of the reunion, the way he'd looked at her as if she were some new treasure he'd discovered—but that had been one single night. And even then, when he'd realized how upset Melanie had been, he'd been quick to pursue her.

To reassure her that there was nothing between Phoebe and him?

She would never know. Just as she would never know how much he still thought of her sister, how often his heart ached with loss.

Phoebe's insecurities, those feelings that had dominated her interactions with her sister most of her life, reared up and grabbed her attention every once in a while, reminding her that Wade had belonged to Melanie.

Never to her.

True, Wade seemed content now. But was it the familiarity of their friendship? His new fatherhood? Guilt at leaving her pregnant and alone? She feared it might be all three.

But he's with me now. He couldn't make love to me like that if he didn't care for me at least a little. Could he? Stop being a pessimist.

The school day dragged. She wondered how Wade's interview went. She checked her mobile phone for messages several times during the day, but he hadn't called. Although she hadn't expected him to, she worried that things hadn't gone well.

He probably wouldn't call her if the interview had not been successful. For all the years that she'd known him, Wade had been an intensely private man about his deepest feelings; she suspected that if he didn't want to talk, prying any information out of him would be next to impossible.

It wasn't until she saw the familiar outline of her little home that her spirits rose. Bridget was in there, with Angie. The sight of her daughter, the feel of that little body snuggled into her arms, was always balm to her sad moments.

Angie was sitting cross-legged on the couch, watching an afternoon soap opera, when Phoebe came through the door. "She was great today," Angie informed her. "I laid her down for her afternoon nap about two so she shouldn't get up again until at least four. I put the paper and the mail on the table."

"Thank you so much," Phoebe said. "I really appreciate you coming on short notice."

"Not a problem." Angie gathered her things. "Wish me luck on my psych test."

"Luck." Phoebe winked and smiled at her as Angie left. She set down her bag of paperwork from the day and slipped out of her shoes, then headed for the kitchen to get a drink.

As she sipped her tea, she glanced through the mail Angie had laid on the kitchen table. She set aside two bills and the grocery store flyer that had coupons in it, tossed three offers for credit cards in the trash, and laid out two envelopes of what looked like personal missives for immediate attention.

The first was a thank-you from a fellow teacher for whom she and her coworkers had thrown a bridal shower. The second bore an unfamiliar return address in California. Curious now, she slit the envelope and extracted a single sheet of paper.

Dear Mr. Merriman,

Mothers Against Drunk Driving (MADD) thanks you for your generous donation in memory of your loved one, Melanie Merriman. May we express our deepest condolences on your loss. Melanie sounds as if she was indeed a special young woman.

With your donation…

Bewildered, Phoebe picked up the envelope and looked more closely at the address. The sender had gotten Wade's name wrong on the envelope: it read Wade Merriman and she hadn't even noticed that it wasn't for her. Additionally, a change of address label had been slapped over the original and she realized it had been forwarded from his father's home in California.

She reread the letter—and suddenly it began to make sense, horrible sense, and the small, fragile bubble of hope she'd allowed herself to feel burst.

Wade had made a donation in Melanie's memory—*in his loved one's memory*—to a charitable organization known nationally for its education programs targeting drinking and driving. His *loved one*. Phoebe registered the hit to her heart as desolation spread through her and tears stung her eyes.

It wasn't that she begrudged the money, or the

thought. A part of her treasured the realization that her sister's name had been so honored. But now there was no way she could pretend that their marriage would be anything more than a convenience.

Now she knew for sure that there was no way Wade was ever going to love her because he was still in love with her sister. She sank down in a chair at the table and reread the letter twice more. Then she realized that if the letter hadn't been forwarded, she never would have known about the donation.

A sob escaped without warning. She clapped a hand over her mouth, but the truth confronting her wouldn't be denied and her efforts to resist the tears were futile. She had known Wade didn't love her. She shouldn't be so upset by this.

But she was. Not just upset, but devastated.

How could she marry him? Her heart wasn't going to be able to take that kind of beating day after day. She'd been kidding herself, believing that she could love him enough to make a marriage work. Even for the sake of her sweet baby girl sleeping upstairs, she couldn't do it.

At that thought, another sob welled up and tears began to stream down her face. Giving in to her misery, she laid her head down on her arms and cried.

Wade let himself into the house, wondering where Phoebe was. The baby monitor on the end table was silent, so she wasn't in Bridget's room. Could she be napping? Doubtful. He had yet to see her sleep during the day. Maybe she had taken Bridget out in the yard.

He crossed the living room and headed into the kitchen—and stopped short as he caught sight of her. She was slumped in a chair with her arms on the table, her head buried. Fear gripped him. "Phoebe! Sweetheart, what's the matter?" He rushed forward. Was she ill? Dear God, had something happened to Bridget? Panic nearly stopped his heart. "God, what's wrong? Is it Bridget?"

He knelt beside her chair and put an arm around her shoulders to hug her to him—and she exploded out of the chair halfway across the kitchen.

"Don't," she said between sobs. "Just—don't." She fumbled in a drawer for a tissue then turned away, her shoulders shaking with misery. "Bridget's fine."

A huge wave of relief swamped him momentarily, only to rush back as he realized she hadn't told him anything about herself. "Then what is it? Are you…" He could barely bear to utter the word. "Sick?"

She whipped back around at that, immediately grasping what he was asking. Her mother had gotten sick and died; so had his. "Oh, no, Wade. There's nothing wrong with me."

Except that there was. Her eyes were swollen from crying, her nose pink. She blotted her eyes and blew her nose while he stood. "Then…what?" he finally managed to ask.

She tried to smile, but her lips trembled and she quickly abandoned the effort. "I can't marry you."

What? "Why?" It was the most obvious question and he was too confused to think of a better one.

She sighed. "I just can't. It wouldn't be fair."

Fair to whom? "What the hell are you talking about?" Heat rose. He knew his tone was too rough, too angry, but— "Dammit, you scared me half to death! I thought something happened to Bridget or you. And now you tell me you won't marry me but you won't tell me why?"

A brittle silence followed the furious torrent of words, but she didn't speak, merely stood there with her eyes averted. And in her stance he read determination. He knew Phoebe and he knew that posture.

But what—? It hit him then. Stunned, he sank into the chair she'd bolted from. "It's because of Melanie, isn't it?"

She sucked in a sharp breath and nodded, and he saw a tear trickle down her cheek.

"Lord God above," he said quietly. Silence

reigned again as he absorbed the information. He'd wondered—no, he'd feared—for more than a year, that she blamed him for Melanie's death. It had kept him from contacting her after the first time they'd made love, and it had cost him the first months of his child's life.

When he'd finally decided to try to talk to her about it, she had been gone. And after he'd found her, after he'd learned about Bridget, his guilt had taken a backseat while he had adjusted to fatherhood and pretended that everything was fine and that Phoebe would love him and that they'd spend the rest of their lives together.

He scrubbed his hands over his face and looked down at the table, unable to stand seeing the pity and regret he knew he would see in her eyes.

A letter lay on the table and his name caught his eye. His first name, anyway. As he scanned it, he realized what it was. The foundation to which he'd made the donation in memory of Melanie had sent a thank-you note.

"I opened it by accident." Phoebe's tone was flat.

"I thought it would be a meaningful wedding gift."

"A *wedding gift?*"

"I'm sorry," he said. "I know there's nothing I can say to ever make it up to you—"

"You don't have to—"

"—and if it helps any, I will never forgive myself for letting Melanie die. If I'd been quicker, I'd have caught her. I've relived that night a thousand times and I know why you blame me." He halted for a moment. "I blame myself, so why shouldn't I expect you to?"

"Wade—"

"Don't." His shoulders slumped. "Just tell me what you want me to do now. Do you want me to leave?" His voice broke. "I will. I hope that you'll let me see Bridget sometimes, but I won't push—"

"Wade!"

At the volume and pitch of her voice, he finally stopped talking abruptly for the first time since she'd shoved away from his embrace.

Looking at the anguished set of his features, hearing the pain in his voice, she suddenly realized what he was thinking. It had nothing to do with lost love. *He was blaming himself for Melanie's death!* A tidal wave of shock, confusion and compassion crashed over her head and she forgot about her own pain.

"Wade," she said. He didn't look at her and she said it again, crossing to the table and touching his arm. "Wade, look at me."

Slowly, he lifted his gaze to hers and she was astounded by the pleading look in his eyes.

"I don't blame you," she whispered. She knelt on the floor beside his chair. "I've never blamed you. Melanie was impulsive. She had an ornery streak a mile wide. Her heart was that big, too, most of the time. She had been *drinking*. Neither one of us is responsible for what happened that night." She paused and put a hand to his face. "I don't blame you," she said again, urgently, as the look on his face eased fractionally.

"Then why?" He swallowed. "Why won't you marry me? God, Phoebe, I know I was a slow learner, but I realized that night at the dance that you were what had been missing from my life." He averted his eyes. "I took advantage of you after the funeral. I have no excuse, except that I had finally figured out that I loved you and I couldn't have walked away from you then any more than I could have stopped breathing."

He stopped speaking again then, and the only sound in the room was his harsh breathing and the hitching breaths she still took in the aftermath of her storm of tears.

Phoebe was frozen, his words hammering at her brain but not making sense. At least, not making sense in her current framework of reality.

"Phoebe?"

She sank down onto her heels and he looked alarmed. "I'm sorry. I shouldn't have—"

"You love me?"

He stopped. Searched her eyes, his own incredulous. "You didn't know?" He snorted. "I thought the whole damned world could see it."

"I didn't know," she confirmed. "I thought—believed that you still…"

"Melanie?"

She nodded. "When I saw the letter, I thought you'd done it because you still missed her, and that it was an accident that it came to this address."

"Oh, sweetheart, no." He put his hands beneath her elbows and stood, lifting her to her feet. "It was supposed to make you *happy*. I wanted to do something special to commemorate our marriage." He paused, looking down at her and she could see him choosing his words with care. "My feelings for your sister were only a crush. Infatuation. Mel and I weren't well suited. You surely could see that. We were over long before that reunion and I never regretted it."

As their eyes met again, she saw the beginnings of hope creeping into his expression. "You love me?" she said again. Stupid, she knew, but she wasn't quite sure she'd really heard it the first time.

His taut expression eased and the hope blossomed into a look that warmed her heart. "I love you," he said. "I've loved you since the night you asked me to dance and I realized I'd been chasing the wrong sister for a long time."

Her eyes filled with tears. "I love you, too," she said. "Oh, Wade, so much…" She smiled tremulously. "Pinch me. I must be dreaming."

"No way," he said. "Either the pinch or the dreaming. This is real, sweetheart. As real as that little girl sleeping upstairs." He gathered her against his body and pressed his forehead against hers. "Marry me, please, Phoebe?"

She tried to nod. "Yes. I would love to be your wife."

"Mother of my children," he prompted.

"Children? As in more than our one?" She slid her arms up around his neck and toyed with the collar of his shirt.

"Definitely more. Bridget would be spoiled stinking rotten if she was an only." He paused. "When did you realize…?"

"That I loved you?" She laughed. "At the risk of inflating your ego to an unforgivable level, I'll tell you. I can't remember when I didn't love you. I worshipped you when I was eight, nine, ten. I idolized you at eleven and twelve. By thirteen I was hopelessly infatuated. It tore me to pieces when you dated Mel."

"I never knew." His tone was wondering. "How could I not have known?"

"I wasn't exactly the most outgoing kid," she reminded him.

"Yeah, but you were always comfortable with me. You were—in love with me," he said ruefully. His expression changed. "God, I could really have blown it, couldn't I?"

She shrugged. "Doubt it."

Within ten minutes, he had her flat on her back in the big bed in her room. *Their* room, she amended silently. Soon she'd be giving herself and everything she had into his care.

Her attention abruptly veered back to the present as one warm, hairy leg pressed between her own legs and Wade's weight pressed her into the bed. She wriggled beneath him and he growled. "Wait."

"For what?" she teased, slipping her hands between them and rubbing his small, flat nipples into hard points.

"Tell me," he demanded, holding himself above her on his forearms, "that you felt it, too, that night we danced. Tell me it wasn't just me."

She slipped her hands down his back and he shuddered when he felt them moving lower, trying to pull him closer. Drawing back, he pushed slowly into the welcoming heat of her body, already soft and slick.

She murmured a sound of pleasure as she shifted her hips to accommodate him. "It wasn't just you." Then he lowered his head and claimed her mouth and she lost track of anything she'd intended to say as he began to move against her.

A short while later, she lay cuddled against his side. Wade was on his back, his arm around her idly caressing the ball of her shoulder, as another thought struck her. "Holy cow. I forgot all about your interview. How did it go?"

His hand stilled for a moment, then resumed its hypnotic rhythm. "Great!" She tilted her head back to see his face and he grinned at her. "I was offered the job."

"And you said yes." It was rhetorical and she was shocked when he shook his head in the negative.

"I said maybe," he said. His expression sobered, a sheepish quality creeping across his face. "I might have fibbed to you a little bit."

"Fibbed?" She was flabbergasted. "You made up the job?"

"No, no," he said hastily. "The job is real, and it's mine if I want it. But it's not in New York. In fact, it's not even on the East Coast."

"Where—? It's in California!" Could she get any more surprised? "Isn't it?"

"Southern California," he specified. "We'd have to move to San Diego if—"

"Yes!" She nearly shouted it in a totally un-Phoebe-like burst of enthusiasm as she pounded on his chest with her free hand. "You said yes, didn't you? We're going back?"

"I said it depended on my wife." He caught her and held her with ease as she flung herself atop him and wound her arms about his neck. "We wouldn't be in Carlsbad," he warned her. "I'd probably need to live somewhere closer to Mission Bay."

"Call them and tell them you'll take it!" She wriggled out of his arms and snatched up the portable telephone, thrusting the handset at him.

Wade laughed. "All right, all right. I'll do it in a few minutes." He paused, setting aside the phone and drawing her back into his arms. "Are you sure? I mean, I know you wanted to stay here and get tenure, and I can keep looking for a job around here if you'd rather not leave."

She detected the slightest trace of diffidence in his tone and her heart melted all over again. "You'd really do that for me?"

"For us," he qualified. "Wherever we decide to

live, I want you to be completely happy with the decision."

She sighed, sliding her hands into his hair and drawing his head down to hers. "Silly man. Don't you know I'd be happy anywhere with you?" She kissed him tenderly. "All I need is you, and our family. Going back to California would be wonderful, but all I really want is to spend the rest of my life with you."

And as he drew her back down to the bed, she realized the dream she'd had for so many years had truly become a reality. "I love you," she murmured.

"And I love you." He kissed her, then slid his hands down her body. "But I have to confess, that's not the *only* thing I want to do with you."

She laughed, too happy for words. Wade, the child they'd made together in love, and a future that looked as rosy as Bridget's cheeks. She thought of Melanie, and for the first time a true sense of peace filtered into Phoebe's heart. She had a hunch that wherever she was, Mel was doing a happy angel dance for her. And charming every male angel within sight.

* * * * *

BETROTHED FOR
THE BABY
by
Kathie DeNosky

KATHIE DeNOSKY

lives in her native southern Illinois with her husband and one very spoiled Jack Russell terrier. She writes highly sensual stories with a generous amount of humour. Kathie's books have appeared on the Waldenbooks bestseller list and received the Write Touch Readers' Award from WisRWA and the National Readers' Choice Award. Kathie enjoys going to rodeos, travelling to research settings for her books and listening to country music. Readers may contact Kathie at: PO Box 2064, Herrin, Illinois 62948-5264, USA or e-mail her at kathie@kathiedenosky.com.

This book is dedicated to my editor,
Tina Colombo. Thank you for your unwavering
support and encouragement. You're the very best.

And a special thank-you to my son, Bryan, for his
help with the Spanish in this book.

Te amo, mi hijo.

One

When Hunter O'Banyon glanced over at the pretty little blonde he'd met only moments ago, adrenaline began to pump through his veins. Her porcelain cheeks were flushed with a mixture of heat and excitement, and he could tell from the sparkle of urgency in her violet eyes that he was in for one hell of a ride.

"I hope you don't mind, but this is going to have to be faster than I'd planned," she said, sounding a little breathless.

Grinning, he nodded. "Bring it on. I can take it as fast as you want to go."

"I like the way you think." Her smile caused his

heart to race like a twelve-stroke engine hitting on all cylinders. "Hang on, big guy. This might get a little wild."

Hunter took a deep breath and braced himself. "Burn it, darlin'."

At the same time as she pushed the gas pedal all the way to the floor, she reached out to flip a switch on the dash. Lights and the keening wail of a siren competed with the sound of spinning tires kicking up a huge cloud of gravel and southwest Texas dust as the pickup truck careened away from the tarmac at Devil's Fork Community Airfield.

When Hunter had discovered there was no commercial air service to the little town, he'd wondered why the pilot of the Cessna Skyhawk he'd chartered to fly him to Devil's Fork from El Paso had laughed like a hyena when Hunter had called it an airport. Now he knew why. The entire thing consisted of an asphalt landing strip that he'd bet barely met FAA standards, a storage shed that leaned precariously to one side and a wooden pole with a tattered wind sock attached to the top just above the United States and Texas flags. As far as he could tell, there weren't even any lights for landing at night. He could only hope the Life Medevac operation looked better.

"By the way, I'm Callie Marshall, the flight nurse on the Evac II team," the blonde said conversationally.

Nice name for a nice-looking woman, he thought

as they approached the edge of town. "I'm Hunter O'Banyon."

"Thank God." She grinned. "When my pager went off, I didn't give you time to introduce yourself, and it suddenly occurred to me that you might not be the man I was supposed to meet."

His heart stalled and he had to clear his suddenly dry throat. When she smiled, Callie Marshall wasn't just pretty, she was drop-dead gorgeous.

"What were the chances of anyone else flying into Devil's Fork?" he asked when he finally got his vocal cords to work.

Her delightful laughter was one of the nicest sounds he'd heard in a long time. "Good point," she said, nodding. "I think you're the first person I've heard of flying into Devil's Fork since I arrived two months ago."

"Somehow that doesn't surprise me." He tightened his safety harness when she turned a corner, seemingly on two wheels. "Did you arrive by plane?"

"No way." She shook her head, causing her ponytail to sway back and forth. "I drove over from Houston. I wasn't about to take one of those puddle-jumper flights in here."

As they sped down Main Street, Hunter decided that if he'd blinked, he might have missed the entire town. Besides the fact that Callie was going so fast it wasn't much more than a blur, the business district was only a few blocks long and there wasn't much more than two or three blocks to the residential section.

"Mary Lou, our dispatcher, said you're from the Miami area. It might take a while for you to get used to Devil's Fork. It's about six hundred miles from the nearest beach and not exactly a hotbed of social activity."

"No kidding." He cringed when they sailed through a four-way stop on the opposite end of town without so much as slowing down. "I knew this place was small, but I expected something a little bigger than this."

"I did, too," she agreed. "After I drove through it the first time, I had a hard time believing there was enough of a call for a medevac operation to be based here. But I was wrong."

Hunter thought back to what he'd read in the file he'd been handed on the business his grandmother had given him to run. "The way I understand it, we're the only emergency service available for sections of five different counties."

She nodded. "The population is so sparse in this part of Texas, it isn't cost-effective for communities to have their own ambulance." Shrugging, she steered the truck onto a dirt-packed road leading up to a large aircraft hangar with Life Medevac Helicopter Service painted on the side. "Besides, if they had a ground unit, it would take too long to reach most of the people and even longer to get them to a hospital. We're their best hope for emergency medical care."

When she drove the truck around the side of the building, Hunter breathed a little easier. The Life Medevac base appeared to be in much better condition than the Devil's Fork airfield. Besides the well-kept hangar, there were two brand-new, top-of-the-line Bell EMS helicopters sitting on brightly painted helipads, and the entire area was ringed with what looked to be state-of-the-art lighting for night takeoffs and landings.

"I'll see you when we get back," she said, jamming the gearshift into Park at the same time she killed the engine and threw open the driver's door. "I have a flight to catch."

"Thanks for the ride," Hunter called, getting out of the truck.

Turning, she gave him another one of her killer smiles. "I almost forgot to tell you—beware of Mary Lou's coffee. She'll tell you it's the best you've ever had, but don't believe it." She grimaced. "It's awful."

As he stood there staring at Callie slowly jogging toward the waiting helicopter, he couldn't put his finger on what it was about her, but something bothered him. Aside from the fact that she'd driven the truck through town as though the hounds of hell were chasing them and she now moved as if she had all the time in the world, there was something about the snug way her navy-blue flight suit fit her around the middle that didn't seem quite right.

But when she disappeared inside the cabin space of the chopper and the door slid shut behind her, he quickly dismissed his concerns as Evac II lifted off the helipad. Although Emerald Larson had assured him that she'd seen to it that all the equipment was up-to-date and exceeded state requirements, he intended to order new flight suits in a color that could be more easily differentiated from other first responders that might be on scene when the Life Medevac crews arrived. And he'd make sure everyone wore the right size.

"You must be Hunter O'Banyon, the new boss of this outfit."

At the sound of the female voice behind him, Hunter turned to face a woman he'd judge to be somewhere in her late sixties or early seventies. With curly snow-white hair, a perfectly round face and a pair of narrow reading glasses perched on her nose, she looked as if she could easily play Mrs. Claus in a Christmas pageant.

He smiled as he extended his hand. "That would be me. And you must be Mary Lou Carson."

"The one and only." Grinning, she firmly shook his hand. "Come on in the dispatch room and rest a spell. I'll pour you a cup of the best coffee you've ever had, then I'll show you your quarters."

Reaching into the bed of the pickup truck, Hunter grabbed his luggage and followed Mary Lou out of the late-August heat and into the air-conditioned office of the hangar. When she led him into the dispatch room, he looked around at the framed military medals hanging on the wall beside the door.

"Did these belong to your husband?" he asked conversationally.

"Some of them." Mary Lou walked over to a small kitchen area on the opposite side of the room to stir the delicious-smelling contents of a huge pot on the electric range. "The rest are mine."

When she walked back over to where he stood, she handed him a cup of coffee, then motioned for him to sit in one of several chairs on the opposite side of a scarred wooden desk. "Take a load off, Hunter."

"What branch of the military were you in?" he asked, sitting down.

"Lester and I were both career Navy." She walked between the desk and a built-in counter filled with radio equipment, a computer and several telephones to settle herself into an old wooden desk chair that looked as if it might have been around since World War II. "He was an aircraft mechanic and I was a nurse. He died in an accident onboard an aircraft carrier not long before we were supposed to retire."

"I'm sorry." Hunter knew all too well what it was like to lose someone unexpectedly.

"Don't be sorry," she said, surprising him. "Lester died doing what he loved most—working on fighter jets. That's the best way any of us can hope to go out of this world." Before he could respond, she shrugged. "That's why I'm a dispatcher here. After my arthritis forced me to stop working the floor in a hospital, I took this job. When people call with an emergency, I sometimes stay on the line and talk them through whatever medical crisis they have until one of our crews arrives. It's almost as satisfying as nursing."

Hunter took a sip of coffee as he considered what Mary Lou said. But as the bitter taste spread over his tongue, he had to force himself to swallow. Quickly setting the cup on the desk, he barely controlled the urge to shudder. What Callie had told him about the coffee being awful had been an understatement. The stuff was as thick as syrup and tasted as though it had been made with quinine.

Coughing, he looked up to see Mary Lou watching him expectantly. He could tell she was waiting for him to tell her how good it was.

"You like your coffee strong, don't you?" he asked, trying not to grimace.

She shrugged. "I like my coffee to be just the way I like a man—strong and the best I've ever had."

If he'd thought her coffee was enough to send his system into shock, her outspokenness finished the job. He couldn't have been more dumbfounded if he'd tried. Unable to think of a thing to say, he waited to see what she'd say next. Unless he'd misjudged her, that shouldn't take very long.

Her knowing smile clued him in on the fact that she'd known her statement would render him speechless. "There's a few things about me you might as well know up front, Hunt. I don't mince words. I say exactly what I think because I'm old enough to get away with it and I've never been one to beat around the bush."

"I can respect that." Hunter had no idea where Mary Lou was going with this, but he could tell she had more on her mind.

"I'm glad to hear you say that, because what I'm going to tell you now might not set real well."

"I'm listening."

"I'm going to treat you like I treat everyone else around here because I'm not impressed by much of anything anymore. And that includes you being Emerald Larson's grandson."

Hunter frowned. He'd specifically asked Emerald not to divulge his relationship to her. For one thing, he didn't need the added pressure of living up to someone's expectations. And for another, he still hadn't fully come to terms with being her grandson.

"How did you learn about—"

"Emerald and I go way back. She hasn't always been on the top of the heap. When she was a teenager, she worked behind the soda counter in my father's drugstore." Mary Lou grinned. "She was like an older sister to me, and we've stayed in touch over the years."

Hunter wasn't particularly happy about having one of Emerald's lifelong friends working for him. He didn't like the idea of not being able to make a move without his manipulative grandmother knowing about it.

"If you're worried about me running to Emerald to report everything you do, don't waste your time," Mary Lou said as though she'd read his mind. "I don't carry tales. If she wants to know what's going on with you, she'll have to ask you herself."

"That's good to hear." Whether he should or not, Hunter believed the woman.

Draining the last of her coffee, Mary Lou placed her cup on the desk and stood up. "Now that we have that out of the way, I'll show you to your living quarters and let you get settled in while I finish up the beef stew I put on for our supper." She pointed to his cup. "Would you like that warmed up?"

He quickly shook his head. "I'm not much of a coffee drinker." He didn't want to hurt her feelings, but if he never drank another drop of the bitter brew, it would be all too soon.

She shook her head. "I don't know what's wrong with you young people. I'm the only one working here who likes coffee."

As Hunter grabbed his suitcase and followed her through a doorway and down a hall toward the back of the hangar, he suspected the others' reluctance to drink Mary Lou's coffee had everything in the world to do with self-defense and nothing to do with not liking coffee.

"This is your office," she said, passing a door on the way to the back of the building. Pointing to a door across the hall, she added, "And this is the on-duty crew's sleeping quarters. We have three crews working rotating twenty-four-hour shifts—two days on duty and four off. Of course, on the outside chance that we get a call while one crew is out, the first two days that a crew is off duty, they're on call."

"What about you? What are your hours?"

"I'm here round the clock. When I'm not dispatching a crew, I'm cooking and handing out advice that nobody seems to listen to." She laughed as she pointed to a door next to the crew quarters. "This is my room. I have a ringer in here that wakes me up when we have a night call or I decide to take a nap."

Hunter frowned. "Who's the dispatcher on your days off?"

She continued walking toward a door at the end of the hall. "On the rare occasions that I take a day off, one of the members of the off-duty crew fills in for me."

"You don't have regularly scheduled time off?" He didn't like the sound of that. Aside from Emerald taking advantage of Mary Lou, he wasn't sure that it was even legal for the woman to be working that much.

"Don't get your shorts in a bunch, Hunter," Mary Lou said as if she'd read his mind. "I don't have family, and working here at Life Medevac is what makes me happy and keeps me going. I love what I do, so don't go getting any ideas about making me take time off on a regular basis, because I won't do it." She opened the door to his room, then, stepping back, pointed to his luggage. "Are all your things in that one suitcase?"

He nodded. "I stored the rest of my things until I find a place in Devil's Fork."

"Good idea." The woman nodded her approval. "Now go ahead and get your gear stowed away while I radio Evac II and find out the status of their patient and what time they estimate they'll get back to base."

Hunter stared after Mary Lou as she breezed out the door and down the hall as if her working without regular days off was a nonissue. But he wasn't so sure. It wasn't just a question of the labor laws. Her age and well-being had to be taken into consideration, as well. She might seem like a dynamo with boundless energy, but working 24-7 would be hard on a much younger person, let alone a woman close to seventy.

As he lifted his suitcase and placed it on the edge of the bed to unpack, he decided there were several things he needed to do right away. Not only did he need to order the correct size flight suits for everyone, he'd have to check into Texas labor laws.

Putting away the last of his clothes, he looked around. It was a good thing he always traveled light. The room was barely big enough for the twin bed, small chest of drawers and bedside table. There was no way he'd have had room for anything but his clothes.

But then, he didn't need a lot of room. For the past five years he hadn't cared how spacious his accommodations had been or even where they'd been located. After working construction so hard each day that he'd been too tired to think or remember, all he'd needed was a place to sleep, shower and change clothes. With any luck, there would be enough work to keep him just as busy at Life Medevac.

At the sound of a helicopter landing outside, he walked down the hall to the dispatch room. "They weren't gone long."

Mary Lou nodded. "Juanita Rodriguez thought she was going to have her baby, but it turned out to be false labor." Smiling, she added, "She's only nineteen and it's her first pregnancy. She and her husband, Miguel, are worried they won't make it to the hospital in time."

"I hear that's a big concern for most first-time parents." A twinge of regret ran through Hunter. Anticipating the arrival of a child was something he would never experience.

But he didn't have time to dwell on the disturbing thought as the flight crew from Evac II entered the dispatch room. Besides Callie, the crew consisted of a sandy-haired man who looked to be in his forties and a fresh-faced kid of about twenty.

"The name's George Smith," the man said, smiling

as he walked over to shake Hunter's hand. Almost as tall as Hunter's own six-foot-three-inch frame, George was built like a heavyweight prizefighter, and if his grip was any indication, as strong as one. "I'm the pilot for the Evac II team." He nodded toward the younger man. "And that kid over there is Corey Timmons, the EMT on our crew."

"It's nice to meet you, Mr. O'Banyon," Corey said, stepping forward to pump Hunter's hand enthusiastically. "We've been looking forward to you taking over."

"Call me Hunter." He wasn't surprised to hear the employees had been looking forward to a change in administration. From the file he'd been given, when Emerald bought Life Medevac, the employees hadn't been paid their wages in several weeks.

Grinning, the young man's brown eyes danced mischievously. "We're glad to see you survived the drive across town with Callie behind the wheel."

Hunter chuckled. "Was there doubt?"

"After flying into Devil's Fork with Crash Jenson at the controls of that little four-seater prop job, we kinda wondered if her driving wouldn't finish you off," George added, laughing.

"If you two keep joking about my driving, I'll stop making those chocolate-chip-oatmeal cookies you love so much," Callie warned good-naturedly as she crossed the room to the kitchen area, where Mary Lou was putting the finishing touches on the crew's dinner.

"We take it all back," Corey said earnestly as he walked over to grab a plate for Mary Lou to fill with a generous helping of stew.

"You bet," George said, nodding vigorously. "We were just joking around, Callie. Whatever you do, don't stop making those cookies." Turning to Hunter, he confided, "You've never tasted anything as good in your entire life as her chocolate-chip-oatmeal cookies."

"I'll look forward to trying them," Hunter said, enjoying the easy banter.

As George moved to get a plate of stew, Hunter watched Callie open the refrigerator to remove a carton of orange juice and once again noticed the way her flight suit fit. The navy-blue fabric was fairly loose everywhere but in her midsection and she looked as if…

A sudden cold feeling of intense dread began to fill Hunter's chest and he had to swallow hard against the bile rising in his throat. Callie Marshall wasn't just carrying a few extra pounds around the middle. She was several months pregnant.

Two

As she walked past Hunter to sit down in one of the chairs in front of Mary Lou's desk, Callie wondered what on earth she'd done to come under such close scrutiny. His intense stare had followed her from the moment she'd walked into the room and caused her skin to tingle as if he'd reached out and touched her.

Shaking her head to clear it, she decided her uncharacteristic reaction to him had to be because her hormones were all out of whack due to her pregnancy. It was the only reasonable explanation she could think of to explain it.

His concentrated stare had probably been nothing

more than the result of noticing her thickening midsection. He was no doubt trying to figure out whether she was just a bit plump or expecting a baby.

Careful to keep her voice low to avoid calling the others' attention to the fact that she'd caught him staring, she smiled as she turned to meet his intense green gaze. "In case you're wondering about my odd shape, I'm four and a half months pregnant."

Running an agitated hand through his dark brown hair, he looked a little uncomfortable. "I…didn't mean to—"

"Don't worry about it." She smiled, hoping to put him at ease. "It's not like it's a big secret. And, as you can see, I'm certainly not trying to hide my pregnancy."

"Your husband is okay with you flying while you're pregnant?" He shook his head. "I'm sorry. It's none of my business."

It was an odd question, but the concern on his handsome face and in his deep voice was genuine. "Don't worry about it. I don't have a husband, so it's a nonissue." She shrugged. "I'm unmarried, uncommitted and quite content to stay that way."

"I didn't mean to pry." He looked more uncomfortable than before.

"It's not a problem. I'm actually looking forward to single motherhood."

He looked as if he intended to say something, but Corey chose that moment to walk over and plop down in the chair beside her. "Have we sucked up enough to get more cookies or do we need to grovel a little more?"

Callie laughed at the likable young EMT. "No, I think you've redeemed yourself enough for another batch of chocolate-chip-oatmeal cookies."

"If you'll excuse me, I think I'll go check out my office," Hunter said suddenly, turning to walk down the hall.

Staring after her new boss, she wondered what had caused his abrupt change. When she'd met him at the airfield, he'd been congenial and outgoing. But within the span of a few minutes his mood had become pensive and troubled. Was he concerned that she would be unable to do her job?

She rose to her feet to follow him into the office and reassure him that she was perfectly capable of carrying out her duties, but the dispatch radio chose that moment to crackle to life.

"Looks like we have another run," Mary Lou said, crossing the room to answer the call.

As Callie listened to the highway patrol officer relay the location of the one-car accident on Interstate 10 and the patrolman's assessment of the driver's injuries, she, George and Corey started for the door. "Tell him we're on the way."

"ETA is fifteen minutes," George said.

"Keep the stew warm," Corey added.

Out of the corner of her eye Callie saw Hunter

reenter the room. His concerned expression reinforced her determination to set his mind at ease. But their talk would have to wait until later. Whether or not he believed she was capable of doing her job, she had an accident victim depending on her for emergency medical attention. And she wasn't about to let her patient down.

Drenched in a cold sweat, Hunter awoke with a jerk and, swinging his legs over the side of the bed, sat up. Propping his elbows on his knees, he cradled his head in his hands as he tried to chase away the remnants of his nightmare.

He hadn't dreamed about the accident in almost six months. But it was just as real now as it had been when he'd lived through it five years ago. He and his fiancée, Ellen Reichert, a second-year resident at the Mount Sinai Medical Center in Miami, had flown into Central America to deliver medical supplies and administer first aid to some of the remote villages hit the hardest by a category-four hurricane. Everything about the trip had been routine and uneventful until he'd circled the landing site for their last stop. That's when all hell had broken loose and the course of his life had changed forever.

The twin-turbine helicopter he'd been piloting had suddenly lost oil pressure, then, before he could get it safely set down, it stalled out. He didn't remember a lot of the details of what happened after that, only that he'd fought the controls with little success. The chopper had ended up tilting precariously in midair, then come down hard on its starboard side.

His first thought had been to make sure that Ellen was all right, then get them out of what was left of the helicopter. But the blood in his veins had turned to ice when he'd called her name and she'd failed to respond. He'd placed his fingers to the side of her neck and, detecting a faint pulse, scrambled to release their seat belts. Pushing the door on the port side of the chopper open, he'd carefully lifted her up through the opening, then carried her a safe distance from the wreckage.

When she'd regained consciousness, they'd both known she didn't have long, and that's when his devastating heartbreak had turned to total despair. She'd told him that she'd been waiting for the perfect time to tell him she'd recently learned she was pregnant. With her dying breath she'd told him how much she loved him and how sorry she was that she had to go, then, closing her eyes, she'd quietly slipped away.

The ensuing investigation into the crash had proven the accident had been caused by mechanical failure and there was nothing he could have done to prevent it. But he'd quit flying that day and struggled for the past five years, feeling guilty because he'd walked away with nothing more than cuts and bruises, blaming himself for living when the woman he'd loved and their future child had died. He'd spent countless hours going over every detail of the accident, wondering if there was something he could have done differently, something that could have lessened her injuries or saved her life. But try as he might, he couldn't think of anything that would have changed the outcome.

He took a deep shuddering breath and tried to relegate the disturbing memories to the back of his mind. There was no doubt why the horrific dream had returned, and he couldn't say he was overly surprised that it had. After discovering that Callie was pregnant, all he'd been able to think about was once again being responsible for the lives of a woman and her unborn child. Even though she wasn't on his flight crew, as her employer it was ultimately his job to see to her safety.

Fortunately her shift had ended right after the Evac II team had returned from transporting the car accident victim to a hospital in El Paso. That meant that he had four days to come up with a convincing argument to get her to ground herself. And unless her crew was called out as backup for Evac III, she and her baby would be safe.

Now all Hunter had to do was figure out a way to keep them that way.

"Give me a second," Callie called when it sounded as if whoever was at her front door would knock it off its hinges with their insistent pounding. Wiping the flour from her hands with her apron, she turned her CD player down and hurried from the kitchen to open the door. "What's so important that—"

She stopped short at the sight of Hunter O'Banyon standing on her tiny front porch. Lord have mercy, but he was one of the best looking men she'd ever seen. He was dressed in a black T-shirt and worn blue jeans. The soft fabrics fit him like a second skin and emphasized the width of his broad shoulders and his narrow hips. When she glanced at his arms, the sight of his bulging biceps stretching the knit sleeves of his shirt sent a shiver of awareness straight up her spine.

Callie gave herself a mental shake. What on earth was wrong with her? And why in the name of heaven was she ogling the man as if he were a fudge-nut brownie with rich chocolate frosting?

"Are you all right?" His expression was one of deep concern.

"Of—" she swallowed hard "—course. Why wouldn't I be?" Other than being embarrassed that her hair was piled on her head in total disarray, her shorts and T-shirt were the oldest things she had in her closet and she was coated with a fine dusting of flour, she was just peachy.

"I knocked for five minutes before you answered the door. I thought something might be wrong." He rubbed his hand over the back of his neck. "Never mind. Do you have a few minutes? We need to talk."

What could he possibly think they needed to discuss? And why did he have to show up after she'd received a phone call from her mother?

At least once a week since telling her mother she was pregnant they'd gone through the same old routine of her mother wanting to know who the father of Callie's baby was and why she was so insistent on keeping the man's identity a secret. Frustrated beyond words with her mother's persistence, by the time Callie had ended the phone call, she'd already measured the ingredients for several dozen sugar cookies and had pulled the box of oats from the cupboard for a double batch of chocolate-chip-oat-meal cookies.

Some women cleaned house when they were upset. Callie baked.

"Do you mind if I come in?" Hunter asked, returning her to the present.

"I'm sorry. Please come in." She stepped back for him to enter her small cottage. "I was just baking some—oh no! My cookies!" Remembering the peanut butter cookies she'd put into the oven just before hearing him pound on the door, she made a beeline for the kitchen with him hot on her heels.

"Damn! When you make cookies, you don't fool around, do you?" he said, looking around.

Taking the baking sheet from the oven, she placed it on the top of the stove, then glanced at the table and countertops. Plates of cookies covered every available surface.

Shaking her head at the sight, she nibbled on her lower lip. She must have been more upset over her mother's phone call than she'd realized.

"Would you like some milk and cookies?" She grinned. "I have plenty."

"No kidding." His deep chuckle caused a wave of goose bumps to sweep over her skin. "What are you going to do with all of them?"

"They won't last long around George and Corey."

She opened a cabinet to get something to store the cookies in, but the feel of Hunter's broad chest pressed to her side as he stepped forward to reach for several of the plastic containers on the top shelf sent a charge of excitement skipping over every nerve in her body. When he handed them to her, then stepped back, she had trouble drawing her next breath.

Unnerved, her hand trembled as she took the containers from him. "Th-thank you."

He gave her a short nod, then moved farther away. "I think I will take you up on that offer of some milk and cookies."

Pouring them each a glass of milk, she set one at the far end of the table and started to sit down at the opposite end. Hunter was immediately behind her, holding the chair, and his close proximity unsettled her so much that she almost turned over her glass.

What in blazes was wrong with her? She not only felt as jumpy as a frightened rabbit, she'd suddenly turned into a major klutz.

When he sat down across from her, he studied the plates of cookies between them. "What do you suggest I start with first?"

"I like the oatmeal cookies, but that's probably because I use chocolate chips instead of raisins," she said, reaching for one of the tasty treats.

He nodded as he took a cookie from one of the plates. "I'm kind of partial to peanut butter myself." Taking a bite, his eyes widened. "Corey and George weren't exaggerating—these are some of the best cookies I've ever tasted."

As they munched on the cookies, Callie wondered what it was he thought they needed to discuss. For the life of her she couldn't think of anything so important that he'd pay her a visit on her day off.

"What did you want to talk to me about?" she asked, hoping the sooner he stated the purpose for his visit, the sooner he'd leave. She desperately needed to regain her composure.

Taking a deep breath, he set his empty glass on the table, then caught her gaze with his. "I'm concerned that your job might be a little too much for a woman in your condition."

She laughed. "Contrary to what you might think, pregnancy is not a disability."

"I understand that," he said, nodding. "But at times I'm sure it's extremely tiring."

"I'm not going to pretend that it isn't." She rose to place their glasses in the dishwasher, then started stacking cookies in the containers for freezing. "But there are also times when we'll go for a day or two without an emergency call and I'm exhausted from sheer boredom. Besides, my obstetrician doesn't have a problem with me working as a flight nurse, so if you're worried that it's too strenuous for me, don't. Corey and George are both very conscientious and won't let me do any heavy lifting. And when we're not out on calls, I make sure to take regular naps."

"Yes, but there's other things to be considered, such as turbulence or pilot error," he said as he handed her plates full of cookies to be stored in the plasticware.

"I trust George. He's a good pilot."

"I'm not saying he isn't."

She snapped the lid shut on the box, then started filling another one. "What *are* you saying?"

He rubbed the back of his neck as if to relieve tension. "Aren't you worried about having to make a rough landing or a possible crash?"

"Not really." She couldn't for the life of her figure out why he was so overly concerned. Every pilot she'd ever known considered flying the safest mode of transportation. "In the event that something like that happens, I'm in no greater danger because I'm pregnant than I would be if I wasn't."

"But—"

"I see no reason why you're so worried about it, but if you think it's that important, why don't you review the employment records and put me on the crew with the best pilot?"

To her surprise, he placed his large hands on her shoulders and turned her to face him. But instead of arguing his point further, he stared at her for several long seconds before he muttered a curse and lowered his head to capture her lips with his.

As his mouth moved over hers in a gentle caress, Callie's pulse raced and her insides began to hum. The last thing she'd expected for him to do was kiss her. But instead of pushing him away as she should have, she reached out and placed her hands on his biceps to steady herself. The feel of his rock-hard muscles flexing beneath her palms sent a shiver of excitement up her spine and caused her knees to tremble.

If she had any sense, she'd put a stop to the kiss right now and demand that he leave. But his firm, warm lips were making her feel things that she'd only read about in women's magazines and romance novels, and she didn't want the delicious sensations to end.

When he wrapped his arms around her and pulled her against him to deepen the kiss, the feel of his superior strength surrounding her sent tiny little sparks skipping over every nerve in her body. Opening for him, she felt her heart skip several beats when he slipped his tongue inside to tease and explore her with a tenderness that made forming a coherent thought all but impossible.

Placing his hand at the small of her back, he urged her forward, but the feel of her round little tummy pressed to his stomach must have brought him back to reality. He suddenly went completely still, then, releasing her, he carefully set her away from him and took a couple of steps back.

"That shouldn't…have happened." He ran an agitated hand through his thick dark brown hair. "I think I should probably leave."

"Don't worry about it."

Embarrassed and more than a little confused by her uncharacteristic behavior, Callie began packing more cookies into the plastic containers. Why hadn't she stopped him instead of clinging to him as if she were desperate for a man's attention?

Hunter O'Banyon might be tall, dark and movie-star handsome, but she was no more interested in him than she was in any other man. But, dear heaven above, could he ever kiss.

Her cheeks feeling as if they were on fire from her sudden wayward thought, she shoved a container of cookies into his hands. "Take these back to the hangar for Mary Lou and the on-duty crew."

"Callie...I—"

If he didn't leave soon, she'd be up all night baking. "It's getting late and I'm sure you need to get back." She walked into the living room and opened the front door. "Thank you for stopping by. I appreciate your concerns and I will give them some thought."

"By the way, I know this is short notice, but I'm holding a staff meeting the day after tomorrow at 10:00 a.m.," he said, looking anything but happy. "Will you be able to be there?"

She shook her head. "I have a doctor's appointment. But I'll stop by after my checkup and someone can fill me in on what was covered in the meeting."

He stared at her for what seemed an eternity before he gave her a short nod. "Good night, Callie," he said, walking out onto the porch.

"Have a nice rest of the evening, Hunter," she said, closing the door behind him.

Walking straight to the kitchen, she stacked the containers of cookies on a shelf in her freezer, then pulled out the ingredients for a batch of brownies. Her phone conversation with her mother had been frustrating and caused her to make several batches of cookies. But Hunter's disturbing kiss was sending her into a baking frenzy, and for some odd reason everything she wanted to make was chocolate.

As she measured cocoa and flour, something she'd heard on a cooking show came to mind and caused her to knock over a cup of sugar. Eating chocolate released the same endorphins in the brain that were released while having sex.

"Not good, Callie. Not good at all."

Hurriedly opening a bag of milk-chocolate chips, she popped a handful into her mouth, and as the rich taste spread over her tongue, she decided that even if chocolate did make her gain too much weight, it was far less dangerous to her peace of mind than Hunter O'Banyon.

As he descended the steps and walked over to the white truck with Life Medevac painted on the side, Hunter shook his head. He didn't blame Callie one damned bit for giving him the bum's rush. Hell, he'd deserved more than that. He'd acted like an oversexed teenager on his first date. But what he was having the devil of a time trying to figure out was why.

Getting into the truck, he started the engine and, backing from the driveway, drove across town. But instead of turning onto the road leading to the Life Medevac hangar, he kept going until the lights of Devil's Fork faded in the distance behind him. He needed to think, and even though he could go into his room for solitude, he'd found that staring at the vastness of a starlit night always helped him put things in perspective.

When he parked the truck and stared out the windshield at the stars above the Apache Mountains in the distance, he couldn't help but wonder what the hell had gotten into him. He'd only stopped by Callie's place to try to talk some sense into her and get her to see the wisdom in grounding herself until after she had her baby. But when he'd placed his hands on her shoulders and looked into her pretty violet eyes, he could no more have stopped himself from tasting her sweetness than he could stop his next breath.

He took a deep breath. Although he wasn't overly proud of it, he hadn't exactly led the life of a monk since Ellen's death. But he'd always been careful to be with women who wanted nothing more from him than mutual satisfaction and had no expectations of their liaison leading to anything more. And Callie Marshall was most definitely *not* that type of woman. Instead of smoke-filled nightclubs, champagne cocktails and a meaningless one-night stand, she was a cozy little cottage, homemade cookies and a long-term commitment.

But come to think of it, he'd been so busy in the past several months that he'd completely abandoned any kind of a social life. And although he was far from being as randy as a seventeen-year-old boy, a man of thirty-two did have certain needs that couldn't be ignored.

He frowned. But he'd never in his entire life found a pregnant woman irresistible.

He stared at a shooting star streaking across the inky sky. He guessed it was only natural that he'd be attracted to Callie even though she was expecting a baby, considering his current state of celibacy. She was a very pretty woman with a killer smile, a delightful laugh and a pair of legs that could drive a saint to sin. Combine all those traits with his neglected libido and it was no wonder he'd felt compelled to kiss her.

Satisfied that he'd discovered the reason for his un-characteristic caveman behavior, he started the truck and headed back toward the Life Medevac base. Now that he had things in perspective, there was no reason that he and Callie couldn't put what happened this evening behind them and move forward as employer and employee. Hell, maybe they could even be friends.

But much later, as he lay in bed trying to will himself to sleep, Hunter couldn't seem to forget the sweet taste of Callie's soft lips or that the blood in his veins had heated considerably when she'd kissed him back. And whether he liked it or not, the very last thing on his mind was friendship.

Three

On the drive back from her appointment with the obstetrician, Callie thought about Hunter's visit and how foolish she'd been. The kiss they'd shared had been very nice, but it didn't mean anything. She knew he'd been frustrated with her refusal to ground herself and he'd been just as surprised by his actions as she had. There had really been no reason for her to get so flustered and read more into it than that.

But she'd spent the rest of the night baking everything from chocolate-fudge-nut brownies to chocolate cake. And by the time she'd gone to bed, the gray light of dawn had begun to chase away the shadows of night.

She shook her head. She hadn't baked that much since she'd discovered she was pregnant.

Thinking back on that day, she could still remember walking out of her gynecologist's office in a total state of shock. She'd always wanted children, but she'd envisioned herself happily married and anticipating the blessed event with the man she loved and who loved her in return. She wasn't supposed to have become pregnant by a man who put social status above a meaningful relationship.

When she'd first met Craig Culbertson, he'd swept her off her feet with his charm and thoughtfulness. But it hadn't taken long for her to discover that he wasn't the man she'd thought he was. He'd hidden his true nature behind a winning smile and charming ways, and by the time they'd parted company, *shallow, self-centered* and *selfish* were the nicest words she could think of to describe the conceited snake.

Then, when she'd discovered she was pregnant a month after their breakup, her disillusionment with Craig had turned to abject fear. One of the deciding factors in her ending their relationship had been the sickening disgust she'd felt when he'd confided in her that at the age of nineteen he'd gotten his girlfriend pregnant and that his twelve-year-old brother was actually his son. He'd told her that once his parents had learned of the pregnancy and discovered the girl wasn't the family's social equal, they'd used their money, as well as their position in Houston society, to gain custody of the baby, adopt him and raise the boy as their own.

A cold chill raced through Callie. She could only imagine the devastation and powerlessness the young mother must have felt at losing all contact with her child. And that was the very reason Callie had made the decision to leave her job as an emergency room nurse at one of the Houston hospitals and take the job as flight nurse with Life Medevac.

If Craig found out about her pregnancy, she wasn't sure he and his parents wouldn't try to do the same thing to her that they'd done to the mother of his first child. Callie hadn't been born into a life of wealth and privilege and therefore would no doubt be considered an undesirable candidate to raise a Culbertson heir. They'd take her to court and she'd come out the loser. She didn't have the kind of money it would take to fight a custody battle against their high-powered lawyers.

She'd come from a middle-class single-parent home where there hadn't been an endless supply of money, and social outings had consisted of making trips to the mall or attending a matinee at the movie theater. And even if her father hadn't been lost at sea during a storm while working on an oil platform in the Gulf of Mexico, her social status wouldn't have been a whole lot different.

As she steered her car onto the lane leading up to

the Life Medevac hangar, she placed her hand on her rounded tummy. She might not have been born with a silver spoon in her mouth, but she loved her little boy with all her heart, and no one was going to take him away from her.

Parking the car, she took a deep breath and forced herself to forget about Houston and the ruthless Culbertsons. She was about to face Hunter O'Banyon and tell him that she'd given a lot of thought to his request that she ground herself. She'd even gone so far as to discuss her physical limitations with her obstetrician, and together they'd concluded there was no reason for her to go on maternity leave for a few more months. Now all she had to do was explain that to Hunter.

"Hi, Mary Lou," Callie said as she entered the dispatch room. "Is Hunter in his office?"

The older woman nodded. "I suspect he's back there compiling a list of everyone's size and the number of new flight suits he's going to order." She laughed. "How do you look in red?"

"We're going to wear red flight suits?"

"That's what he says." Mary Lou looked thoughtful. "Come to think of it, though, our crews will be more easily identified among other emergency personnel at an accident scene."

"It does get confusing sometimes when some of the other services wear the same shade of dark blue that we do," Callie agreed.

"Did everything go okay at the doctor's office?" Mary Lou asked. Since learning of Callie's pregnancy, the woman had taken it upon herself to monitor Callie's progress and well-being.

Smiling, Callie nodded. "The obstetrician did a sonogram and said the baby's size is right on target for a four-and-a-half-month fetus." She laughed. "But I doubt that I can get away with blaming my five-pound weight gain on my son."

"No, that would be due to all those cookies you bake," Mary Lou said, grinning.

As Callie walked down the hall to Hunter's office, she decided that Mary Lou was right. If she didn't stop baking, there wouldn't be a flight suit big enough to accommodate her expanding form, whether she was pregnant or not.

Knocking on Hunter's office door, she waited a moment before entering the office. "Do you have the time to fill me in on what took place at the staff meeting or should I come back later?"

He shook his head and pointed to the brown leather chair in front of his desk. "Have a seat. I've been waiting for you."

"That sounds ominous."

"Not really." His intense green eyes held hers as she lowered herself into the oversize armchair and tried not to notice how good-looking he was or that the sound of his deep voice had caused her insides to start humming. "Before I can order the new flight suits for everyone, I need to know if you've given any more thought to my suggestion that you ground yourself until after your baby is born."

"Yes, I have." She met his questioning gaze head-on. "I even discussed your concerns with my obstetrician this morning."

"And?"

Hunter held out little hope that she'd changed her mind, but since it had been the uppermost thing on his mind for the past two days, he had to know.

"The doctor and I both agreed that as long as I avoid heavy lifting, eat a healthy diet and get plenty of rest, there's no reason that I can't continue as a flight nurse on the Evac II team."

"But—"

"But nothing." Her determined expression warned him that she wasn't going to budge on the issue. "I'm not only capable of doing my job, I need the money I'll make between now and when I give birth to pay for the doctor and hospital."

He had to concentrate hard to keep his mind off the fact that she had the prettiest violet eyes he'd ever seen. "And there's nothing I can say to change your mind?"

"No. But as I told you the other night, if my continuing to fly bothers you that much, pair me with your best pilot. That should eliminate some of your concerns about pilot error."

Hunter took a deep breath, then slowly released it as resignation set in. "I anticipated your decision and I've already made arrangements for you and Corey to be switched to Evac I."

"That's your team." If the dismay on her pretty face was any indication, he'd shocked her.

Not at all happy about the situation, he nodded. "George and Mike—the Evac III pilot—are good, but I'm better."

"Don't you think your assumption that you're a better pilot is a bit arrogant?" She didn't look any happier with his decision than he was.

He shook his head. "Not in the least. It's a matter of experience. I have more flight hours in a Bell helicopter than George and Mike combined. Until he retired from the Air Force a couple of years ago, George flew Sikorskys. And Mike flew Apaches for the Army. I've flown a Bell almost exclusively for the past twelve years." He stopped short at adding that if he'd been behind the controls of a Bell the day of the accident, instead of a reconditioned military chopper given to the hurricane relief organization for aid missions, his fiancée would probably still be alive.

"When does this reassignment take place?"

"Effective immediately." Glancing down at the list of everyone's flight suit sizes, he asked, "What size flight suit do you think you'll need until after you have the baby?"

As he watched her thoughtfully nibble on her lower lip, sweat popped out on his forehead. The memory of Callie's softness and sweet taste when he'd kissed her was doing a real number on his neglected libido.

Giving him the size she thought she'd need to accommodate her advancing pregnancy, she asked, "Was there anything else discussed during the staff meeting that I should know about?"

He sat back in his desk chair. "Mary Lou served your cookies, and everyone agreed that if you ever decide to give up nursing, you should open a bakery shop."

She gave him a half smile as she stood up. "I don't think that would be a good idea. I only bake when I'm…" She stopped suddenly and shook her head. "It doesn't matter. What's my new schedule?"

Hunter rose to his feet. "Instead of coming in this evening, you'll need to be here day after tomorrow."

"At the usual time? Or did you change that, too?"

"Six in the evening," he said, nodding. When she turned toward the door, he said, "By the way, the other night I noticed you have a loose board on one of the porch steps. You'd better have your landlord fix it. You don't want to run the risk of falling."

"If I had a landlord, I'd have him take care of the repair." She shrugged one slender shoulder. "But since I bought the place when I moved to Devil's Fork, I guess I'll have to buy a hammer and a few nails and see what I can do about it myself."

For reasons he didn't care to contemplate, he didn't like the idea of her trying to make the repair herself. "I'll be over this evening to fix the step."

"Don't worry about it." She edged toward the door. "Upkeep is part of a homeowner's job. I don't think hammering a couple of nails into a board will be all that difficult."

Hunter figured he knew what the problem was and, rounding the desk, walked over and put his hands on her slender shoulders. He realized he'd made a huge error in judgment the moment he touched her. An electric charge zinged straight up his arms, and he had to fight an overwhelming urge to draw her closer.

"Callie, about the other night—"

"Please, don't." She shook her head. "It was just a simple kiss and I'm sure it didn't mean anything more to you than it did to me."

Whether it was a matter of stung pride, a bruised ego or the fact that he hadn't been able to forget how soft and yielding she'd been in his arms, her statement hit like a physical blow and he was determined to prove her wrong. "Darlin', that kiss was anything but simple." Slowly lowering his head, he felt as though he just might drown in her violet eyes. "And I think you know it as well as I do."

The moment his lips touched hers, it felt as if a spark ignited somewhere deep inside of him and heat spread throughout his entire body. If he had any sense at all, he'd call Emerald Larson, tell her that he'd changed his mind about taking over the air-ambulance service and put as much distance as he could between himself and Callie Marshall.

But instead of setting her away from him and apologizing for acting like an oversexed teenager, Hunter slid his arms around her and pulled her to him. Callie's soft, petite body nestled against his much larger frame sent blood racing through his veins and caused his heart to pound hard against his rib cage.

When her perfect lips parted on a soft sigh, he took advantage of her acquiescence and deepened the kiss. Slipping his tongue inside, he tasted the sweetness that was uniquely Callie and reacquainted himself with her tender inner recesses.

To his satisfaction, she circled his waist with her arms and melted against him as he gently coaxed her into doing a little exploring of her own. But with each stroke of her tongue to his, the fire that had begun to burn in his belly spread lower and his body tightened with desire faster than he could have ever imagined.

Shocked by the intensity of his need, he eased away from the kiss. Staring at the confusion on her pretty face, he had a feeling he looked just as bewildered.

"I, um, think…it might be a good idea…if we didn't do that again," she said, sounding suspiciously breathless.

"I think you're right." Releasing her, he rubbed at

the tension gathering at the base of his neck. Why did he turn into a Neanderthal every time he was around her? "I'll…see you later this evening…when I come by to repair the step."

She hurried over to the door. "It's really not necessary. I can handle fixing the—"

"I said I'd take care of it." He shook his head. "I can still fly a helicopter with a swollen finger. But if you smash your thumb, you'll have trouble starting an IV or splinting a broken limb."

She stared at him for several more seconds before she nodded, then quickly walked out of his office.

As Hunter watched Callie leave, he closed his eyes and counted to ten, then twenty. Why the hell couldn't he have left well enough alone? What on God's green earth had he thought he was going to prove, besides the fact that he had all the finesse of a bulldozer? Hadn't he sorted through what happened the other night and come to a reasonable conclusion for his attraction to her?

He hadn't been with a woman in almost a year, and that was long enough to make any normal adult male ready to crawl the walls. But even as he thought about finding a willing little lady to help him scratch his itch, he rejected the idea. A one-night stand might help him with his basic needs, but a meaningless encounter couldn't fill the void of companionship in his life.

Shaking his head, he walked back to his desk and sank into his chair. He wasn't looking for any kind of romantic relationship and neither was Callie, but he saw no reason why they couldn't be friends. They were both new in town, alone, and she needed someone to help out with the upkeep on her house from time to time.

Now if he could just keep that in mind and stop grabbing her like a caveman and kissing her until they both needed CPR, everything would be just fine.

As he sat there trying to convince himself that he could do just that, the phone rang. Checking the caller ID, he groaned when he recognized one of Emerald Larson's private numbers.

Switching the speakerphone on, he greeted his grandmother. "Hello, Emerald."

"Good afternoon, Hunter. How is my oldest grandson?"

He almost laughed. He wasn't fool enough to think that the old gal had called him just to say hello and shoot the breeze. Emerald Larson had a purpose behind everything she did. And that included placing a phone call to one of her grandsons.

"I'm doing okay. How are you?"

"Planning a little dinner party for my grandsons and their wives for the end of next month." She paused. "You will attend, won't you?"

"Sure," Hunter said, suddenly feeling more alone than he had in his entire life.

He'd only learned about his brothers a few months

ago, and although they'd formed a bond of friendship that he knew would stand the test of time, Caleb and Nick had both recently married. And that made Hunter the odd man out. Unfortunately he'd always be the odd man out. Marriage and family weren't in the cards for him. Not now. Not in the future.

Loving someone only opened a person up to more pain and heartache than it was worth. His mother had loved Owen Larson and ended up suffering a lifetime of loneliness for her efforts. Owen had run out on her, to leave her facing motherhood alone, and never looked back when he returned to Harvard after sweeping her off her feet during his spring-break in Miami. Then, Hunter had damned near lost his mind from the guilt of surviving the helicopter crash that had taken the lives of Ellen and their unborn child.

No, the emotional investment and risks that went along with loving someone weren't worth the high price a man had to pay.

"Hunter, are you still there?"

"Sorry." He took a deep breath. "What was that you were saying?"

"I said I'm on my way back to Wichita from Houston and I thought I would stop by to see you and my old friend Mary Lou."

He should have known that she wouldn't be able to resist checking up on him from time to time. She'd done the same with his brothers and the companies she'd given them. Why should he be any different?

Even though she'd given him Life Medevac to run as he saw fit, it still came under the umbrella of Emerald Inc., and she hadn't become one of the richest, most successful businesswomen in the world by sitting back and letting others oversee her holdings.

"When will you be here?" he asked, barely resisting the urge to cuss a blue streak.

"My pilot said we should be landing at the Devil's Fork airfield in five minutes."

Rubbing the tension at the base of his neck, Hunter sighed heavily. "I'll be there in a few minutes to pick you up."

"There's no need." He could envision her waving her bejeweled hand dismissively. "I had a limousine service send a car down from Odessa to drive me to the Life Medevac hangar."

"Then I guess I'll see you shortly," he said, resigned to his fate of spending the afternoon with his indomitable grandmother.

Fifteen minutes later, when he met the limousine in the Life Medevac parking lot, Hunter wasn't surprised to see Luther Freemont, Emerald's trusted personal assistant, standing ramrod-straight beside the open back door of a sleek black limousine. "Hey there, Luther. How's it going?"

"Very well, sir," the man answered, as formal as

ever. Once he helped Emerald from the backseat of the limo, he gave Hunter a short nod. "It was nice seeing you again, sir."

When his grandmother slipped her hand in the crook of Hunter's arm and started walking toward the office entrance, he noticed that her assistant got back into the limo. "Do you think old Luther will be all right out here on his own? After all, this place is to hell and gone from a corporate office."

"Poor Luther, he's a proper gentleman and very set in his ways." Emerald laughed. "He doesn't quite know what to make of you and your brothers."

"The feeling's mutual."

"And he's not at all sure what to think of southwest Texas."

Hunter opened the door and waited for her to precede him into the building. "Is Luther always such a tight…uptight?"

As she laughed, her silver-gray eyes twinkled merrily. "Yes, he's always very formal."

"I'll bet he was just a barrel of laughs when he was a kid," Hunter said as he escorted Emerald into the dispatch room.

He introduced her to the on-duty Evac III team as they passed through on the way to his private office, but purposely avoided calling her his grandmother. He still wasn't entirely comfortable thinking of her as a family member, nor did he need the added pressure that went along with others knowing he was her grandson.

"Where's Mary Lou?" she asked, seating herself in the chair in front of his desk.

"When she found out you were dropping by, she decided to run into town to pick up something for refreshments. She'll be back soon."

"Good. I haven't seen her in quite some time and I'm looking forward to catching up."

As they stared at each other across the desk, Hunter couldn't help but think how out of place Emerald Larson looked. She was professional elegance from the top of her perfectly styled silver hair to the soles of her Italian pumps. His office furnishings were light-years away from the opulence she surrounded herself with at Emerald Inc. headquarters.

"A few months ago, when you learned I'm your grandmother and I told you about your father, you weren't as vocal about your feelings as your brothers, Caleb and Nick."

She gave him a look that he had no doubt intimidated the hell out of anyone facing her in a corporate boardroom. But he wasn't one of her loyal lackeys and she was on his turf now.

"I'm here to clear the air once and for all," she said bluntly.

"Do we have to?" he asked before he could stop

himself. He knew for certain she wouldn't want to hear what he thought of her interference in his life.

"Yes." There was a steely determination in her voice, and whether he liked it or not, he knew come hell or high water she was going to have her say. "I'm sure you'd like to know why I insisted that your mother keep her silence about your father's identity until I was ready to tell you myself."

He glared at the woman who until three months ago he'd known only by reading about her in newspapers and national magazines. He hated dancing to her tune. But as his mother had pointed out before he'd left Miami, if he hadn't taken Emerald up on her offer of giving him one of her companies to run, the sacrifices she'd made to ensure his birthright would have been in vain. Keeping his father's identity a secret from her close-knit Irish family had caused a breach that had never been reconciled.

Hunter clenched his back teeth together so tightly his jaw ached. "I'm still having a problem with that. What gave you the right to coerce my mother into signing a paper stating that she wouldn't tell anyone— not even me—who my father was?"

"I know you're bitter about the way I handled everything," Emerald said patiently. "I'd probably feel the same way. But believe me, it was the best for all concerned parties."

Anger, swift and hot, burned at his gut. "For who? You or your son?"

"I never once considered the effect it would have on me or Owen." She shrugged. "My only concern was you and your mother."

"What you did to my mother, as well as to Caleb's and Nick's mothers, amounts to blackmail." He hadn't meant to sound so harsh, but the truth wasn't always pretty.

To his surprise, Emerald didn't seem the least bit offended by his accusation. "You see it as blackmail. I saw it as protecting my grandsons and their mothers from the hazards of dealing with the paparazzi and a corruptive lifestyle." She sighed. "I was determined to see that you and your brothers didn't turn out to be anything like your father. Owen might be alive today if I had given him more of my time and attention instead of everything he thought he wanted."

Hunter took a deep breath in an attempt to bring his temper under control. "Did he even know that he'd gotten three women pregnant?"

For the first time since meeting the mighty Emerald Larson and learning that she was his grandmother, Hunter watched her lower her head as if she might be ashamed of her philandering offspring. He could almost feel sorry for her. Almost.

"Yes, Owen knew he had three sons. But, as usual, he relied on me to bail him out of taking responsibility for his actions." When she raised her eyes to look at him there was unapologetic defiance in their gray depths. "I'll admit that I've made a lot of mistakes and have more than my share of regrets, but whether or not you approve of my methods to insure you boys were nothing like him, you can't deny that it worked. And I didn't exactly coerce your mother into signing the agreement to remain silent about your father. I just made it clear that should word get out that I'm your grandmother, I would have to deny it in order to protect you from the media frenzy it would create."

Hunter could see her reasoning, but that didn't change the fact that she'd waited thirty-two years before she'd clued him in on who had fathered him or that all that time she'd had private investigators reporting his and his brothers' every move. "Why did you wait so long to tell us?"

"I wanted all three of you to gain some life experiences of your own instead of having to live down your father's reputation of being an international playboy," she said pragmatically. "That would have been a huge burden for all of you. Not to mention how it would have affected you to learn that you had a multimillion-dollar trust fund and would eventually inherit a sizable part of my business holdings."

As Hunter mulled over what she'd said, he couldn't help but agree with her. Handling the knowledge that he'd become an overnight millionaire and owner of his own business was hard enough to grasp at the age of thirty-two. He couldn't imagine the effect it would have had on him at a much earlier age.

But before he could comment, Emerald added, "And before you ask, it was extremely hard for me to read about your accomplishments in a private investigator's report while you were growing up and not be there to see them for myself." She leaned forward as if to emphasize her point. "What I did and the way I went about it I did out of love. Believe me, nothing would have pleased me more than to have had a traditional grandmother's relationship with you and your brothers. But I had to give that up in order to protect you."

Thinking it over, Hunter realized that as difficult as it had been for him growing up not knowing who his father was, it had to have been much harder for Emerald. She'd known all about him and his brothers but hadn't been able to let any of them know how she felt.

"I guess all we can do now is move forward," he said, thinking aloud.

"I believe that would be wise," Emerald agreed. "Taking over the Life Medevac Helicopter Service is a good start for you, and I expect you to do quite well." She surprised him when she rose from the chair and rounded the desk to kiss his cheek. "It's time to get back to what you do best—flying helicopters and helping those in need—and leave the past behind,

Hunter. It's history and can't be changed. But the future is an unwritten page and sometimes found where you least expect it."

Four

"If you don't stop letting Hunter O'Banyon kiss you, you're going to be as big as a barn," Callie muttered, poking another snickerdoodle into her mouth as she measured the ingredients for a double batch of choco-late-chocolate-chip cookies.

The minute she'd arrived back home from her meeting with Hunter, she'd walked straight into the kitchen, put on her apron and started baking. Five dozen snickerdoodles, a double batch of sugar cookies and a pan of brownies later, she still hadn't been able to forget how his lips had felt on hers. Warm, firm and deliciously male, his mouth could very easily be clas-sified as a lethal weapon. At least for her.

Spooning chocolate dough onto cookie sheets, she wondered what there was about Hunter that caused her to abandon every ounce of common sense she possessed. All he had to do was touch her and she clung to him like a piece of plastic shrink-wrap on a hot plate.

She slid the pan of cookie dough into the oven and set the timer. Then, sitting down at the table while she waited on the cookies to bake, Callie stared off into space.

It wasn't uncommon for a woman in her second trimester to find herself feeling more sensual than ever before, but she didn't think her pregnancy hormones could account for the compelling attraction she experienced with Hunter. With just a look he could make her heart flutter. And when he touched her, she practically melted into a puddle at his feet. She hadn't had that kind of reaction to Craig, and he was her baby's father.

Lost in thought, it took her a moment to realize someone was knocking on her door. Hurrying to remove the pan of cookies from the oven, when she walked into the living room and opened the door, she found Hunter squatted down beside the steps. He had replaced the loose board with a new one and was pounding nails into the wood with no more than a couple of whacks with a hammer. She swallowed hard when she noticed how his bicep and the muscles in his forearm flexed with each blow.

"That should last a while," he said, straightening to his full height. "And it'll be a lot safer for you."

When she finally found her voice, she nodded. "Thank you."

He wiped the sweat from his forehead on the sleeve of his T-shirt. "Is there anything else that needs fixing or that you'd like me to take a look at while I'm here?"

"I can't think of anything." She motioned toward the door. "Would you like to come in to cool off and have a glass of iced tea?"

Smiling, he nodded. "That sounds like a winner." He put the hammer and a small sack of nails in the back of his truck, then climbed the steps to Callie's cottage. "It's not as humid here in southwest Texas as it is in Florida, but it's still hotter than hell."

Callie laughed as they walked inside the house. "It's late August. What do you expect?"

"Good point," he said, grinning.

When they walked into the kitchen, she poured them each a glass of iced tea. "Having lived close to the Gulf all my life, I'm not used to all this dry heat."

"Thank God for air-conditioning."

"Amen to that." She smiled as she placed her hand on her rounded stomach. "I've been hotter this summer than I've ever been in my life."

"It's no wonder you're hot, with the oven on all the time." Chuckling, he looked at the plates of cookies and brownies sitting on the counter. "I see you've been at it again."

She smiled wanly. There was no way she was going to tell him that just the thought of him kissing her could send her into a baking frenzy.

He reached for a brownie. "What are you going to do with all this stuff?"

Thinking quickly, she shrugged. "Schools are always having bake sales. I thought I'd donate some of the things I've baked for their fund-raisers. And after the baby is born, I doubt that I'll have a lot of time, so I've frozen a lot of what I've made."

"Good idea." He grinned. "I'm sure Corey will appreciate that."

"I'm sure he will. He eats constantly but never seems to fill up." She frowned. "Do all boys eat like they have a bottomless pit for a stomach?"

"Pretty much." Hunter reached for one of the chocolate-chocolate-chip cookies on the baking sheet she'd removed from the oven earlier. "My mom said that once I hit puberty, I ate everything in sight."

"I guess that's something I have to look forward to." Callie smiled at the fluttering in her stomach. It was as if the baby knew she was talking about him.

"You're having a boy?"

She nodded. "That's what the sonogram indicates."

"When are you due?"

"Around the first of the year." She turned to spoon cookie dough onto a baking sheet. "Of course, that doesn't mean he won't decide to come a couple of weeks early or late."

"That would be anywhere from a week or so before Christmas to mid-January."

She wondered why Hunter was taking such an interest in when she'd give birth, until it occurred to her that he would need to find someone to cover her shifts at Life Medevac. "I'm planning on taking maternity leave at Thanksgiving and being back to work no later than mid-February. Mary Lou suggested that I bring the baby to work with me and she could watch him when I go out on a call. Is that all right with you?"

He nodded. "But are you sure it's a good idea to wait that long to take your leave?" He frowned. "I don't mean to offend you, but won't it be difficult climbing in and out of the helicopter when you're that…far along?"

"No offense taken. I know I'll be quite large." She slipped the pan of cookies into the oven, then turned to face him. "If I see that it's a problem, I'll…take my leave earlier than…I'd planned."

He took a step toward her. "Are you all right?"

Laughing, she nodded. "It's just the baby moving. He seems to be particularly active today."

"Does it hurt?" He looked and sounded genuinely concerned.

"No. If anything, it tickles." She lovingly placed her hand on her stomach. "At this stage of pregnancy it's like having a butterfly flapping its wings inside of me. Later on, I'm told it will feel like I have a prizefighter in there."

"I'll bet that does feel weird." When the timer on the oven went off, he reached for a hot pad. "Why don't you sit down and put your feet up?"

"I'm fine."

Hunter pointed to one of the kitchen chairs. "Sit."

He could tell she wasn't happy about it, but while she sat down and propped her feet up in one of the other chairs, he removed the cookies from the oven. "Damn! That's hot!" he cursed when the back of his hand touched the top of the oven.

She was at his side in a flash. "Let me see."

Reluctantly letting her examine his hand, he tried to ignore how nice her soft palms felt holding his calloused one. "It's nothing."

"It's already starting to form a blister," she said, reaching for a bottle of some kind of clear lotion.

"What's that?"

"Aloe vera. It will stop it from hurting and help it heal faster." She flipped the top of the bottle open, then glanced up at him and grinned. "And don't worry, it won't make you smell like a flower."

As he watched her gently spread the clear gel on the small burn, a warmth began to fill his chest. It had been a long time since he'd had a woman fussing over him. And whether it was wise or not, he liked the feeling more than he cared to admit.

"That should take care of it," she said, closing the bottle.

Amazed at how much better it felt, he flexed his hand. "That stuff really works. Thanks."

"Not…a problem."

She sounded slightly winded, and he figured their close proximity had the same effect on her that it had on him. He was having the devil of a time trying to keep from taking her in his arms and kissing her senseless.

"I think I'd better be going."

"How much do I owe you for fixing the step?" she asked, reaching for her purse on the table.

"I ate enough cookies and brownies to more than pay for the job."

He edged toward the door. If he didn't get out of there soon, he was going to take her in his arms—and that could spell disaster to his good intentions. And he'd have succeeded, too, if she hadn't touched him.

"Hunter, stop being so darned stubborn."

Her small hand resting on his forearm sent a wave of heat streaking throughout his entire body. Without a single thought to the consequences or that he'd promised himself he'd be able to keep his hands to himself, he pulled her into his arms.

"Darlin', friends help each other all the time." He

kissed her forehead. "And they don't ask for anything in return."

She stared at him for several long seconds before she shook her head. "I'm not sure that you and I could ever be just friends. And right now I'm not looking for anything more."

"That makes two of us, Callie." He brushed her perfect lips with his. "But I think as long as we keep that in mind, we'll be just fine." He kissed her soundly, then forced himself to set her away from him and walk to the door. Turning back, he smiled. "I'll see you at work tomorrow evening, *friend.*"

"Where's Corey?" Callie asked when she arrived at work the next evening. "I didn't see his truck in the parking lot."

"He called to say he'd be a few minutes late," Mary Lou answered as she opened the container of brownies Callie had placed on the table by the coffeepot. Removing a double-fudge-and-nut chocolate square, she took a bite and shrugged. "I told him that if we get a call before he reports for his shift, I'd give him a talkin' to he won't soon forget."

Callie frowned. "It's not like Corey to be late. Did he say what's up?"

"He said he and his girlfriend were on their way back from talking to her parents up in Odessa. He should be here in about a half hour or so." Mary Lou lowered her voice and leaned forward. "Can you keep a secret?"

"Of course."

The older woman grinned. "Corey is going to be a daddy in about seven months."

"You're kidding." Callie laughed. "He's not much more than a boy himself."

Mary Lou grinned. "I've always said he's twenty-two going on ten."

"What's up?" Hunter asked, walking into the dispatch room.

Callie's heart came to a skittering halt, then took off double time. If she'd thought he looked good in jeans and a T-shirt, it was nothing compared to the way he looked in his flight suit. The one-piece coverall emphasized the impossible width of his muscular shoulders and narrowness of his trim waist.

"Just some girl talk," Mary Lou said, winking at Callie.

"Which one of us guys are you dissecting?" Hunter asked, grinning.

His comment had been for both she and Mary Lou, but when his gaze caught Callie's, she felt warm all the way to her toes. If he wanted to, she had a feeling Hunter O'Banyon could charm a little old lady right out of her garters with that smile of his.

And he thought they could be *just* friends? She

almost laughed. The way he was looking at her, there was a better chance of elephants roosting in trees.

"Don't worry, big guy." Mary Lou cackled. "We weren't taking you to task for anything. This time."

He arched one dark eyebrow. "This time?"

"We were discussing when Corey would show up," Callie added.

Hunter's skeptical expression turned to one of understanding. "Corey had some important personal business to take care of up in Odessa. He'll be here as soon as he can."

"You know what's going on, don't you?" Callie guessed.

"He came by yesterday evening to ask me and Mike what we thought he should do about the situation," Hunter said, nodding.

"That little skunk told me I was the only one he'd talked to about it," Mary Lou said, obviously put out that the confidence wasn't as big a secret as she'd thought. "Just wait until I—" Mary Lou stopped abruptly when the emergency phone rang.

Callie listened as Mary Lou asked several questions in Spanish. Great. Corey wasn't back yet and on the Evac II team he'd been the only one fluent in Spanish.

"Come on, Callie. We don't have time to wait for Corey," Hunter said, heading for the door. "As it is, we're going to have to race the stork to the hospital."

"Is it Juanita Rodriguez again?" Callie asked,

thankful that Hunter had obviously understood Mary Lou's end of the conversation and would be able to interpret for her.

He nodded as they climbed into the helicopter and put on the headsets that would enable them to communicate over the engine noise. "She's definitely in labor this time. From Mary Lou's questions, I could tell that Juanita's water broke and she's home alone."

"Where's her husband Miguel?"

"He's in El Paso at a National Guard meeting this weekend. We can radio his armory and have him meet us at the hospital."

While Hunter started the engine, Callie strapped herself into one of the jump seats in the back and listened to Mary Lou's voice give the coordinates for the Rodriguez ranch to Hunter. They had about a fifteen-minute flight to reach their destination, then another thirty minutes on to El Paso. Mary Lou was going to stay on the phone with Juanita until they got there, and hopefully Baby Rodriguez would wait to make his or her grand entrance into the world until after they made it to the hospital.

When they lifted off, Callie began to mentally run through emergency birthing procedure on the outside chance that she would have to deliver Juanita's baby, and it took a moment for her to realize Hunter had spoken to her. "I'm sorry. What did you say?"

"I asked if you've delivered a baby before." His

deep baritone coming through the headset was oddly intimate and sent a shiver straight up her spine.

She gave herself a mental shake. Hearing Hunter's voice through the headset was no different than when she'd communicated with George or Corey on a flight.

"I've delivered a few babies—one of them in the back of a taxicab when the E.R. doctors were busy treating victims from a bus accident."

"But you don't speak or understand Spanish?"

She sighed. "No."

They fell silent, and in what seemed record time, Hunter was setting the helicopter down in a field next to the Rodriguez ranch house.

Removing her headset and unfastening her seat belt, Callie grabbed one of the medical cases containing sterile dressings, latex gloves and other medical supplies and hurriedly slid the side door back. She bent slightly to avoid the rotor blades, then, once she was clear of the helicopter, she jogged the short distance to the house. Fortunately the front door was unlocked, and she walked inside without so much as a second thought.

"¡Por favor ayúdeme!"

Callie followed the frantic cries and found Juanita in one of the bedrooms. Drenched in sweat, the young woman was practically hysterical and instead of working with the contractions she seemed to be fighting them.

"¡El bebé está listo!" Juanita repeated, clutching at Callie's hands.

"What's she saying about the baby?" Callie asked Hunter when he appeared in the narrow doorway.

"She said the baby is ready."

"Tell her that I need to check to see how close she is to having the baby," Callie said, slipping on a pair of sterile latex gloves.

While Hunter assured Juanita that everything was going to be all right, Callie checked to see how many centimeters the woman had dilated. "The stork is going to win this one," she said, reaching into the medical case for clamps, a sterile drape and antiseptic. "The baby's head is crowning."

As she arranged the medical supplies she would need for the birth of Juanita's baby, Callie listened to Hunter reassure the woman. She had no idea what he was telling her, but it seemed to calm Juanita as well as send warmth throughout Callie's body. She'd always thought Spanish was a beautiful language and she didn't think she'd ever heard a more sexy sound than Hunter's deep voice flawlessly pronouncing the words.

"Do you have any kind of experience being a breathing coach?" Callie asked as she prepped Juanita for the delivery.

He shook his head. "No. We covered it briefly in EMT training, but that's it."

"You'll do fine." Using the two-way radio clipped to the epaulet on the shoulder of her jumpsuit, she advised the hospital in El Paso of the situation, then turned her full attention on the task at hand. "Tell Juanita to breathe, then show her how. She's tensing up instead of relaxing her pelvic floor and allowing the baby to pass through the birth canal."

"*Respira,* Juanita. *Respira.*"

When Hunter showed the young woman what he meant, she trustingly stared into his eyes and began to concentrate on doing as he requested. Once she stopped fighting the pain, she rapidly progressed to the pushing phase of the delivery. Moving into position to lift her shoulders when it came time to push, he continued to reassure her that everything was going to be all right.

"*Todo será bien,* Juanita."

"Tell her to stop the shallow breathing and start pushing," Callie said, showing the woman how to position her hands on her knees for leverage.

Encouraging Juanita to push with all her might, he supported her shoulders, and after only a couple of tries, the baby's dark head emerged from the young woman's lower body. Hunter watched Callie quickly and efficiently suction the infant's nose and mouth before it was time for Juanita to push the rest of her baby out into the world.

With one more mighty push from Juanita, the baby slid out into Callie's waiting hands. Without being prompted, the baby girl opened her mouth and wailed at the top of her tiny lungs.

"*Mí bebé,*" Juanita murmured tearfully.

"You have a beautiful daughter, Juanita," Callie said, placing the baby on her mother's stomach.

Awed by the miracle he'd just witnessed, the moment was so bittersweet Hunter couldn't have pushed words past the lump clogging his throat if his life depended on it. Although he was happy for the Rodriguez family and their new addition, he'd never know what it was like to watch his own son or daughter come into the world. After losing Ellen and their unborn child, he never intended to put himself in the position of loving someone and taking the risk of losing them. He'd been down that road before and had barely survived. There was no way in hell he could go through that again.

"Hunter, could you please hold the baby while I get Juanita ready for transport?" Callie asked, breaking into his disturbing thoughts.

The last thing he wanted to do was hold a baby. He knew for certain it would only compound his sense of loss and regret that he'd never hold his own child. But before he could protest, Callie placed the baby in his arms. As he stared down at the red-faced little girl wrapped in a soft white blanket, instead of the sorrow he expected, Hunter couldn't help but marvel at how small she was, how perfect.

Gently touching her little hand, he was thoroughly amazed when the baby curled her perfectly formed tiny fingers around one of his. "She's holding on to me."

"Babies do that," Callie said, smiling.

He watched Callie and Juanita exchange an indulgent glance. Apparently there was no language barrier when it came to women's opinions of men. It must be universally accepted that men didn't have a clue about these things. But that was okay with him. Men didn't understand women, so he supposed that made the genders pretty equal.

While Callie radioed the hospital to report a successful, complication-free birth, Hunter contemplated how they were going to get Juanita into the helicopter without Corey. He wasn't about to let Callie lift anything heavier than her nurse's bag or the baby, and the door and hallway were too narrow to get the stretcher into the bedroom. That left only one alternative.

"Are we ready for transport?" When Callie nodded, he handed her the baby. "You take your nurse's bag and the baby while I carry Juanita to the chopper."

"That would probably be best," Callie said, lifting the nylon bag's webbed strap to her shoulder. "You'd probably have to carry her to the front door before you could put her on the stretcher anyway."

Telling Juanita what was taking place, Hunter scooped her slight body into his arms and carried her out to the helicopter. Once he placed her on the stretcher and Callie handed her the baby, Juanita and her new daughter both drifted off into a peaceful sleep.

The flight to El Paso was uneventful, and once they

had Juanita and her new daughter safely checked in to the hospital, Callie and Hunter boarded the helicopter and headed back to the Life Medevac base.

"You did a wonderful job of calming Juanita down," Callie said as she stared through the windshield at the vast blue sky ahead of them. Riding in the front seat next to Hunter on the trip back to Devil's Fork, she enjoyed the view of the rugged Texas mountains that she missed when riding in the back with a patient.

"It didn't show that I had no idea what I was doing?" he asked, grinning sheepishly.

Smiling, she shook her head. "Not at all. Juanita is young and had no idea what to expect when her contractions started. Factor in that she was home alone and miles away from help and it was no wonder she was frightened half out of her mind. You were able to put her at ease and that made it a lot easier for her."

He shrugged. "I just did what I thought would help." They were both silent for some time before he asked, "Who's going to be with you when you have your baby?"

It was the last thing she'd expected him to ask. "Are you volunteering for the job?"

"Hell no."

She laughed at his horrified expression. "But you're a great labor coach."

He grunted. "Only because Corey wasn't there to take over for me. I'm the pilot, remember?"

"You're also a certified EMT."

"Only because my grandmother strongly suggested that it would be a good idea since I was taking over an air-ambulance service." He shrugged. "Besides, whether or not you and the father of your baby are together, I'm sure he'll want to be there when his son is born. He can be your breathing coach."

A cold chill ran the length of her spine at the thought of Craig Culbertson being anywhere near her or her child. "I can assure you, he won't be anywhere around when I give birth."

"Maybe he'll change his mind."

"It's not an issue."

Hunter was quiet for a moment, then turned his head to give her a questioning look. "He doesn't even know he's fathered a child, does he?" His mouth flattening into a disapproving line, he shook his head. "Forget that I asked. It's none of my business."

She hadn't discussed with anyone—not even her mother—why she'd made the decision not to tell Craig about the baby. But she needed to make Hunter understand, without divulging too many details, why she felt she had no choice but to keep her silence.

"Believe me, it's for the best." Placing her hand protectively over her son, she shook her head. "Even if I told him about the baby, he wouldn't care."

"Don't you think you owe him the chance to prove you wrong?"

"No. He's too selfish and self-centered to care about anyone or anything but himself."

Hunter stared straight ahead and she could tell he was thinking over what she'd said. "There must have been some substance to the man or you wouldn't have become involved with him," he finally said.

Callie sighed heavily. "In the past several months I've spent countless hours wondering why I allowed myself to be fooled by his insincerity."

She could feel Hunter's intense gaze as surely as if he'd reached out and touched her. "And?"

"I came to the conclusion that he was the consummate charmer who was more interested in the chase than in a meaningful relationship."

"I know the type," Hunter said disgustedly. "Let me guess—he asked you out several times and you turned him down. That's when he pulled out all the stops and did everything in his power to convince you that he was wild about you."

"That's exactly what happened. I became a challenge that he was determined to conquer." She took a deep breath. "And like a fool, I allowed him to wear down my resistance and charm me into believing that we could have a future together."

When Hunter took her hand in his to give it a gentle squeeze, a warmth like nothing she'd ever known filled her all the way to her soul. "Don't be so hard on yourself, darlin'. It's not the first time a woman has been taken in by a player. And it's sad to say, but it won't be the last."

She knew he was right, but that didn't make her feel any less foolish for allowing it to happen, especially since she was now facing motherhood alone. "Then you understand my reasoning for keeping my pregnancy a secret?"

"Not entirely." He released her hand, then, remaining silent for several long seconds, he finally added, "Don't you think you should at least give him the opportunity to redeem himself? I know if I was in his shoes, I'd definitely be angry if I discovered a woman had denied me the right to know my own son."

Callie knew for certain she couldn't take the chance of telling Craig. But she wasn't ready to outline her reasons to Hunter. "He'd only view the baby as an inconvenience, and my child deserves better than that."

"Do you ever intend to tell your son who his father is?"

"He'll be better off not knowing."

"Every kid has a right to know who they are and where they came from," he said forcefully. His tone left no doubt that he felt very passionately about the subject. "He'll grow up wondering if every man he passes on the street is the one responsible for his existence."

"Why do you feel so strongly about this?"

She watched him take a deep breath, then slowly release it. Just when she thought he was going to tell her it was none of her concern, he spoke. "I grew up not knowing anything about my father, and it wasn't until just recently that I even learned who he was—after he'd been dead for six months."

"Oh, Hunter, I'm so sorry." She began to understand why he felt it was so important that she inform Craig about the baby. "Your mother didn't tell him about you?"

"He knew." There was an edge to his voice. "He just chose to ignore the fact that he'd fathered three sons with three different women." Hunter gave her a meaningful glance. "But the point is, they gave him the opportunity to know about us. He was the one who made the decision to stay out of our lives."

"But she didn't tell *you*," Callie guessed.

He shook his head. "She had her reasons and she knew that one day I would learn who he was. But that didn't make it any easier on me when I was growing up or stop me from resenting the fact that I wasn't given the choice to know anything about the man."

She could understand why Hunter felt the way he did, but her circumstances were different. If she told Craig about the baby, there was a good chance that he and his parents would try to separate her and her son the way they'd done that poor girl and her baby twelve years ago. And that was a chance Callie wasn't willing to take.

"I will tell my son about his father when I feel he's ready," she said carefully. "But until that time we'll be just fine on our own."

Five

For the next few days Hunter couldn't stop thinking about the conversation he'd had with Callie on the way back from El Paso. There'd been something in her voice that had alerted him to the fact there was more to her refusal to tell her baby's father about the pregnancy than she was letting on. He couldn't quite put his finger on what that something was, but it was serious enough that she felt silence was her only option.

Hunter's heart stalled. Could the man have been abusive?

Fury stronger than he could have ever imagined coursed through his veins. He wasn't a violent man by nature, but just the thought that the jerk might have mistreated Callie in any way was enough to make Hunter ready to tear him limb from limb.

Suddenly needing to move before he put his fist through the wall, Hunter grabbed his sunglasses and, taking his ball cap from a hook beside his office door, jammed it onto his head. He felt as if he had enough adrenaline coursing through him to bench-press a 747 fully loaded with passengers and cargo. What he needed was some good, hard physical labor to help him work off his anger. And he knew exactly what he was going to do.

As he drove to the lumber yard, he mentally reviewed all the things in need of repair or replacement at Callie's place. Besides the steps he'd fixed a few days ago, he'd noticed the place could use a coat of paint and a new deck at the back door to replace a badly deteriorating concrete stoop.

Purchasing everything he needed to make the improvements, Hunter scheduled a delivery for the lumber to build a new deck, then loaded his truck with a new extension ladder, several buckets of paint, brushes and scrapers. Satisfied that he had everything he needed, he headed toward Callie's house at the edge of town.

He'd thought about talking to her before he started buying supplies and making plans, but if her protest over the simple repair he'd made to the step was any indication, she would have refused his offer. And whether she liked it or not, he wasn't taking no for an

answer. In the case of the back stoop, it was a matter
of safety.

When he parked the truck and positioned the ladder
against the side of the house, he wasn't surprised when
she came out to glare at him. "Why on earth are you
making so much noise and what are you doing to my
house?"

With her shoulder-length blond hair in delightful
disarray, her eyes soft with sleep and her feet bare, she
looked as if she'd just crawled out of bed. She also
looked sexy as hell.

"Good morning to you, too." He grinned as he
grabbed one of the scrapers. "Did you stay up late last
night making cookies?"

"As a matter of fact, I did."

"What kind?"

She shook her head. "Don't change the subject.
What are you doing here at the god-awful hour of
seven-thirty in the morning? And why is that ladder
propped against the side of my house?"

"One thing at a time, darlin'," he said, climbing the
ladder. "Contrary to popular belief, seven-thirty isn't all
that early. Did you know the lumber yard and hardware
store here in Devil's Fork open every morning at six?"

Glaring at him, she propped her fists on her shapely
hips. "Since I've never had occasion to go into either
establishment, no, I didn't know that."

He scraped off a long strip of peeling paint close to

the peak of the roof. "The other day I noticed that the paint on this place had started to crack and peel."

"So you just decided to take it upon yourself to paint my house?" Clearly fit to be tied, she looked mighty damned cute standing there in an oversize pink T-shirt and a pair of mint-green camp shorts, tapping her bare foot against the hard-packed dirt.

"You can't do it," he said as he continued to remove strips of weathered paint from the board siding. "And it needs to be done before winter sets in."

"It could wait until after I have the baby."

He shook his head. "You'll be too busy once the baby gets here. Besides, I might as well do something constructive on my days off."

"But I can't afford this right now."

"You don't have to pay for it."

"Yes, I do."

"I've already taken care of it."

She made a noise that sounded suspiciously like a growl. "Tell me how much you've spent and I'll pay you back."

He grinned. "Nope."

"Are you always this—" she stopped as if searching for the right word "—this meddlesome?"

He stopped scraping to stare down at her. "Are you always this stubborn when someone is trying to help you?"

Rubbing her temples with her fingertips, she shook

her head. "I do appreciate you trying to help. But I can't afford all the improvements right now and I can't let you pay for them."

"Consider it a housewarming gift," he said, sending more flakes of paint falling to the ground.

"That's absurd." She frowned. "You're newer in town than I am."

He chuckled. "Minor technicality."

"I can't let you do this."

"You can't stop me." He climbed down the ladder, then, placing the scraper on the tailgate of the truck, walked over to stand in front of her. "Look, there are things around here that need attention and you're not able to do them in your condition."

She rolled her eyes. "I've told you before, I'm pregnant, not disabled."

"Whatever. You can't do them and I need something to keep me busy on my days off."

He could tell he was wearing down her resistance when she sighed heavily. "Yes, but it isn't fair for you to pay for the materials to make improvements to my house."

Unable to resist taking her into his arms, he smiled as he pulled her to him, then pushed the brim of his ball cap up out of the way. "If it bothers you that much, why don't we strike a deal?"

She looked suspicious. "What kind of agreement are you talking about?"

"I'll do some work around your house and you can make me a few home-cooked meals." He used his index finger to raise her chin until their gazes met. "Does that sound fair?"

"Not really. I still think that I'm getting the better end of this deal."

Her soft body pressed to his was playing hell with his good intentions, and before he could stop himself, he lowered his mouth to hers. "Throw in a couple dozen brownies—" he brushed her perfect lips with his "—some chocolate-chip-oatmeal cookies—" she parted for him on a soft sigh "—and we'll call it even," he finished as he deepened the kiss.

The combination of Callie's sweet taste and the fact that she was kissing him back sent blood surging through his veins and had his lower body tightening with a need that threatened to buckle his knees. Never in all his thirty-two years had he been aroused as fast or as completely as he was at that very moment.

But when she raised her arms to his neck and tangled her fingers in the hair at his nape, her feather-light touch caused a jolt of hunger to fill every fiber of his being and the need to touch her became overwhelming. Sliding his hand beneath the tail of her T-shirt, when his calloused palm met the satiny skin along her side, his heart thumped hard against his ribs. They'd been so embroiled in their argument over him doing repairs to her house that he hadn't paid attention to the fact that she wasn't wearing a bra.

When he cupped her full breast, then gently slid the pad of his thumb over her tight nipple, her moan of pleasure mingled with his groan of frustration. What the hell did he think he was doing?

Not only was he making out with his flight nurse for God and everybody to see, she was pregnant with another man's child. He wasn't looking for a lasting relationship with any woman. And Callie wasn't a woman who engaged in meaningless flings.

Reluctantly removing his hand from beneath her shirt, he broke the kiss to stare into her wide violet eyes. "Darlin', I think you'd better go back in the house and I'm going to get back to work."

Her porcelain cheeks colored a deep rose and she backed away from him. "I'll be…gone for…a little while," she said, sounding out of breath. "I need to go…to the grocery store."

He frowned. "What for? Your cabinets and freezer are full of food."

She took several steps backward. "I have to see if the store carries fifty-pound bags of flour."

Repositioning his ball cap, Hunter watched her turn and hurry around the side of the house toward the front porch. He'd never seen a woman bake as much as Callie. Maybe it was some kind of hormonal nesting thing.

He shook his head as he grabbed the scraper from the back of the truck and climbed the ladder. Whatever it was, as long as she was inside the house baking and he was outside painting, there wouldn't be any more encounters like the one they'd just shared. And if he repeated it enough times, he just might start to believe it.

When she heard someone knocking on the front door, Callie glanced at the clock on the stove. Hunter couldn't possibly have driven out to the Life Medevac hangar, showered and changed clothes, then driven all the way back to her place in such a short time.

After he'd finished the arduous task of scraping away the peeling paint, he'd told her he was going to go back to the hangar and clean up while she finished dinner. Although she couldn't imagine what it would be, he must have forgotten something.

Wiping her hands on a towel, she checked the pot roast she'd put in the oven earlier, then hurried to open the door. "I'm afraid dinner isn't quite…" Her voice trailed off as icy fear froze her vocal cords and filled every cell in her being.

"Hello, Callie." Craig Culbertson flashed his practiced smile as he brushed past her. "Since you didn't know I was coming for a visit, I didn't expect you to make dinner for me. But I'm sure whatever you're cooking up will be delicious."

"Wh-what are you doing here?" she asked, gripping

the doorknob so hard she wouldn't be surprised if she left her fingerprints embedded in the metal.

"I've missed you." He looked around her small, tidy living room. "What were you thinking when you left Houston for this? It's not even as nice as that minuscule apartment you had."

She ignored his insult and repeated her question. "Why are you here, Craig?"

Turning to face her, his charming smile disappeared; it was replaced with an expression of utter disgust. "Good God! You're pregnant."

Drawing on every ounce of courage she'd ever possessed, she squared her shoulders and placed a protective hand on her stomach. "Yes, I am."

"It's mine, isn't it?" he asked, his tone accusing.

Knowing full well that he wouldn't believe her, she shook her head. "No. The baby belongs to—"

"Me."

Callie had never been so relieved to see anyone in her entire life as she was when Hunter walked through the open door and put his arm around her shoulders. Nor had she ever been as shocked when she heard his claim to be her baby's father.

"This is Craig Culbertson from Houston," she said, silently thanking Hunter for intervening. "Hunter O'Banyon is my—"

"Husband," Hunter interrupted, giving her a look that asked for her to trust him.

"You're married?" Craig shook his head. "You can't be. Your mother said you only moved here a couple of months ago. That's not nearly long enough to find yourself a husband and get knocked up."

"I take exception to the phrase 'knocked up' in reference to my wife's pregnancy," Hunter said, his voice hard as granite.

"Sorry." His tone was anything but apologetic, but Craig apparently decided that Hunter meant business and wasn't one to be trifled with, because he immediately began to backpedal. "It was just an expression, no offense intended."

A fresh wave of fear coursed through Callie as she thought about her last conversation with her mother and how she'd tried to get Callie to tell her who the baby's father was. Had her mother inadvertently hinted to Craig that Callie might be carrying his child?

"Why did you call my mother?" she asked, surprised that her voice was fairly steady considering the state of her nerves.

Craig gave her the smile that she used to think made him look endearingly handsome. Now it only made her feel ill.

"When I discovered your old phone number was no longer in service, I remembered your mother's name, looked up her number and called her to ask how to get in touch with you." He shrugged. "She was reluctant to tell me about your move to Texas until I told her that we'd been seeing each other before you left and how much I missed you. That's when she suggested that if I was ever in the Devil's Fork area that I should look you up. I decided to clear my calendar for the rest of the week and make the drive out here to no-man's-land to see how you're doing."

Callie did a slow burn. She wasn't as angry with her mother as she was with Craig. He'd obviously fed her mother a line about how much he cared, and her mother had fallen for it. Unfortunately Nancy Marshall had never met Craig and had no idea what a snake he was. He wasn't interested in how Callie was doing. His ego was still smarting from the fact that Callie had been the one who'd rejected him instead of the other way around.

"Actually your mother and I talked for some time and I found her to be a very nice lady," Craig added solicitously.

"Oh, really?" Callie shook her head. "It's amazing to me that you carried on a lengthy conversation with my mother when you never would take the time to meet her when you and I were seeing each other."

"You've always been close with your mother, haven't you, Callie?" Craig asked.

She gritted her teeth. "You know I have."

"That's the main reason I find it odd that she didn't know anything about your marriage." He rocked back on his heels as he pointed to Hunter. "It seems to me that she would be the first one you told about your marriage to O'Banyon."

When the timer on the stove went off, indicating that the pot roast was done, Callie reluctantly left the two men standing in her living room glaring at each other. She had no idea what was going to take place or how to deal with it. Hunter's expression from the moment he'd walked through the door had been dark and foreboding. And Craig, as was his usual fashion when he felt threatened, had become arrogant and condescending.

Removing the roast from the oven, she hurried back into the living room before punches started flying. "Craig, I'm sure you have better things to do with your time than stand here debating my marital status."

He shook his head. "Not really. But I will take you up on that offer of dinner."

"I didn't—"

Hunter pulled her to his side and pressed a quick kiss to her lips. "I'm sure we have enough for three, don't we, darlin'?"

Had Hunter lost his mind? The last thing she wanted to do was spend more time in the presence of a snake like Craig Culbertson.

"Well, yes, but—"

"Good." Hunter turned to Craig. "Why don't you have a seat while I help my wife finish getting things on the table?"

Craig gave her a triumphant smile as he plopped down on the end of the love seat. "I think I'll do that."

As soon as she and Hunter entered the kitchen, she turned on him. "What on earth were you thinking?" she demanded, careful to keep her voice low. "I want him out of this house, out of this state and out of my life. For good."

Hunter nodded. "That's the plan."

She looked at him as though he might not be the sharpest knife in the drawer. "And having him stay for dinner is the way to do that?"

"I believe so."

Taking in a deep breath, Hunter still couldn't believe that he'd claimed to be Callie's husband and the father of her baby. But when he'd walked up the porch steps and heard the disgust in Culbertson's voice and the fear in Callie's, Hunter had done the only thing he could think of that didn't involve putting his fist in the man's nose.

"Would you care to explain your reasoning?" she asked as she reached for a pair of oven mitts. "Because I'm having a really hard time understanding."

When he noticed how badly her hands trembled, he took the mitts from her and removed a roasting pan from the oven. Placing it on a hot pad, he tossed the mitts on the counter, then cupped her cheeks with his palms. "The first thing I want you to do is calm down, Callie. I give you my word that as long as I have breath left in my body, I won't let him do anything to harm you or the baby. Is that clear?"

She gazed at him for several long seconds, and the fear he saw in her eyes just about tore him apart. "Yes," she finally said, nodding.

"Good." He reached into the cabinet for a platter. Handing it to her, he explained. "It's clear that Culbertson needs some convincing that you and I are married."

"That came as a surprise to me, too," she said, slicing the roast.

He rubbed the tension building at the back of his neck. "Then it's unanimous, because I was pretty damned shocked about it myself. But it's the only thing I can think of that might make him leave you alone. And that's what you want, isn't it?"

"Absolutely." There wasn't even a heartbeat's hesitation in her voice, and Hunter had no doubt that she didn't want Craig Culbertson anywhere near her.

"The way I see it, if we can convince him how happy we are and how much we're looking forward to our first child, he'll get the message, go back to Houston and you'll never hear from him again." He carried the platter of pot roast over to the small kitchen table while Callie set another place. "Now all we have to do is get a few things straight."

"Like what?"

He removed three glasses from one of the shelves, filled them with ice, then reached for a pitcher of iced tea sitting on the kitchen island. "He'll want to know how we met, when we got married and what we're going to name the baby."

She stared at him openmouthed. "We don't have time to coordinate all that."

Thinking quickly, Hunter said, "Just tell me what you intend to name your son and when you discovered you were pregnant. I'll take care of the rest. Just follow my lead and agree with the line I feed Culbertson."

"This is never going to work," she said, plunking a bowl of mashed potatoes onto the table. "There are too many ways he can trip us up."

Hunter caught her by the shoulders and turned her to face him. "Trust me, Callie. Unless you can think of something else, this is the only way."

He watched her close her eyes, take a deep breath, then opening them, she gave him the information he requested. "You'd better be right about this, Hunter. I won't let him take my baby away from me."

"There's no way in hell, darlin'," he said, giving her a quick hug.

Hunter's heart twisted at the fear he'd heard in her soft voice. He wanted to know what had caused her to be so terrified that Culbertson would try to get custody when the man clearly had no use for children. But that would have to wait until later. Right now they had to con the man into leaving Callie alone for good.

* * *

By the time dinner was over, Callie's nerves were stretched to the breaking point. Sitting between the two men, she'd listened to them discuss everything from baseball player stats to the size of engine they preferred in their vehicles. She wasn't sure whether to be relieved or disappointed that the subject of her and Hunter's marriage had yet to come up.

But that hadn't stopped Hunter from playing his part as the devoted husband to the hilt. Throughout dinner he'd given her smiles that threatened to melt her bones and he'd found every excuse imaginable to touch her. She'd caught Craig taking it all in with great interest, but not once had he asked any of the questions she knew for certain had to be running through his mind.

"Why don't we have dessert in the living room?" Craig asked when Callie rose from her chair to slice pieces of German chocolate cake for them.

"Go ahead and have a seat in there while I help Callie clear the table," Hunter said, rising to gather their plates. "We'll join you in a few minutes."

"It's not going the way we planned," she whispered when Craig left the room.

"Be patient, darlin'." Hunter rinsed the dishes to put in the dishwasher, then measured grounds from one of the canisters for a pot of coffee. "If he doesn't get around to asking, I'll bring up the subject myself."

"I should have never let you talk me into this." She shook her head at her own foolishness. "I'm sure he can see right through this little farce."

"Don't worry. Everything is going to be just fine."

As she allowed Hunter to carry the tray she'd arranged with dessert plates, cups and saucers and a carafe of coffee into the living room, she prayed he was right. Her nerves couldn't stand much more. She already had an almost uncontrollable urge to preheat the oven and start measuring sugar and flour.

"I have a question for you two," Craig said when he placed his empty dessert plate back on the tray. "If you're married, why doesn't Callie wear a wedding band?"

Sitting beside Hunter on the love seat, she had just taken a sip of milk from the glass she'd brought with her from the kitchen and it was all she could do to keep from choking at his blunt question. Panic seized her. She'd been right. Craig knew they were only pretending. Now what were they going to do?

"She had to take her wedding ring off when her fingers started getting a little puffy," Hunter said without missing a beat. He took her left hand in his and brought it to his lips to kiss her ring finger. "Once she has the baby, it will be right back where it belongs."

A wave of tingling heat traveled up her arm, then spread throughout the rest of her body at the loving gesture. She was glad that Hunter had been able to think fast because at the moment she wasn't sure she could think at all.

"When and where did you meet?" Craig asked.

Hunter held up his hand. "See that little scar on my palm? I had to go to the emergency room in Houston when I had a run-in with a fish hook. As soon as I saw Callie, I knew she was the woman for me." Giving her a smile that made her insides feel as if they'd turned to warm pudding, he lightly kissed her cheek. "We were married a few days later and pregnant a few weeks after that."

"Why the rush?" Craig asked, sounding more than a little suspicious.

"Once I see what I want, I don't let it get away from me." Hunter put his arm around her shoulders and held her close to his side. "I'm afraid you're going to have to face facts, Culbertson. She's with me now and I'm not about to let her or our baby go."

Callie watched Craig. She knew him well enough to know that he wasn't entirely convinced. There was a huge hole in their story, and although he hadn't asked again why she'd failed to tell her mother about her marriage to Hunter, Callie knew it was on his mind. But gaining strength from the man holding her so possessively against him, she decided that if the matter came up again, she'd simply tell Craig that she didn't have to explain herself to him or anyone else.

"Well, I suppose I should be going," Craig said as

he rose to his feet. "As always, your cooking was delicious, Callie."

When Hunter stood, then helped her up from her saggy love seat, she began to believe they might have pulled off the ruse. Craig would be leaving town and, with any luck, she'd never have to see or hear from him again.

"Have an enjoyable trip back to Houston," Hunter said as they all walked to the door.

Craig shook his head. "Oh, I'm not leaving the area for several more days. While you two were finishing dinner, I checked the phone book and found a little bed-and-breakfast just up the street." His smirk made Callie want to scream with frustration. "I thought I'd stick around for a while and take in the sights." He laughed as he opened the door. "It's been my experience that you can learn a lot from talking to the locals in a town the size of Devil's Fork."

As Craig walked down the steps and out to his sleek red sports car, Callie felt like crying. How could her life have gotten so out of control in such a short time?

Turning to Hunter, she sighed heavily. "Any more bright ideas?"

He didn't look any happier about the turn of events than she was. "The way I see it, we don't have a whole lot of choice. I'm going to have to move in with you until that sorry excuse for a human being leaves town."

Six

Two hours later, after helping Callie clean up the kitchen, Hunter found himself trying to fold his six-foot-three-inch frame into a comfortable sleeping position on her lumpy love seat. Muttering a word he reserved for extreme situations, he sat up, propped his elbows on his knees and cradled his head in his hands. What the hell had he gotten himself into? And why?

If he'd kept his mouth shut, he'd be sleeping on a fairly comfortable, albeit narrow, bed at the Life Medevac hangar instead of torturing himself on the most uncomfortable piece of furniture known to man. And he for damn sure wouldn't be locked into playing house for the next week with a woman that he was already finding it all but impossible to keep his hands off.

But even as he castigated himself for getting involved, he knew he'd done the right thing. After meeting Culbertson and listening to Callie explain how he and his parents had used their money and influence to take the baby away from the first girl Craig had gotten pregnant, Hunter knew as sure as he knew his own name the Culbertsons wouldn't think twice about trying to do the same thing to Callie.

Shaking his head, Hunter couldn't believe how arrogant they were. What gave them the right to take a baby from his mother simply because Culbertson blood ran through the child's veins? What kind of people thought that it automatically made the mother unfit just because their bank account dwarfed hers?

As he sat there thinking about how ruthless and selfish they were, he realized that if Emerald Larson had wanted to, she could have taken him and his brothers away from their mothers at any time. She certainly had more money and power than the Culbertsons ever dreamed of having and she would have had very little trouble gaining custody of her grandsons.

But instead of viewing the three of them as possessions, Emerald had cared enough to content herself with watching Hunter and his brothers grow up in pictures and P.I. reports in order to ensure they turned out to be as normal and well-adjusted as possible. And for the first time since learning the details of his parentage he began to appreciate the sacrifices that had been made by Emerald on his behalf.

Any lingering traces of anger he still carried from being denied the right to know who his father was dissipated. Although Hunter would always have a problem with any man walking away from a woman when she needed him most, he came to the conclusion that Emerald and her philandering son weren't entirely responsible for the anger and confusion he'd grown up with.

It had been Marlene O'Banyon's choice to agree to Emerald's terms. And although Emerald hadn't required that his mother remain single, Hunter sometimes wondered if she'd signed the confidentiality agreement secretly hoping that one day Owen Larson would come to his senses and return to Miami for her and Hunter. But Owen had never laid eyes on any of his children, nor had he seen their mothers again. And with his death in a boating accident somewhere in the Mediterranean eight months ago, it was never going to happen.

Of course, his mother had no idea that old Owen had sown more than just one wild oat. Although she was the first woman he'd gotten pregnant, she certainly hadn't been the last. Hell, Hunter doubted that Emerald was completely certain that he, Nick and Caleb were Owen's only offspring.

But that was immaterial now. The fact of the matter was, in light of the way the Culbertsons had dealt with a similar situation, he understood and could even commend his grandmother for handling everything the way she had.

Lost in thought, it took a moment for Hunter to realize that Callie had gotten out of bed and was tip-toeing her way through the living room into the kitchen. "Can't sleep?" he asked, careful to keep his voice nonthreatening so as not to frighten her.

Her startled cry was loud enough to wake the dead. So much for trying not to frighten her.

"It's just me, Callie."

"Dear heavens, you scared me out of a year's growth," she said, clutching something to the front of her robe.

"I'm sorry." He switched on the lamp at the end of the love seat. "I didn't mean to…" He stopped to stare at her when he realized what she was carrying. "What the hell are you doing with your apron at—" he checked his watch "—midnight?"

"I'm too keyed up to sleep," she said defensively. "I thought I'd find something to do."

He frowned. "So you're going to start cooking?"

She breezed past him to enter the kitchen. "Everyone deals with stress in their own way. Some people drink. Some eat. I bake."

That explained why she'd made enough baked goods to stock a chain of grocery stores, he thought as he followed her. She'd been scared witless since learning she was pregnant that Culbertson would find out about the baby. Now that he had, it appeared that Callie would be making enough cookies to feed every man, woman and child in the whole damned state.

"Our shift starts in a little less than eighteen hours." He yawned. "Don't you think it would be a good idea to be well rested when we go to work?"

She shook her head as she reached for a set of measuring cups and the canister of flour. "Don't worry about me, I'll be fine. You're the one who needs rest to pilot the helicopter. Go back into the living room and get some sleep."

"That's easier said than done," he muttered.

"I promise I won't make much noise," she said, knocking over the cup of flour she'd just measured.

"That's not the problem." He pulled out a chair and sat down at the table. "I'm too tall."

"Excuse me?"

She looked thoroughly confused and so darned cute standing there in her nightclothes and apron, he had to force himself to remember what they were talking about. "The love seat is roughly fifty inches long and I'm six foot three. You do the math."

Her eyes widened. "Oh, dear. I'm sorry. I hadn't thought of it being too short for you." She shook her head. "But it's not a problem. You can take my bed and I'll sleep on the love seat."

"Like hell." He wasn't about to sleep on a comfortable bed while she endured that instrument of torture in her condition.

"Why not?" she asked as she cleaned up the flour she'd spilled. "I'm at least ten inches shorter and shouldn't have nearly as much trouble getting comfortable."

"You're pregnant."

"And you're bossy." She grinned. "But I'm trying not to hold that against you."

Her pretty smile sent a wave of heat straight through him, and he could think of several things he'd like for her to hold against him—every one of them soft, warm and deliciously feminine. He swallowed hard. Thinking along those lines could only accomplish one of two things. It would either get him in a whole lot deeper than he was comfortable with or drive him completely insane. And he wasn't altogether sure that he hadn't already crossed the line in both areas.

"I can sleep in one of the chairs and—"

"Wake up with a terribly stiff neck," she interrupted, dropping an egg on the counter. "Darn." Grabbing a paper towel, she cleaned up the mess. "If I'm going to be flying with you, I not only want you well rested, I'd like for you to have your full range of motion."

"I can manage in the chair." He stood up and started toward the living room, but her soft hand on his back stopped him dead in his tracks and sent a jolt of electric current throughout his system.

"I think we're overlooking the obvious here," she said, turning to measure more flour into a bowl. "I'll probably be up for hours before I'm relaxed enough to go to sleep. There's no reason for you to be uncomfortable when there's an empty bed that you could be sleeping in. And if I want to go to sleep before you get up, I'll be careful not to wake you when I lie down."

She had a point. It was pretty silly for him to try to sleep in the chair when he could be stretched out. But just knowing that she'd eventually be getting in bed with him was enough to send him into orbit.

"I guess that could work," he said, thinking aloud. "And we're both adults. There's no reason we can't handle this." And maybe if he repeated it enough, he'd start to believe it.

"Exactly." She waved her hand toward the other room as she reached for a spoon and promptly knocked over a container of baking powder. "You're distracting me. Now go to bed and let me get started on these cookies."

Yawning, he scratched his bare chest and headed for her bedroom. Hopefully he'd be out like a light as soon as his head hit the pillow. And if he believed that, he was sure somebody had a piece of beachfront property in the middle of Arizona that he'd be fool enough to buy.

* * *

A couple of hours after Hunter went to lie down in her bed, Callie turned off the light in the kitchen and quietly walked into the bedroom. Making several dozen cookies had helped, but her nerves were still on edge and she expected they would remain that way until she was certain Craig was out of her life for good.

As she removed her slippers, then turned to pull back the cover, she forgot all about her current problem with Craig and focused on the sight of Hunter's broad back. From the muted moonlight filtering into the room through the sheer drapes she could see that he was lying on his stomach with the sheet covering him from the waist down.

Her heart stalled and she swallowed hard as the sight of all that delicious masculine skin reminded her of earlier in the kitchen when she'd first seen his bare chest. The play of his perfectly defined chest muscles beneath a light sprinkling of dark hair had fascinated her beyond words and distracted her to the point she'd been about as coordinated as a bull in a china shop.

How on earth was she going to be able to sleep with all that raw masculinity mere inches away? And why did her double bed suddenly seem as though it had shrunk to the size of a cot?

Wishing she had bought a two-bedroom house instead of a charming one-bedroom cottage, she shook her head as she jammed her feet back in her slippers.

She'd go into the kitchen, grab a handful of chocolate chips and lie down on the love seat.

"Are you going to stand there the rest of the night or are you going to get into bed?"

She jumped at the sound of Hunter's voice and her cheeks heated with embarrassment at being caught staring at him. Thank heavens there wasn't enough light in the room for him to see her guilty expression. "I…didn't want to…disturb you."

He rolled to his back and gazed up at her. "I wasn't asleep."

"What's wrong?" The way he'd been yawning before he'd gone to bed, she'd have thought he'd be asleep before he had a chance to close his eyes. "Is the mattress too soft for you?"

"No, it's quite comfortable."

She frowned as she gingerly sat down on the side of the bed. "Then what's the problem?"

"I've been thinking—"

"I'm not altogether sure I want to hear this," she interrupted warily. "The last time you shared your thoughts is what got us into this mess."

"Are you going to take off your robe and lie down?"

She swallowed hard. It would have been hard enough to stretch out beside him if he'd been asleep. But awake? Just the thought caused a tingling sensation to skip over every cell in her body.

"That's what you've been thinking about?"

"No." His deep chuckle sent a shiver straight up her spine. "But you've been going on adrenaline all evening, and I think it would probably be a good idea for the baby's sake if you tried to relax."

Callie knew he was right. But she wasn't sure that was going to be an option, especially with him so close.

"Are you going to keep me guessing or are you going to tell me what you've come up with this time?" she hedged.

He shook his head. "Not until you lie down."

Exasperated beyond words, she shook her head. "I think it would be best if I slept on the love seat."

"Why? You aren't afraid of sleeping in the same bed with me, are you?" She couldn't see much of his expression in the darkened room, but she'd heard the laughter and good-natured challenge in his voice.

"Don't be silly," she lied. "I just think since we're clearly attracted to each other, it might not be a good idea."

"Remember, we're both adults," he said softly. "I give you my word that nothing is going to happen that you don't want to happen."

It shouldn't be a problem, she told herself as she stood up to remove her robe. She wasn't sure why, but she trusted him. And she knew for certain she didn't have to worry about herself. The last thing she wanted or needed was to become involved with another man.

When she slipped into bed, he turned to his side,

propped his elbow on the pillow and rested his head against his palm. His proximity sent a delicious little thrill from the top of her head all the way to the tips of her toes. She did her best to ignore it.

"I think we should get married."

His voice was low and intimate, and it took a moment for her to realize what he'd said. When she did, her heart slammed against her ribs.

"You can't be serious."

When she started to get out of bed, his hand on her arm stopped her. "Think about it, darlin'. It won't take much effort on Culbertson's part to discover that we aren't married or that I've never been to Houston."

"And this just occurred to you?" She rubbed at her suddenly throbbing temples. "Why did I let you talk me into this? I told you it wouldn't work."

"That's why I'm suggesting we get married," he said patiently. "It doesn't matter when we got married, we'll still be husband and wife."

"I can't see where that would do anything but add one more complication to an already impossible situation." A sudden thought caused a chill to race through her, and she had to take a deep breath in order to get words passed the tightness in her throat. "He could ask for a DNA test to prove paternity."

"He might, but something tells me he won't."

Her breath caught on a soft sob. If he and his parents learned that her son had been fathered by Craig, the

Culbertsons were the kind of people who would intervene and take her baby away from her—not because they loved the child, but because they viewed him as one of their possessions. They'd find an excuse to find her unworthy or unfit to raise their heir, the same as they'd done that poor girl twelve years ago.

"There's no way out of…this." A chill ran the length of her spine. "They're going to take my child away from me and there's nothing I can do to stop them."

Hunter reached out to wrap his strong arms around her and cradle her to him. "Not as long as I'm around to stop them, they won't."

"I can't see how—"

"Taking a child away from a single parent isn't as difficult as it is from a married couple."

"Yes, but the Culbertsons are quite wealthy and can hire the best lawyers. And I'm sure they'll see that the case is heard by a judge who travels in the same social circle they do." She placed her hand over her stomach. "We'd be fighting a losing battle."

"Let them hire whoever they want or get whatever judge they think will go along with their request." He kissed her forehead. "It's not like I don't have a few connections of my own."

Pulling back to look at him, she shook her head. "I'm not sure who you think you know, but it's going to take more than a connection or two to keep them from taking my son."

"You might be surprised." He gently brushed a strand of hair from her cheek with his index finger. "Let me worry about dealing with the Culbertsons and their lawyers. I'm going to do some checking, but I suspect there's more to his visit than what he's saying."

Anger and frustration filled her. "This is the very reason I detest rich people. They think that because they have money it gives them the right to do anything they please."

"Not all people of means are like the Culbertsons, Callie," he said quietly. "My father's family had money, but there was never a threat of them taking me or my brothers away from our mothers."

Remembering their conversation on the trip back from El Paso, Callie bit her lower lip to keep it from trembling as a fresh wave of fear coursed through her. "I'd say your father's family is the exception, not the rule."

"Maybe, but I'm betting it's closer to being the other way around." He lightly ran his palm up and down her arm, sending a wave of tingling warmth to every part of her. "At any rate, I promise you have nothing to fear from the Culbertsons as long as I'm around."

"I hope you're right," she said, hiding a yawn behind her hand.

He kissed the top of her head. "We'll talk more in the morning. Right now we both need to get some rest."

Within moments his deep, even breathing signaled that Hunter had fallen asleep. But, as tired as she was, Callie couldn't stop thinking about the threat that Craig posed or Hunter's offer of marriage.

Everything he said made perfect sense and could very well solve her problem. But friendship only went so far. She couldn't believe he was willing to enter into something as serious as marriage simply to help her. What did he expect to get out of it for himself? And what would happen if they were successful in keeping the Culbertsons from taking her baby away from her? How long before Hunter asked for an annulment or a divorce?

Thoroughly exhausted from the tension of Craig's unexpected visit and the speculation of what would happen if she did go along with Hunter's insane suggestion, Callie felt herself begin to drift off to sleep. But instead of having nightmares of her baby being taken away from her by Craig and his family, she dreamed of marriage to a tall, dark-haired, handsome man with a sexy-as-sin voice and devastating kisses.

The feel of thin, downy-soft hair against her cheek, the steady beat of a heart beneath her ear and the scent of clean masculine skin assailed Callie's senses as she floated in the surreal world between sleep and wakefulness. When a pair of strong arms tightened around her, she smiled and snuggled against the hard male body beside her.

"Good morning, sleepyhead."

The sound of Hunter's voice caused her eyes to fly open and had her tilting her head to meet his incredible green gaze. She was lying with her head pillowed on his broad chest and her arm thrown over his flat belly. But it was the realization that her leg was draped over his muscular thigh—his bare muscular thigh—that sent a shiver of excitement up her spine and had her wondering if she'd be able to draw her next breath.

"H-how long have you been awake?"

"About an hour."

Goose bumps shimmered over her skin at the vibration of his rich baritone rumbling up from deep in his chest. But it was the feel of his hard arousal straining at his briefs that had her gingerly moving her leg away from his. They were treading in dangerous territory and it would definitely be best to put some distance between them.

"Where are you going?" His warm breath stirred the fine hair at her temple and caused her heart to skip several beats.

"I, um, should probably get up and cook something for breakfast."

He held her firmly against him when she tried to pull from his arms. "I've got a hunger, but it's not for food."

A delightful heat like nothing she'd ever known began to flow through her veins at his candid comment.

"I—it wouldn't be a good idea to complicate things more than they already are."

His deep chuckle caused the warmth inside of her to pool in the pit of her belly. "Darlin', kissing isn't complicated." He brushed her lips with his, sending a delightful tingling sensation all the way to her toes. "It's one of the purest forms of pleasure a man and woman can share."

The sound of his voice, his provocative words and the feel of his calloused palm caressing her side through her thin cotton gown were like a drug and she suddenly had a hard time remembering her own name, let alone why it would make their current situation more difficult. But she ceased thinking at all when his mouth settled over hers and he tenderly traced the outline of her lips with his tongue.

"This is…insane," she murmured, trying to draw some much-needed air into her lungs.

He nibbled kisses along her jawline to the sensitive hollow below her ear. "Do you want me to stop?"

"I should demand that you stop and get out of my house immediately."

His lips blazed a trail down her neck to her collarbone. "But you aren't going to do that?"

With a myriad of delightful sensations coursing through her, she had to concentrate on his question. "N-no."

"Why not?" he asked as he ran his palm back down

her side, then slipped his hand beneath the hem of her gown.

His fingers sliding along her bare skin made breathing all but impossible and caused the heat in her lower belly to intensify. "Wh-what you're doing...feels too good."

"Do you want me to stop?"

Unable to think clearly, she shook her head. "Don't you dare."

He caressed her hip, then her ribs as he slowly moved his hand up her body. "Are you aware of what's going to happen if I continue?"

When he covered her breast with his hand, then chafed her puckered nipple with the pad of his thumb, need coursed through her to settle deep in the most feminine part of her. "W-we'll make love."

His hand continued to caress her overly sensitized skin. "Is that what you want, Callie?"

Staring into his dark green eyes, her heart pounded hard in her chest. From the moment they'd first met there had been a magnetic pull drawing them together, a chemistry they'd both tried but found impossible to deny. And with each kiss the tension between them had heightened until it had become a force that was impossible for either of them to fight.

Whether it was her pregnancy hormones that caused a desire stronger than anything she'd ever known or something more, she didn't want him to stop. She wanted to feel the warmth of Hunter's kisses and the passion of his loving touch.

"It's pure insanity. But yes, I want to make love with you, Hunter."

Seven

At Callie's admittance that she wanted to make love with him, Hunter's heart slammed against his rib cage so hard he was surprised it hadn't jumped right out of his chest. Throughout the night he'd lain with her in his arms, and with each tick of the clock her soft body and sweet womanly scent had increased the tension he'd been fighting from the moment he'd laid eyes on her. But when she'd awakened and stared up at him with her sexy violet eyes, he'd become harder than he'd ever been in his life and could no more have stopped himself from tasting and touching her than he could stop the sun from rising in the east each morning.

But as much as he wanted to sink himself deep inside of her, to hear her call his name as he pleasured her, he couldn't bear the thought that she might regret one minute of what they would share. "Are you sure that making love is what you really want, Callie?"

His heart stalled and he found himself holding his breath when she closed her eyes and remained silent for several long seconds. Then, to his relief, she opened her eyes and nodded her head.

"I think I'll go into total meltdown if we don't."

Taking a deep breath, he tried to slow the liquid fire racing through his veins. "I know I should have asked this before things went this far, but would your doctor be okay with our making love?"

Her porcelain cheeks colored a pretty pink as she nodded. "The obstetrician has given me the go-ahead for normal activity with no restrictions. And that includes lovemaking."

Hunter couldn't believe the level of relief that washed over him. If she'd told him there was even the slightest possibility of a problem or the tiniest bit of discomfort for her, he'd have found some way—no matter how difficult—to walk away. But knowing there was nothing to prevent them from having a pleasurable and satisfying experience sent a fresh wave of heat straight to his groin.

Unfortunately it was short-lived. He hadn't planned on spending the night with Callie, let alone making love with her, and protection hadn't even crossed his mind when he'd left the hangar yesterday evening. But he was thinking about it now. Or, more accurately, the lack of it.

But as he gazed at the woman in his arms, he realized there was no possibility of him making her pregnant. And truth to tell, it wouldn't matter to him if she wasn't already expecting a child.

The thought of Callie carrying his baby appealed to him more than he could have ever imagined and should have scared the living hell out of him. It was something he didn't understand, wasn't entirely comfortable with and, at the moment, didn't intend to analyze. All that mattered was bringing her pleasure, cherishing her as she was meant to be cherished.

Without a moment's hesitation he gathered her close and covered her mouth with his. Her soft lips molded to his with a hungry desperation that matched his own and sent fire racing through his veins with the swiftness of a raging river.

When she parted for him to deepen the kiss, Hunter thought his head might come right off his shoulders as she boldly stroked his tongue with hers and engaged him in an erotic game of advance and retreat. She was letting him know that she felt the passion as deeply as he did, that she wanted him as much as he wanted her.

Breaking the kiss, he nibbled his way to the base of her throat as he reached for the hem of her gown.

"Lift your hips, darlin'," he whispered against her satiny skin.

When he'd whisked away her panties and thin cotton gown, he quickly removed his boxer briefs, then tossing the garments to the floor beside the bed, gathered her back into his arms. At the feel of her satiny skin against him, desire raced through his veins, and he had to fight an almost uncontrollable urge to cover her with his body and sink himself deep inside of her.

His entire being pulsed with the urgent need to claim her, but he was determined not to rush things no matter what his body demanded. "You feel so soft...." He trailed kisses down the base of her throat, then past her collarbone to the slope of her breast. "So sweet."

As he teased her with a light swirling motion, the fire of need in his belly grew when she threaded her fingers in his hair and pulled him closer. Arching her back, she gave him better access to the hardened tip, and taking her into his mouth, he chafed her with his tongue and caressed her with his lips.

"P-please, Hunter."

"Not yet, darlin'." Moving his hand down her side to her hip and beyond, he cupped her at the apex of her thighs. "I want to make sure you're ready for me."

"If I was any more ready...I'd burn to a crisp." Her voice sounded wispy and breathless and he had no doubt she was as turned-on as he was.

Parting her, he stroked her, then touched her intimately. Her moist warmth and moan of pleasure assured him that she needed him as much as he needed her.

"I want you to promise me something," he said as he continued to stroke her.

"Anything." He watched her close her eyes and catch her lower lip between her teeth a moment before she whimpered, "You're driving me…crazy."

Her response to his touch heightened his own passion, and he had to take several deep breaths in order to force himself to slow down. "I want you to promise me that if there's even the slightest bit of discomfort, you'll tell me."

"I promise." When she opened her eyes to gaze up at him, the desire in the violet depths robbed him of breath. "Please…make love to me, Hunter."

Unable to deny either one of them any longer, he nudged her knees apart and levered himself over her. As he moved his lower body into position, he settled his mouth over hers at the same time he pressed himself forward.

Slowly, carefully, he pushed into her, and the feel of her tight body melting around him as he sank deeper and deeper had him clenching his teeth as he struggled for control. But when she raised her hips for more of him, the slender thread of his restraint snapped and he buried himself completely within her feminine depths.

With every muscle in his body taut with the need to complete the act of loving her, Hunter forced himself to remain completely still. She needed time to adjust to him and he needed time to savor the feeling of being completely one with the most desirable woman he'd ever known.

Gathering her close, he kissed her sweet lips. "I'm going to try to go slow, but I want you so damned much I'm not sure that's an option."

Her smile caused the fire threatening to consume him to flare out of control. "I want you just as much."

He held her gaze with his as he eased his hips back then forward, thrusting into her again and again. As he felt her respond by meeting him halfway, he increased the rhythm with each stroke, and in no time he felt her body tighten around his, signaling that she was poised to find her release.

When she wrapped her legs around his waist to hold him close, the pressure in his body increased tenfold and it was all he could do to hold himself in check. But he wasn't going to find his satisfaction without her, and sliding his hand between them, he touched her as he thrust into her one last time.

Her moan of pleasure and the quivering of her tiny inner muscles rippling around him as she found her satisfaction triggered his own completion. Heat and light flashed behind his tightly closed eyes as he surrendered to the storm, and feeling as if his world had been reduced to just the two of them, he emptied himself deep inside of her.

As Hunter slowly drifted back to reality, an emotion filled his chest that he didn't dare put a name to. He'd never experienced anything as amazing as what he'd just shared with Callie. Her passionate response to his touch had excited him in ways he'd only dreamed of and he felt more alive than he had in years.

"Are you all right?" he asked when he finally found the strength to move to her side.

"I-I'm fine."

A slight crack in her voice had him rising up to look down at her beautiful face. The tears he saw welling up in her eyes scared him as little else could. If he'd hurt her in any way, he'd never forgive himself.

"Callie, darlin', what's wrong?"

"Nothing. Making love with you was one of the most beautiful experiences I've ever had." She cupped his cheek with her palm, and her smile lit the darkest corners of his soul. "Thank you."

Weak with relief, he shook his head. "I should be thanking you. You were incredible."

When she hid a yawn behind her delicate hand, he kissed the top of her head. "You were up pretty late and it's still early. Why don't we take a nap, then we can talk over breakfast." He hadn't much more than gotten the words out before her shallow breathing signaled that she'd drifted off to sleep.

As he watched the predawn shadows in the room melt away with the light of day, Hunter held Callie close and thought about what they would be talking about later. After the accident and Ellen's death, he'd never intended to ask another woman to marry him. But these were a different set of circumstances. He and Callie wouldn't be marrying for love. They would be doing the only thing he could think of that might discourage Craig Culbertson from trying to take her baby away from her.

He closed his eyes and tried to think of some other way to help Callie. From the time he'd gone to bed until she'd entered the bedroom a couple of hours later, all he'd been able to think about was how they could stop Culbertson and his family.

Hunter had no idea what the man's motive was, but he must have learned about Callie's pregnancy from her mother and shown up to confirm his suspicions that he was the father. Considering the disgust in his voice when he'd accusingly asked her if the child was his, Hunter was surprised that Culbertson hadn't jumped at the chance for someone else to take responsibility. But he hadn't, and Hunter had every intention of pulling out all the stops to find out why. And he knew exactly who to contact to help him start making inquiries into the matter. He'd get the name of a discreet private investigator from Emerald's trusted assistant, Luther Freemont, and see what they could dig up on Culbertson.

If he'd wanted to, Hunter could have asked outright for Emerald to intervene on Callie's behalf and he had no doubt that she would have. But that wasn't his style. Whether it was pride or bullheaded stubbornness, he fought his own battles. He'd offered to help Callie and he'd be the one to see the matter through to the end.

Another reason he didn't want to get Emerald involved was that he wasn't ready for anyone—and especially Callie—at Life Medevac to learn of his relationship to the indomitable Mrs. Larson. For one thing, he had yet to prove himself with the business she'd given him to run. And for another, Callie had trust issues with anyone who had money. If she were to discover that he was Emerald Larson's grandson and had been given a trust fund large enough to make a dent in the national debt, as well as being in line to inherit part of Emerald Inc., she'd automatically assume he was like the Culbertsons and refuse his help. And that was something they both knew she couldn't afford to do.

Gazing down at her sleeping so peacefully in his arms, he fleetingly wondered if getting married would pose a threat to either of their hearts. But he immediately dismissed the concern. They wouldn't be marrying for love, and as long as they kept things in perspective and their emotions in check, there shouldn't be a problem for either of them.

Satisfied that he had everything under control,

Hunter relaxed and closed his eyes. They'd stay together as long as it took to settle this business with Culbertson once and for all, then evaluate the best way to handle the dissolution of their marriage.

An unexpected twinge of regret tightened his chest at the thought, but he ignored it. He and Callie were friends now and they would remain friends once they parted ways. And that's just the way it had to stay.

"Where's your husband, Callie?"

Callie went perfectly still at the sound of the familiar voice. Needing a refill on her prenatal vitamins, she'd stopped at the drugstore on her way to start her shift at Life Medevac. She didn't have the time nor the desire to deal with the likes of Craig Culbertson.

"Not that it's any of your business, but Hunter owns the air-ambulance service and had some paperwork to deal with," she said, heading back to her car.

She could pick up the vitamins another time. Right now she wanted nothing more than to put as much distance between her and Craig as humanly possible.

But before she could get the driver's door open, he caught her by the arm. "What's your hurry? Surely you have enough time to talk to an old friend."

Extricating herself from his grasp, she turned to face him. "We aren't friends and never will be. Now if you'll excuse me, I need to get to work."

His knowing smirk was enough to make her want

to scream. "If your husband owns the business, going in late shouldn't be a problem for you."

She reached for the handle on her car door. "I need to be there on time to relieve the on-duty crew."

He shook his head as he placed his hand on the driver's door to hold it shut. "What you need to do is answer a few questions."

"No, I don't."

"Oh, I think you do." He reached out to trace his index finger down her cheek. "It seems that none of the people here in town knew anything about you and O'Banyon being married. In fact, Mr. Jones over at the grocery store was quite surprised to hear the news."

A cold chill slithered up her spine at Craig's touch. She must have had blinders on not see that his charm was a weapon, not an endearing quality. How could she have ever found herself attracted to such a reptile?

Batting his hand away, she shook her head. "Don't ever touch me again."

"You used to like for me to touch you, Callie," he said, trying to affect an injured look.

"That's ancient history." She tried to remove his hand where he held the car door. "All I want from you now is to be left alone."

His eyes narrowed and a sneer replaced his wounded expression. "Now is that any way to talk to your baby's daddy?"

"Just because you can fertilize an egg doesn't make

you father material. That takes someone special." She jerked the car door from his grasp and started to get in. "Someone who is actually capable of loving a child."

"Like O'Banyon?"

"Yes. Exactly like Hunter."

His sarcastic laugh caused her to clench her fists until her knuckles ached. "Why don't you give up the charade, Callie? We both know you're no more married than I am. If you come back to Houston now, maybe I'll forget that you and O'Banyon tried to dupe me into believing the baby belongs to him." He shrugged. "Who knows? I might even be persuaded to let you have visitation rights."

Fear so strong it threatened to the buckle her knees ran through her. "As long as I have breath left in my body, you won't take my child away from me," she said, doing her best to keep her voice steady.

His knowing smile made her skin crawl. "That remains to be seen, my dear."

As Callie got into the car, her hands shook so badly that it took a couple of tries before she was able to fit her key into the ignition. Everything she'd feared for the past several months was coming true.

As she backed the car from the parking space and drove the short distance to the Life Medevac hangar outside of town, her body trembled and tears ran unchecked down her cheeks. For reasons she didn't have time nor the inclination to analyze, all she could think

of was getting to Hunter. She knew it made no sense
at all considering the short time they'd known each
other, but with him she felt more secure than she had
in her entire life. And although she hated being vulnerable and dependent in any way, his reassuring presence
gave her strength.

Parking her car at the side of the hangar, she hurried
into the dispatch room. Thankfully the on-duty crew
and Mary Lou were occupied with a game of Texas
Hold 'Em poker. She knew she looked more than a
little upset and she didn't particularly want to endure
a barrage of questions from Mary Lou.

"Is Hunter in his office?" she asked as she breezed
past them.

"He's been in there all afternoon making phone
calls," Mary Lou answered without looking up from her
cards.

When Callie came to Hunter's office, she didn't
even hesitate as she opened the door and walked into
the room. Craig might think he had the upper hand, but
she wasn't going to stand by and let him take her son
away without a fight. And if that meant entering into
a marriage with a man she barely knew, then that's
exactly what she was going to do.

"If you're still willing to marry me, my answer is yes."

Eight

Hunter was on his feet and rounding the desk in a flash. Callie looked as if she'd seen a ghost, and the tears streaming down her cheeks just about tore him apart.

"What's happened?"

When he took her into his arms, she burrowed into his embrace. As she told him about meeting up with Culbertson and the man's arrogant attitude, pure fury burned at Hunter's gut.

"Do you honestly think we would have a chance of stopping him if we were married?" she asked, trembling against him.

"There's not a doubt in my mind, darlin'."

If he could have gotten his hands on Culbertson at

that very moment, Hunter would have choked the life out of him for putting her through that. The man was without question the sorriest excuse for a human being he'd ever had the misfortune to meet, and it was going to give him great pleasure to deal the arrogant jerk a good dose of reality.

Hunter had spent the entire afternoon on the phone with Emerald's personal assistant, Luther Freemont, and the private investigator Emerald Inc. hired for running background checks on potential employees for Emerald's various companies. After speaking with the man at length, Hunter was confident that if there was anything they could use to combat Culbertson's attempt to gain custody of Callie's baby, the P.I. would find it.

And on the outside chance that Culbertson was squeaky-clean—which Hunter knew damned good and well he wasn't—he and Callie would establish themselves as a married couple with a stable home life that no lawyer, judge or social worker could argue wasn't perfect for raising a child.

"I don't want you spending any more time worrying about Culbertson or what he's going to do," Hunter said as he soothingly rubbed at the tension along her spine.

She leaned back to look at him, and the anxiety he saw in the depths of her expressive eyes caused his gut to twist into a tight knot. "Th-that's easier said than done."

"Do you trust me, Callie?"

"Yes." There wasn't so much as a hint of uncertainty in her answer.

"I give you my word that everything is going to work out." He gave her a reassuring smile. "By the time this is settled, Craig Culbertson will be running back to Houston like a tail-tucked dog."

"I hope you're right."

"I am."

He sealed his promise with a kiss, and by the time he raised his head, his body was as hard as a chunk of granite. Taking a deep breath, he rested his forehead against hers. He had no idea how she'd managed to get under his skin so quickly, but there was no denying that he found her to be the most exciting woman he'd had the good fortune to meet in the past five years. And the thought of making love to her every night, then holding her as she slept, was enough to send a laser of heat straight through him.

"Why…are you willing…to do this for me, Hunter?" she asked, every bit as breathless as he was. "What's in this for you?"

He'd asked himself the same question at least a dozen times and the answer had been surprisingly simple. "Even though my father's family is well off, my grandmother felt that my brothers and I would be much better off being raised by loving mothers who taught us a solid set of values, instead of giving us everything we wanted, like she'd given our father." He grinned. "Her logic must have worked, because we all turned out to be well-adjusted and productive, instead of selfish and hopelessly irresponsible like her son."

"Your grandmother must be a very special, very wise lady."

"She's definitely one of a kind," he said evasively, thinking that was an understatement. "But the point is, I believe every kid deserves the same chance she gave me and my brothers."

"In other words, you're doing this for the sake of my son?"

Hunter nodded. "I know you'll be a great mom and raise him with the love and guidance he needs. He wouldn't get that from Culbertson and his family."

She shook her head disapprovingly. "He'd turn out to be just like Craig—hedonistic, selfish and shallow."

"Exactly." Hunter kissed her forehead. "And to answer your second question, the only thing I expect to get out of our marriage is the satisfaction of knowing that I stopped that from happening."

"How long—"

Placing his finger to her lips, he shook his head. "Let's take it one day at a time. After we take care of this business with Culbertson, then we'll discuss how we want to handle…things." He had no idea why, but he couldn't bring himself to say the word *annulment* or *divorce*.

He watched her nibble on her lower lip as she gazed

at him for several seconds. "Does that mean you'll be moving in with me for a while?"

"Husbands and wives usually live together, darlin'." He grinned. "Of course, you could always move into my room here at the hangar."

For the first time since walking into the room she smiled. "I don't think that would work very well considering you have a twin-size bed."

"Oh, I think it might work out real well." Sharing any bed with Callie sounded good to him. He brushed her lips with his. "When we aren't making love, I can hold you close while we sleep."

He watched a spark of awareness replace the worry in her violet eyes. "That might work for a time. But what happens when my tummy is as big as an overinflated balloon?"

"Good point," he said, wondering what it would feel like to have her baby moving under his hands. A sharp pang of regret that he'd never feel his own child move inside her knifed through him, but he did his best to ignore it. Suddenly feeling as if he might be drowning, he added, "Maybe your bed would be best."

"When do you want to do this?"

He laughed, relieving some of his tension. "If it had been left up to me, we wouldn't have gotten out of bed this morning."

Her cheeks coloring a pretty pink fascinated the

hell out of him. "I meant, when do you think we should get married?"

"I know." He gave her a quick kiss, then stepped back before he gave in to temptation and took her down the hall to test out his narrow bed. "How does tomorrow afternoon sound?"

"Impossible." The sound of laughter in her sweet voice was like a balm to his soul. "Besides the fact that we'll be on duty, there's a three-day waiting period in the state of Texas from the time we obtain a license until we get married."

"I happen to know there isn't a waiting period in New Mexico." He took her by the hand and led her over to the door. "And remember, I'm the boss. I can have the Evac II crew come in on standby for the day while you and I make a trip up to Carlsbad."

She looked a little dazed as they walked out into the hall. "This is all happening so fast."

"Things will slow down after tomorrow." He put his arm around her slender shoulders and held her to his side. "Now put on your best smile, darlin'. We have an announcement to make to our coworkers."

"Do you, Calantha Marshall, take this man to be your lawful wedded husband? To have and to hold…"

The rotund judge droned on, but Callie had no idea if he recited the words of the traditional wedding ceremony or if he was trying to auction off a pile of dirt.

She was way too nervous to think of anything but the fact that she'd not only let Hunter talk her into marrying him, they were actually going through with it.

When the Honorable Juan Ricardo cleared his throat and looked at her expectantly, she swallowed hard and forced herself to concentrate on what he'd asked. "I do," she said, surprised that her voice sounded fairly steady considering the state of her nerves.

Judge Ricardo nodded his approval, then turned to Hunter and asked the same question.

Giving her a smile that curled her toes inside her cross trainers, Hunter's voice was strong and sure when he answered. "I do."

"Do you have a ring?" the judge asked, giving Hunter an expectant look.

Callie's cheeks heated as Hunter shook his head. They were probably the most ill-prepared couple to be getting married that the judge had ever seen.

"As soon as she said she'd marry me, I didn't want to take the time to pick out a ring," Hunter said, giving the man a conspiratorial grin. "I was afraid she might change her mind."

Judge Ricardo chuckled. "Then, by the power vested in me by the state of New Mexico, I pronounce you husband and wife. You can kiss your bride, son."

When Hunter took her into his arms to seal their union, his kiss caused her head to spin and her knees to feel as if they were made of rubber. Raising his head, he gazed at her for several long seconds before he turned and thanked the judge, then took her hand in his and led her out of the courthouse.

As they got into the Life Medevac truck for the drive back to Devil's Fork, she still couldn't believe how quickly everything had taken place. "What in heaven's name have we done?"

When he reached out and covered her hand with his, a sense of well-being coursed through her. It was completely unexpected and caused her to catch her breath. Dear heavens, was her attraction to Hunter more than a case of overactive prenatal hormones?

Being a registered nurse, she knew that due to an imbalance in hormone levels, during the second trimester some expectant mothers felt more sensual and sexy than they'd ever felt in their lives. She'd naturally assumed that was the reason she'd given in to desire and passion when she'd made love with Hunter. But now? Could she actually be falling for him?

No, that wasn't possible. She'd only known him a short time, and although her attraction to him was stronger than anything she'd ever felt, that didn't mean she loved him.

"You're awfully quiet," he said, bringing her hand to his lips to kiss the back of it.

Thinking quickly, she smiled. "I was contemplating whether to keep my last name, hyphenate it or change it to yours."

He nodded. "I did an Internet search this morning and found a Web site with a list of things that a bride needs to do after the wedding. Changing her personal documents and identification was on the list." He gave her a seductive smile. "It's up to you, darlin'. But I think Callie Marshall-O'Banyon or just Callie O'Banyon sounds pretty good."

"Since our marriage is only temporary, I suppose it would make more sense to hyphenate."

"Then Callie Marshall-O'Banyon it is."

"For now."

"Right. For now."

As they rode in relative silence on the way back to Devil's Fork, Callie couldn't help but wonder why the thought that her name change wasn't going to be permanent caused her to feel a deep sadness. She'd known up front that they were only getting married in order to thwart Craig's efforts to take her baby away from her. So why was she feeling so darned melancholy?

But as she analyzed her reaction, she supposed it was only natural to feel a bit depressed. She'd always thought that once she got married and took her husband's name it would be for the rest of her life. Of course, that had been when she'd been idealistic and thought the only reason she would ever marry was for love.

Glancing over at Hunter, she couldn't help but think that he had all the qualities she'd ever dreamed of in a husband. He was kind, considerate and, above all, caring. Very few men would have cared enough about an unwed mother keeping her baby to give up their freedom indefinitely.

Sighing, she stared out the windshield of the truck. She wasn't sure what lay ahead of them once they returned to Devil's Fork or how long they'd be husband and wife. But there wasn't a doubt in her mind that no matter what happened, she could count on Hunter being right there beside her to face whatever Craig Culbertson tried to do.

When Callie and Hunter walked into the Life Medevac dispatch room, Mary Lou and the on-duty crew gave them a standing ovation. "Congratulations!"

Grinning like a Cheshire cat, Mary Lou stepped forward. "We've all talked it over and we're giving you two the night off."

"Yeah, we decided you couldn't have a decent wedding night here at the hangar with all of us hanging around," Corey chimed in. His knowing smile made Callie's cheeks heat with embarrassment.

"I'm taking over for you, Hunter," George said. "And Mark, the Evac III paramedic, is coming in to take over for Callie."

"What about standby?" Hunter asked. "We have to have a crew on call in case we have overlapping runs."

"We've got that covered," Mary Lou said, stepping between them. She slipped her arms through theirs and started walking them toward the door. "The rest of the guys are going to take care of that. Now I think you should go back to Callie's place and spend the rest of the night having a little honeymoon fun."

Callie felt as if the heat in her cheeks would burst into flames at any moment. She might have known that Mary Lou would cut to the chase and tell them exactly how she thought they should be spending the evening.

"Hunter?" She felt bad about everyone giving up their day off to cover for them. The least he could do was put up a token protest.

But his sexy grin sent a streak of heat thrumming through her veins and spoke volumes of what an excellent idea he thought the Life Medevac staff had come up with. "Sounds good to me," he said, nodding. He took her hand in his and led her through the door, then, turning back, added, "We'll be back at eight tomorrow morning to finish out our shift."

When they walked into her house several minutes later, Callie took a deep breath and turned to face Hunter. "I don't feel right about this."

He frowned as he reached to take her into his arms. "We're married, darlin'. Making love is something husbands and wives do."

She shook her head and tried to remember what she'd been about to say. With him holding her close, it seemed to short-circuit her thought process. "I was talking about our coworkers giving up their day off."

"Why?" He bent his head to nibble at the sensitive skin along the column of her neck. "I thought it was a nice gesture."

"It...is." A shiver of excitement slid up her spine when he kissed his way to the wildly fluttering pulse at the base of her throat. "But they have no idea...that we aren't making...a lifetime commitment."

Raising his head, he held her gaze with his as he cupped her cheek with his large palm. "Don't worry about it, Callie. We're committed to each other now and for as long as it takes to make sure Culbertson never bothers you again."

"But—"

"Giving us the night off was something they wanted to do, and they know we'll do the same thing for them when they need time off."

His deep, smooth voice and the look in his dark green eyes quickly had her forgetting her guilt or the reason for it. The feel of his hands sliding the length of her back sent shivers of delight coursing through her, and it suddenly didn't matter why they'd gotten married or that it wasn't forever. God help her, but she wanted to spend the night in Hunter's arms again, wanted to feel his hands on her and the sense of being cherished as he made their bodies one.

She would have told him, but when his mouth settled over hers, the contact was so tender it caused tears to flood her eyes and robbed her of the ability to speak. He deepened the kiss, and as his tongue stroked hers, the mating was filled with promises of things to come. He wanted her and he was letting her know in no uncertain terms how much.

When he swung her up into his arms and walked into the bedroom, their lips never broke contact, and as he gently lowered them both to the bed, Callie's heart skipped several beats. With his legs tangling with hers, the strength of his arousal pressed against her thigh and had her own body responding with wanton pulses of need.

His lips clung to hers a moment before he raised his head to smile down at her. "I want you so damned much I can taste it."

"And I want you just as much." Her body tingled with such need she trembled from it. "Please, make love to me, Hunter."

His slumberous look thrilled her to the depths of her soul as he rose from the bed to remove their shoes and socks, then, taking her by the hand, he pulled her to her feet. Bringing her hands to rest on his chest, he gave her a smile that caused her knees to wobble.

"Let's do this together, darlin'."

Excited by the prospect of removing his clothes, Callie rose up on tiptoes to kiss the skin just above the neck band of his red T-shirt at the same time she tugged the tail of it from the waistband of his jeans. Sliding her hands under the soft cotton garment, she felt his muscles contract as she slowly pushed the shirt up along his lean sides. When he raised his arms to help her, she allowed him to pull the garment over his head and toss it aside.

"Your body is perfect," she said, lightly running her fingertips over his well-defined pectoral muscles.

When she traced circles around his flat male nipples, he sucked in a sharp breath. "As good as having your hands on my chest feels, it's my turn."

Reaching for her, he gently pulled the blue scrunchie holding her ponytail free and threaded his fingers through the shoulder-length strands. "Your hair is like fine threads of golden silk."

He tilted her head for a quick kiss, then with painstaking care worked the three buttons at the top of her oversize polo shirt through the buttonholes. Slowly, carefully lifting it up and over her head, his gaze held hers captive as he reached behind her to unfasten her bra. By the time he slid the silk and lace from her shoulders to toss it on top of their shirts, their breathing sounded as if they'd both run a marathon.

The look in his eyes warmed her all over as he filled both of his hands with her breasts and chafed the sensitive tips to harden peaks with his thumbs. "You're so beautiful, Callie."

He dipped his head to capture one of her nipples with his mouth, and she had to brace her hands on his shoulders to keep from melting into a puddle at his feet.

He teased first one, then the other tight nub with his tongue, and it felt as if her blood turned to warm honey as tendrils of desire threaded their way through her limbs to pool with an aching emptiness between her thighs. When he finally raised his head, the hungry look in his dark green eyes stole her breath.

Without a word, she reached for his belt and quickly worked the leather through the metal buckle. But when she popped the snap at the top of his jeans, she forced herself to slow down. Glancing up at him, she smiled as she traced her fingernail along each metal tooth of his bulging zipper. "This looks a bit uncomfortable. I think you'd probably feel better if we got you out of these."

"I don't *think,* darlin', I *know* I'd feel better," he said, his voice sounding raspy.

Easing his fly open, she pushed the jeans down his lean hips, then past his muscular thighs and calves. When he stepped out of them, she trailed her hands along his hair-roughened skin on her way back up to his navy-blue boxer briefs. She loved the way the sinew flexed and bunched at her touch.

"Is that better now?"

His sexy grin sent heat spiraling straight to her core. "Oh, yeah," he said, reaching for the waistband of her maternity jeans.

His heated gaze held hers captive as he slid his fingers under the elastic. His warm palms felt wonderful brushing against her skin as he knelt to push the jeans down her legs, then slowly skimmed his hands along her legs on his way back to her silk panties. Touching her between her legs, he applied a light pressure against the most sensitive spot on her body, sending waves of pleasure radiating through her.

"Does that feel good, Callie?" he asked when a tiny moan of pleasure escaped her.

Unable to form a coherent thought, all she could do was nod.

When he stood up, his gaze captured hers, and as if by unspoken agreement they both reached for the last barriers separating them. Never losing eye contact, together they disposed of his boxer briefs and her panties.

Callie's eyes widened at the sight of his magnificent body. When they'd made love the other morning there hadn't been enough light for her to see his physique. But as she gazed at him now, she marveled at how perfectly made he was.

His wide shoulders, chest and thighs were well defined by muscles that she somehow knew hadn't been honed by working out at a gym. As her gaze drifted lower, past his lean flanks, her breath caught at the sight of his proud, full erection. He was impressively built, thoroughly aroused and, as she lifted her eyes to meet his, looking at her as if he thought she was the most beautiful creature on earth.

"You're amazing," he said, his voice thick with passion.

"I was thinking the same thing about you." She might have felt a bit unsure about her expanding shape had it not been for the gleam of appreciation in his eyes and the reverence she detected in his voice.

Reaching out, she tentatively touched him. Shivers of hot, hungry desire streaked through her when she circled him with her hand and his warm, thick strength surged at her touch. Measuring his length and the softness below, she glanced up at him when a groan rumbled up from deep in his chest. His eyes were closed and a muscle ticked along his jaw as if he'd clenched his teeth against the intense sensations her touch created.

"Does that feel good, Hunter?"

When he opened his eyes, the feral light in the green depths caused her to shiver with a need stronger than anything she'd ever experienced before. But when he cupped her breasts, then lowered his head to circle each nipple in turn with his tongue, swirls of heat coursed through her and she abandoned her exploration to place her hands on his shoulders for support.

"P-please…"

"What do you want, Callie?" His warm breath on her sensitized skin made her feel as if she'd go up in flames at any moment.

"You."

"When?"

"Now!" He was driving her crazy and he wanted to play twenty questions?

Chuckling, he raised his head and, wrapping his arms around her, pulled her to him. The instant soft female skin met hard masculine flesh, Callie moaned with pleasure.

"Let's get in bed while we still have the strength," he said hoarsely.

When he helped her into bed, then stretched out beside her, waves of sheer delight danced over every cell in her being at the feel of his calloused palms caressing her ribs and the underside of her breasts. Feeling as if she were burning up from the inside out, she pressed her legs together in an effort to ease the empty ache he'd created there. He must have realized what she needed because he reached down to gently cup her, a moment before his fingers parted her to stroke the tiny nub of hidden pleasure. Waves of heat streaked through her and she felt as if she'd go mad from wanting.

Raining kisses along her collarbone, then up the side of her neck, he moved his finger deeper to stroke her inside. "Is this where you want me, Callie?"

"Y-yes."

"Do you want me there now?"

"Hunter...please—"

"Just a little bit more, darlin'," he said as his relentless fingers continued to stroke her inner core.

"I can't…stand anymore."

When he moved his hand away, he immediately nudged her thighs farther apart with his knee and eased himself into position. He covered her lips with his, and Callie closed her eyes at the exquisite feel of his blunt tip against her a moment before she felt him slowly, surely slip inside.

"Look at me, Callie."

When she opened her eyes, his heated gaze held hers as he set an easy pace, and all too soon she felt her body straining for sweet liberation from the tension he'd created within her. He must have noticed her tightening around him because he steadily increased his thrusts until the coil of need within her snapped and she was cast into the realm of intense pleasure. She heard him call her name at the same time his big body stiffened, then quivered inside of her as he found his own release.

Wrapping her arms around Hunter's broad back, she held him close as her body pulsed with sweet satisfaction. When their bodies began to cool, she bit her lower lip to keep from crying. She'd done the unthinkable. She'd fought against it from the moment they'd met, but there was no sense denying it any longer.

She'd fallen in love with Hunter O'Banyon.

Nine

The next morning, when Hunter and Callie walked into the dispatch room, Mary Lou pointed to a slip of paper on her desk. "Hunter, you have a message from someone by the last name of Barringer." She shook her head disapprovingly. "He wouldn't tell me what the nature of his business was. But he said it was important that you call him as soon as possible." She pointed to a huge box over in the corner. "And the new flight suits you ordered were delivered yesterday afternoon."

"Good," Callie said, walking over to gaze into the box. "I can barely zip the one I have now."

Recognizing the name of the private investigator

he'd hired, Hunter nodded. "While I return his phone call, why don't you and Callie sort through the new flight suits and match them against the list of everyone's sizes." He walked over to kiss Callie's cheek. "I'll be back in a few minutes to help."

Her cheeks colored a deep rose and he didn't think he'd ever seen her look prettier. "Mary Lou and I can handle this. Go make your phone call."

"I can sure tell the two of you are newlyweds," Mary Lou said, laughing. "If you can't be away from her long enough to make a phone call, you've got it bad."

Hunter had no idea why, but he couldn't seem to stop smiling as he picked up the slip of paper with Barringer's number on it and walked down the hall toward his office. Maybe it was because the investigator was reporting back so quickly. But he had a feeling that it had more to do with the fact that he'd just spent the most incredible night of his life with his amazing wife.

Callie was the most responsive, sensual woman he'd ever met, and he couldn't wait for the end of the day when their shift ended and they could get back to her place. Unless they were called out for a standby run, they had four days to resume their honeymoon and he had every intention of making the most of their time off. His body tightened at the thought and he cursed the fact that they had eight hours before they were off duty.

When he closed the office door behind him, he took several deep breaths to calm his runaway libido, then walked over to the desk and dialed Barringer's number. He'd no sooner given his name to the man's secretary than Joe Barringer came on the line.

"I've discovered several things about Culbertson that I think you'll find very interesting," he said without preamble.

"You've got my attention," Hunter said, sinking into the desk chair.

"Craig Culbertson is broke. He's gambled away the trust fund his grandfather left him and it appears that he's started siphoning money out of the one set aside for his son."

"But aren't his parents in control of that money?" Hunter asked. He could've sworn that Callie told him the Culbertsons had adopted Craig's son and raised the boy as their own.

"They were," Barringer said. "But there was a stipulation in his grandfather's will that when Craig reached the age of thirty, he gained control of that fund, as well."

"Anything else?" Hunter asked, wondering how he could use the information to help Callie. So far, he hadn't heard anything worthwhile.

"Yes. It appears that provisions have been made for future children."

Hunter sat up straight in his chair. He had a feeling

he was about to learn the motive behind Culbertson's visit to Devil's Fork. "What kind of provisions?"

"Just a second." It sounded as if Barringer was shuffling papers a moment before he added, "Any future offspring of Craig Culbertson will have a million-dollar trust fund set up and—"

"Let me guess," Hunter said. "Culbertson is the administrator."

"You got it." The disgust in Joe Barringer's voice was evident. "His grandfather must have expected Culbertson to sow more wild oats. Instead of leaving him the lion's share of his estate, the old man stipulated that the majority of his money would be held in trust for future heirs." He paused as if consulting his notes. "And Culbertson has to have custody of each child before a trust will be set up in his or her name."

"That explains a lot," Hunter said, thinking aloud.

"Something else you might find interesting—Culbertson has some pretty shady characters breathing down his neck for past gambling debts. I'm not sure he can wait for Ms. Marshall to give birth. He needs the money now," Barringer finished.

"What about his parents? Can't he go to them for the money?" To Hunter, that would be the obvious choice if the man was in that kind of trouble.

"Harry and Alice Culbertson have pretty much washed their hands of their son," Barringer said. "They've bailed him out several times, and from what I can gather, they put their foot down the last time and told him that was it. They wouldn't pay off any more gambling debts."

"In other words, he's desperate for cash and if he can stall his bookies until Callie has her baby, he'll have one more trust fund to steal from," Hunter said, shaking his head at the man's foolishness.

"That's about it. If I find out anything else, I'll give you a call," Barringer added. "But I think you have the most relevant information now."

When Hunter ended the connection, he immediately called the bank, Luther Freemont, Emerald's assistant, then the bed-and-breakfast where Craig Culbertson was staying. Satisfied that he had everything under control, as soon as the fax came in from Emerald Inc. headquarters, he left the office and walked back into the dispatch room.

"I have some business I need to take care of," he said, putting his arms around Callie. "When I get back from town, there's something I need to tell you."

Concern lined her forehead. "It sounds serious."

"Nothing for you to be worried about, darlin'." Not caring that Corey and Mary Lou were avid spectators, he gave her a quick kiss. "I'll be back as soon as I can."

"If we need you, we'll page you," Mary Lou said, pouring herself a cup of her god-awful coffee.

As Hunter drove into Devil's Fork, he couldn't wait to confront Culbertson. He was about to make the man an offer Culbertson couldn't afford to turn down. And within the next couple of hours Hunter fully expected for Craig Culbertson to be headed back to Houston and out of Callie's life for good.

"I have to admit, your demand that we have this meeting came as a bit of a surprise, O'Banyon."

Seated in a booth at the back of the Longhorn Café, Hunter stared across the table at the most despicable human being he'd ever had the displeasure to meet. With his slick good looks, sophisticated air and boyish smile, Hunter could understand why women would find Craig Culbertson attractive.

But Hunter knew the type. Guys like Culbertson used their assets to hide their true nature, and Hunter never thought he'd ever admit it, but the man seated across from him was even lower than Owen Larson. As irresponsible as Owen had been about impregnating women, then leaving them to face single motherhood alone, he'd never used his offspring as pawns to bail himself out of a jam.

"I'm going to make you a one-time offer, Culbertson. And if you're as smart as you try to lead people to believe, you'll take it."

"Oh, really?" The man's sneering expression made Hunter want to reach across the table and grab him by the throat.

"I'm going to write you a check for five hundred

thousand dollars, then you're going to sign a document relinquishing all rights to Callie's baby." Hunter knew the moment he mentioned the money that he had the man's attention. "You'll leave town and never bother Callie or her child again."

"What makes you think I can be bought off that easily?" Culbertson asked, not even bothering to sound offended by Hunter's demands. "And who's to say that once I sign that paper, I won't discover that your check is no good?"

"Believe me, the check is good." Leaning forward, Hunter lowered his voice to a menacing growl. "And I happen to know that if you don't get your hands on some money, and damned quick, your life won't be worth spit."

Culbertson paled visibly. "What makes you say that?"

"It's amazing what a good P.I. can uncover, like the bookies coming after you for your gambling debts." Hunter removed the fax he'd received from Emerald Inc.'s legal department from one of his pockets and shoved it across the table. "This is a confidentiality and custody agreement. Sign it, accept my check and clear out of town or run the risk of not only losing the trust fund that would be set up for Callie's baby but your life, as well."

"Is that a threat, O'Banyon?"

Hunter shook his head. "Not at all. Although I'd like

to take you apart limb by limb, I won't have to do a damned thing. Your bookies will take care of that for me." He held up his hand to get the waitress's attention. "I'm going to order a cup of coffee. By the time I'm finished with it, you'd better have signed that document or the offer is rescinded and you can take your chances with the bookies and the court system."

After the waitress brought Hunter's coffee, Culbertson gave him a cocky grin. "Why should I settle for half a million? If I wanted to, I could get custody of Callie's brat in a heartbeat and end up with a full million at my disposal."

"I wouldn't count on that." Hunter gave the man a confident smile. "For one thing, Callie and I really are husband and wife. That will go a long way in her favor."

"Oh, that's rich," Culbertson laughed. "You own a run-down air-ambulance service in Nowheresville that I'm sure barely makes ends meet and you expect me to believe that my lawyers and good friend Judge Howell would rather see a child raised by you and Callie than in the lifestyle I could provide."

Hunter took a sip of the coffee, then slowly set his cup back on the saucer. "You don't get it, do you, Culbertson?"

"What's to get? I can tie this up in court for years and I know for certain Callie doesn't have that kind of money." His expression condescending, he shook his head. "And I seriously doubt that you do either."

"You might be surprised who could tie who up in court." Hunter laughed harshly. "Besides, I doubt that your bookies would want to wait that long before they start taking their money out of your worthless hide."

Hunter could tell that he'd given Culbertson something to think about. But the man was more arrogant and self-absorbed than Hunter had given him credit for.

"What if I say half a mil isn't enough? What if I want more?"

"It's up to you." Hunter took a healthy swallow of his coffee. "But I'm getting close to finishing this coffee. If you haven't signed that paper by the time I get done, Callie and I will see you in court." He grinned. "That is, if there's anything left of you by the time the case comes up on the docket."

When Hunter started to pick up his cup, he watched Culbertson glance at the contents, then eye the document in front of him. "And you're sure the check is good?"

Hunter nodded. "I can guarantee it."

"How do I know I can trust you?"

"That's something you'll just have to take on faith," Hunter said, lifting his cup. He almost laughed out loud when Culbertson quickly took an ink pen from the inside pocket of his sports jacket and hastily scrawled his name on the designated line of the document before Hunter could take the last sip of the coffee.

Shoving the paper back at him, Culbertson glared at

Hunter as he folded it and put it in his pocket. "You're welcome to Callie and her brat. Now where's my money?"

Hunter removed a check from a zippered pocket on his flight suit, then, before he could stop himself, he reached across the table and grabbed Culbertson by the front of the shirt. Pulling him forward until they were nose to nose, he made sure there was no mistaking the menace in his voice. "Don't ever let me hear you use that tone of voice again when you refer to my wife or our baby. You got that?"

"You really love her, don't you?"

"Yes, I do." When Hunter realized what he'd said, he released Culbertson's shirt and shoved him away. Then, sliding out of the booth, he tossed the check on the table. "Now get the hell out of Devil's Fork and don't let me see you again."

As he walked out of the café and got into his truck, Hunter's heart pounded hard in his chest and he had to force himself to breathe. He loved Callie.

When he'd lost Ellen, he'd vowed never to love another woman and run the risk of losing her. But as much as he'd cared for his fiancée, his feelings for her couldn't compare to the depths of what he felt for Callie. In the past couple of weeks he'd felt more alive than he had in his entire life and he knew for certain that if he lost her he'd never survive.

How the hell had he let himself get in so deep?

When had it happened? And why hadn't he seen it coming?

Somewhere between that wild ride from the airfield when she'd picked him up the day he'd arrived in Devil's Fork and yesterday when they'd exchanged wedding vows he'd let go of the past and reached for the future. A future with Callie and her son.

Steering the truck out onto Main Street, he shook his head. He wasn't fool enough to think that just because he realized he loved her they could work things out and make a go of their marriage. At the time he'd suggested they get married, she'd had just as many reservations, if not more, than he'd had. And the sole reason they'd married in the first place was to keep Culbertson from taking her baby away from her. Now that he was no longer a threat, their reason for staying together was gone.

He took a deep breath as he turned onto the drive leading up to the Life Medevac hangar. He knew that Callie cared for him. Her response to his kisses and the passion they shared when they made love was proof of that. But did she love him?

She'd told him that she trusted him, but that didn't mean she wanted to stay with him for the rest of her life. And he distinctly remembered her telling him the first day they met that she was quite content to remain single.

He also recalled Callie had a problem with anyone

who had money. How would she take it when she discovered that she was married to a man with a multimillion-dollar bank account and who stood to inherit a
sizable portion of Emerald Inc., the multibillion-dollar
enterprise his paternal grandmother had built from the
ground up?

As he parked the truck, got out and walked toward
the hangar, he wasn't sure how things would turn out for
them. But he had every intention of finding out. He'd tell
her how he felt, explain everything about himself and
pray that she understood and loved him anyway.

"I was just about to page you," Mary Lou said,
hanging up the phone.

"There's been an accident on the Thompson ranch
and they need us there as soon as possible," Callie
added as she breezed past him on the way out the door.

"Where's Corey?" he asked, following her.

"Right here, boss," Corey called, running after them.

When they were all strapped into their seats, Hunter
revved the helicopter's engine and took hold of the
stick. He wasn't happy about having to postpone his
talk with Callie, but it couldn't be helped. They had an
accident victim waiting on them and that took prece-
dence over matters of the heart.

After stabilizing the compound fracture on Carl
Thompson's leg and transporting him to the hospital
in El Paso, Callie was more than ready to get back to

base. It had taken everything she and Corey could do to convince the man that he wasn't on a joyride and couldn't sit up to look out the window during the thirty-minute flight.

"I hope old Carl isn't overly accident-prone," Corey said as they climbed back into the helicopter.

Callie nodded. "If it had taken much longer to get here, I would have radioed for a doctor's order to give him a sedative."

"Well, that's something you won't have to give me," Corey said, taking off his headset and settling back in his seat. "I intend to catch a few winks on the flight home."

When Corey closed his eyes and fell silent, Callie turned her attention to Hunter. As she watched, he put on his headset and flipped switches on the control panel. Her heart skipped a beat and she had to remind herself to breathe. If she lived to be a hundred, she didn't think she'd ever see a man look as sexy as he looked in his flight suit and aviator sunglasses. But then, she thought he was sexy no matter what he did or didn't wear.

She took a deep breath. As hard as she'd fought to keep from loving him, he'd managed to get past her defenses and fill a void in her life that she hadn't even known existed.

Unfortunately that didn't mean they could have a future together. He'd made it quite clear that he was only marrying her to help her retain custody of her son and that once the threat from Craig was over, so was their marriage. Besides, pretending to be happily married and anticipating the birth of a child was one thing. Permanently accepting the role of loving husband and expectant father was something else entirely.

Her chest tightened as she thought of her life without Hunter. She didn't want to think about not being able to see his handsome face every day, hear his hearty laughter or feel the warmth of his touch. But did she have the nerve to tell him how she felt and that she wanted to stay married after her current problems were resolved?

"Damn!" Hunter's vehement curse coming through her headset broke through her disturbing introspection.

"What's wrong?"

"We've got some weather moving in that I don't like," he said, pointing to a bank of clouds.

As she listened to him radio for a weather report from the control tower at the El Paso airport, she was relieved to hear the storm front was moving away from them. She'd never been overly frightened by heavy turbulence in an airplane, but she wasn't sure she wanted to experience it in a helicopter.

"Looks like we're in the clear," he said, lifting off the helipad and steering the helicopter back toward Devil's Fork.

"Did you get your business taken care of this morning?" she asked conversationally.

He nodded. "When we get back to base, we have some things we need to discuss."

"That sounds rather ominous." She wasn't sure from the serious tone of his voice that she wanted to hear what he had to say.

"Don't worry, darlin'. It's not as bad as it sounds."

His endearment reassured her, and they flew in companionable silence for some time before Hunter rattled off a string of blistering curses, ending with a word that most men saved for extreme circumstances.

"I'm almost afraid to ask, but what was that for?" she asked.

"The winds have shifted and we're about to fly right into the middle of that weather front," he said as a gust of wind buffeted the helicopter.

As Hunter fought the stick, Callie tightened her shoulder harness and did her best not to scream when they swayed precariously. Praying they were close to the Life Medevac base, her heart sank when she glanced out the side window and saw the jagged peaks of the mountains.

"I hope like hell I can find a place to set down," Hunter said as he continued to struggle with the controls. "We need to ride this out on the ground."

"That sounds like a good idea to me," she readily agreed.

Glancing over at Corey, she couldn't believe he was still asleep. No wonder Mary Lou complained about trying to wake him up when their crew had a night run to make.

"This is going to be risky," Hunter said, sounding as if his teeth were clenched. "I want you and Corey to hang on tight."

She gripped the sides of the jump seat. "I don't know how, but Corey is still asleep."

"Does he have the shoulder harness buckled?"

"Yes. But he disconnected his headset."

"That's okay," Hunter said tersely. "All that matters is that he's strapped in."

Callie felt as if her heart was in her throat. She knew enough about helicopters to know that landing in a mountainous area was tricky under the best conditions. But during a storm with strong wind gusts it was going to be extremely hazardous.

She felt the helicopter suddenly lurch to one side, and closing her eyes, she prayed as hard as she could while she waited for whatever happened next.

When Hunter spotted a relatively level area at the base of one of the mountains, he clenched his teeth and used every ounce of strength he had to hold the chopper as steady as possible. Fleeting images of another emergency landing and the devastating outcome flashed through his mind. But this time would be different. He was determined that this time the woman he loved and her unborn child would be safe and unharmed.

When the skids bumped the ground hard, then bounced up to come down again with a bone-jarring thud, Hunter killed the rotor engine and released the latch on his shoulder harness. Saying a silent prayer of thanks to the powers that be for a safe, albeit rough, landing, he climbed into the cabin area to check on his passengers.

Taking Callie into his arms, he held her close. "Are you all right?"

She clung to him as she nodded. "Y-yes."

Turning to Corey, Hunter asked, "What about you? Are you okay?"

Pale as a ghost, his eyes wide with shock, the young man nodded. "Wow! That was one hairy landing. Where are we?"

Hunter looked out the starboard windows at the surrounding mountains. "About halfway between El Paso and Devil's Fork."

The adrenaline high he'd been on since realizing they were on a collision course with the storm began to wane, and Hunter felt as if his muscles had turned to jelly. Reaching for the microphone clipped to the epaulet on Callie's flight suit, he radioed Mary Lou to advise her of the situation. Then, after assuring her they were all okay, he told her they would start back as soon as the storm let up.

Unable to stop thinking about how close he'd come to reliving the nightmare he'd been caught up in five years ago and not wanting Callie to see that his hands were beginning to shake, he made up a lame excuse about doing a systems check and climbed back into the pilot's seat.

He was vaguely aware that Callie and Corey were discussing Corey's sleeping habits, but Hunter paid little attention to the conversation. He was too busy thinking about what could have happened if he'd been unable to land the chopper safely.

What would he have done if he'd lost Callie the way he'd lost Ellen? How could he have lived with himself?

He took a deep breath, then slowly released it. The answer was simple. He couldn't. And with sudden insight he knew exactly what he had to do.

As soon as they returned to the hangar, he'd hand Callie the document Culbertson had signed, tell her she was free to pursue an annulment, then terminate her employment at Life Medevac.

Ten

By the time she, Hunter and Corey returned to the hangar, it was time for their shift to end, and Callie was more than ready to turn over the watch to the Evac II crew and go home. Her nerves were still jangled from narrowly escaping a crash landing and she needed to talk to Hunter. He hadn't said more than a handful of words since the incident, and she could tell something was bothering him.

Well, that made two of them. While they'd waited out the storm, Corey had chattered about everything from being hard to wake up to his pregnant girlfriend and their impending wedding, but Callie hadn't paid much attention. She'd been too preoccupied with thoughts of her baby and how close she'd come to losing him.

"I've got a couple of things to take care of here at the office," Hunter said, walking up behind her. "If you don't mind, I'll be over a little later."

Turning to face him, her smile faded at his serious expression. "Is there a problem?"

He hesitated before shaking his head. "No. I'm just not looking forward to the paperwork I have to do."

"We left my car here last night and I need to get it home anyway. I'll see you in an hour or so." When he gave her a short nod and started to turn to walk back down the hall to his office, she asked, "What would you like for dinner?"

"Don't worry about anything for me. I'm not hungry." Then without another word he disappeared down the hall.

She'd only known him for a couple of weeks, but that didn't matter. There was no doubt in her mind that something was terribly wrong, and she had every intention of finding out what it was.

But a hangar full of people wasn't the best place to have a heart-to-heart talk with her husband, and Callie decided that biding her time would be her best option. When Hunter came over, she'd find out what was bothering him, then tell him her news. She was going to grant his wish and ground herself, at least until after her son was born. And, unless she changed her mind, there was the strong possibility that she might give up being a flight nurse permanently.

As she drove the short distance to her house, she placed her hand on her rounded stomach. She knew it would take Hunter some time to find a replacement for her, but that couldn't be helped. Effective immediately, she was resigning her position at Life Medevac to concentrate on becoming a mother and being there for her son as he grew up.

Parking his truck in Callie's driveway, Hunter sat for several minutes staring at her little house. In the past couple of weeks he'd been happier visiting the cozy little cottage than he'd been in five long years, and it was tearing him apart to think that after tonight he would no longer be welcome there.

But what he was about to do was best for all concerned and he knew that Callie would eventually understand that. And even if she didn't, he could at least sleep at night knowing that he'd done everything in his power to protect her and the baby.

When he got out of the truck, he gripped the folder with the papers he was about to give her and slowly climbed the steps to knock on the door. As soon as he got this over with, he had every intention of driving out to that spot he'd found a few days after he'd arrived in Devil's Fork where he could stare at the stars. Maybe if he stayed there long enough, he'd come to terms with the fact that to protect the woman and child he loved with all his heart, he had to give them up.

"Why did you knock?" Callie asked when she opened the door and stood back for him to enter. "Why didn't you just come on in?"

Standing there with her silky blond hair down around her shoulders, flour streaked across her blue maternity top and the prettiest smile he'd ever seen, she was causing his heart to twist painfully in his chest and she didn't even know it.

Walking past her into the living room, Hunter waited until she closed the door, then turned to face her. "We have to talk."

Her smile faded. "Does this have something to do with what happened this afternoon? Because if it does—"

"We were damned lucky this afternoon," he said, cutting her off. He hadn't meant to sound so harsh, but it was taking every ounce of strength he had not to take her in his arms and abandon the course of action he knew he had to take.

"Hunter?"

She extended her hand and took a step toward him, but, shaking his head, he moved away. He knew beyond a shadow of doubt that if she touched him, he'd lose his internal battle. And it was one he knew that he had to win.

"I think you'd better sit down for this," he said, tempering the tone of his voice.

Sinking onto the love seat, she stared up at him with troubled eyes. "You're beginning to frighten me."

"I don't mean to." He took a deep breath and opened the folder in his hand to remove the document that Culbertson had signed earlier in the day. Handing it to her, he explained what he'd learned from the private investigator and about his meeting with Culbertson. "You won't be hearing any more from Craig Culbertson. He's gone back to Houston and won't bother you or your son again."

She gave him a disbelieving look. "You paid him off?"

Hunter shrugged. "I guess you could call it that."

"My God, I can't allow you to do that. That's an exorbitant amount of money."

"Too late, darlin'. It's already done."

Staring at the paper for several seconds, when she looked up at him, she shook her head. "You can't afford this and I can't possibly pay you back."

"I'm not asking you to," he said firmly. "Consider it a baby gift."

"A baby gift is a set of bibs or a high chair. It's certainly not as extravagant as half a million dollars to get someone to leave me alone."

"Don't worry about it. I'm not."

"Hunter, please—"

When she started to rise from the love seat, he shook his head. "I'm not finished yet. Now that the threat from Culbertson is over with, you're free to petition the courts for an annulment."

She sucked in a sharp breath. "Is that what you want?"

It was the last thing he wanted, but he couldn't tell her that. "I believe that was our agreement."

Standing up, she walked over to him. "You didn't answer my question."

"It doesn't matter what I want." He handed her the folder. "After you take a look at this, I'm sure you'll agree that an annulment is for the best."

When she scanned the termination of employment papers he'd drafted and the severance check for a year's wages, she glared at him. "Why am I being fired? And why are you giving me so much money?"

"Because it's the only way I can think of to keep you from flying. There's enough money that you should be able to pay for the birth, as well as stay home with your son for several months." He'd known she wouldn't be happy about it, but that couldn't be helped. It was for her own good and his peace of mind.

"This won't keep me from flying," she said, tossing it onto the coffee table. "I'm an experienced flight nurse. If I wanted to, I could get a job with another air-ambulance service. But I've decided—"

"You'd better not." Before he could stop himself, he reached out to take her by the upper arms. "What happened today was just a glimpse of what could happen every time you climb into a helicopter to make an emergency run. Promise me you'll find a job in a hospital somewhere."

"Hunter, why…are you…doing this to me?" she asked haltingly.

He closed his eyes for a moment, and when he opened them, the tears on her porcelain cheeks caused a pain to knife through him that threatened to knock him to his knees. He didn't like talking about the accident, but he had to make her understand why he couldn't bear the thought of her flying.

"Five years ago I was behind the controls of a helicopter that went down in Central America. It was a mechanical problem and there wasn't a damn thing I could do to stop the crash from happening. I lost my fiancée and our unborn child that day." Wrapping his arms around Callie, he pulled her to him. "I can't and won't let that happen to you."

"That's why you've wanted me to ground myself from the day you got here."

Unable to get words past the cotton lining his throat, he nodded.

Leaning back, she looked up at him. "Why, Hunter? Why can't you let that happen again?"

"Because I love you, dammit." Realizing what he'd said, he immediately released her, stepped back and, reaching up, rubbed the tension gathering at the back of his neck. "Whenever you get ready, stop by the hangar and clean out your locker."

"Are you finished saying what you came here to tell me?"

Fully expecting her to demand that he leave, he started for the door. "Yes."

"Good." She walked up to him and stabbed her finger at his chest. "Now you're going to listen to me."

"I won't change my mind."

Her violet eyes sparkled with anger. "I don't care. You've had your say and I'm going to have mine."

He guessed it was only fair, but it didn't make standing there wanting to hold her and knowing he couldn't any easier. "All right. Make it quick."

"Number one, I'll take as long as I want to tell you what I think. And number two, you need to stop being so bossy and learn to listen." She waved one delicate hand toward the door. "From the minute you walked in here I've been trying to tell you something and you wouldn't let me get a word in edgewise."

"I can't see that it will make a difference."

She folded her arms beneath her breasts and tapped her bare foot against the floor. "Why don't you sit down and hear me out before you start making judgments."

He shook his head. "I don't think—"

"Sit!"

Lowering himself into the armchair, he gazed up at

her. She was working up a full head of steam and he didn't think he'd ever seen her look more beautiful. But then, when a man loved a woman the way he loved Callie, there was never a time when she didn't look beautiful to him.

"If you had let me talk earlier, I could have spared us both a lot of anguish." Standing in front of him, she propped her hands on her hips. "I was going to tell you that after what happened today, I realized that I no longer want to be a flight nurse. So you can take that termination notice and your severance check and stick them where the sun doesn't shine."

Suddenly feeling as if a heavy weight had been lifted from his shoulders, he sat up a little straighter in the chair. "You don't want to fly anymore?"

"No, I don't." She placed her hand on her stomach. "What happened today reminded me of what's important."

Hunter couldn't believe the degree of relief coursing through him. "You have no idea how glad I am to hear you say that."

"And something else." She began to pace. "What gives you the right to tell me what I should do about our marriage? Did it ever occur to you that I might not want an annulment?"

He couldn't believe that she might want the same thing he did—to try to make their marriage work. Almost afraid to hope, he asked cautiously, "You don't?"

"No. An annulment is the last thing I want." She shook her head. "Although, at the moment I'm questioning my sanity and the reason why I love you, you big lug."

Hunter couldn't have stayed in that chair if his life depended on it. Jumping to his feet, he took her into his arms and held her close.

"Thank God!" Giving her a kiss that left them both gasping for breath, when he raised his head, he felt as if his soul had been set free at the love he saw shining in her pretty eyes. "I want to live the rest of my life with you, darlin'." He placed his palm over her rounded stomach. "And if you're agreeable, I'd like to be a father to your baby."

"I'd like that very much." Tears filled Callie's eyes as she reached up to touch his lean cheek. When she'd come to Devil's Fork, she'd had no idea that in running from her past, she'd find her and her son's future. "You're a special man, Hunter O'Banyon."

"I don't know about that, but I promise I'll be the best husband and father I can be," he said, kissing her. "And the first thing I'm going to do for my new family is add a couple of rooms onto the house." He nibbled tiny kisses to the hollow below her ear. "Or, if you'd like, I can build us a new home with lots of bedrooms for babies, as well as guest rooms for grandmothers to visit."

"Could we afford something like that?" Shivering

with desire, she closed her eyes when Hunter cupped her breast to tease her taut nipple through the fabric of her shirt. "You had to spend a lot of money to get rid of Craig."

When his hand stilled, she opened her eyes to look at him. "What?"

"There's something else you don't know about me," he said, looking a bit uncomfortable.

"You mortgaged Life Medevac to pay off Craig," she guessed, hating that he'd put his business in jeopardy for her sake. "Don't worry, I'm a registered professional nurse. After the baby's born, I'll see what jobs are available."

"That won't be ne—"

"I promise I'll make sure the job is on the ground," she hurriedly reassured him.

"But, darlin'—"

"There might be a traveling nurse's position with the tricounty health department. At any rate, I'll be able to help with the loan payments and I can cut a few corners here and—"

His deep chuckle sent a streak of heat straight to her core as he placed his hand over her mouth. "Now which one of us isn't letting the other get a word in edgewise?"

She playfully touched the tip of her tongue to his palm and watched his eyes darken to forest-green. "I love you," she murmured, letting her lips brush his calloused skin.

He shuddered against her a moment before he took his hand away. "I love you, too, Callie." His expression turned serious. "But there's something more I need to tell you about myself."

Her heart stalled at the apprehension she detected in his voice. "What is it?"

"Remember me telling you about not knowing who my father was until just a few months ago and that his family had money?"

She nodded. "That's when you found out you have two brothers and your grandmother's reason for keeping your father's identity a secret."

"Right." His wide chest rose and fell against her breasts as he drew in a deep breath, and she could tell he was reluctant to say more.

"Surely it can't be all that bad."

He shook his head. "Most people wouldn't think so, but you might feel differently."

"Why do you say that?"

"Because you're not overly fond of wealthy people." He gave her a sheepish grin. "Darlin', I'm rich." He shook his head. "Actually I'm not just rich, I'm filthy rich."

"You're what?" Of all the things that had run through her mind, his being wealthy wasn't one of them. He certainly didn't act like any of the wealthy people she knew.

"When my grandmother finally told me and my

brothers who our father was, she also informed us that we each have a multimillion-dollar trust fund and will one day inherit part of a multibillion-dollar enterprise."

Callie's mouth dropped open and she couldn't have strung two words together if her life depended on it. When she finally found her voice, she asked, "Who is your grandmother?"

He smiled. "Emerald Larson."

"*The* Emerald Larson?"

"The one and only," he said nodding. "I hope you won't hold that against me."

She shook her head. "I can't believe...I mean, you never acted any differently than anyone else and I had no idea—"

He silenced her babbling with a kiss, and by the time he raised his head, she couldn't have cared less how much money he had or who his grandmother was. All that mattered was the man she loved more than life itself was holding her securely against him.

"Hunter, I don't care how much money you have or if you have any at all. I love you and that's all that matters."

"And I love you. Never doubt that." His smile heated her from the top of her head all the way to her bare toes. "By the way, what do you have planned for the end of next month?"

"The same thing I have planned for the rest of my life—loving you." He nuzzled the side of her neck, sending shivers of delight skipping over every cell in her body. "Why?"

When she kissed the strong column of his neck, he groaned and swung her up into his arms. "It doesn't matter. Right now I can't think past taking you into the bedroom and getting started on the rest of our lives."

"I like the way you think, flyboy." Circling his wide shoulders with her arms, as he carried her into the bedroom, she whispered close to his ear, "I love you, Hunter."

"And I love you, Callie." Gently lowering her to the bed, he stretched out beside her, then gathered her into his arms. "And I intend to spend the rest of my life showing you just how much."

Epilogue

As Emerald Larson watched her three grandsons and their wives circulate among the guests at the dinner party she'd put together in their honor, she gave herself a mental pat on the back for a job well done. She'd specifically chosen the companies she'd given each of them to run, as well as arranged for them to meet the women she'd known would be perfect for them, and she couldn't have been more pleased with the results of her efforts.

Glancing at her youngest grandson, Caleb, she smiled fondly. He'd proven to be a genius with his innovative and creative approach to management and had not only improved morale at Skerritt and Crowe

Financial Consultants, he'd increased productivity by fifty percent in just a few months. Along with his wife, Alyssa, he was building a solid reputation as a force to contend with in the financial world.

Turning her attention to her middle grandson, she couldn't have been more proud. Upon his return to the Sugar Creek Ranch, Nick had not only reclaimed his birthright, he'd courageously faced his nemesis and found vindication after thirteen long years. With the help of his wife, Cheyenne, Emerald had no doubt that his plans to turn the cattle company into a free-range operation would meet with complete success. And in the spring, when their first child was born, they'd finally realize their dream of raising a family in that big, charming ranch house under the wide Wyoming sky.

When her gaze landed on Hunter, her oldest grandson, Emerald sighed contentedly. He'd been the one she'd worried about the most. After losing his fiancée and their unborn child, he'd given up flying the helicopters he loved and built a wall around his heart that she'd feared might never come down. But when he'd arrived to take over running the Life Medevac Helicopter Service, he'd not only recaptured his love of flying, he'd met Callie, a young expectant mother whose love had helped him let go of the past and healed his wounded heart.

"You wanted to see me, Mrs. Larson?" Luther Freemont asked, walking up beside her.

As a personal assistant, Luther was highly efficient, his loyalty unsurpassed. But as a man, he was the biggest stuffed shirt she'd ever met.

"I want to thank you for helping me accomplish my goal," she said, continuing to watch her grandsons and their wives. "Our efforts have worked quite well, don't you think?"

"I'd say they've been a resounding success," Luther agreed with her.

"I rather enjoyed watching my grandsons prove themselves with the businesses I gave them to run, as well as helping them find the loves of their lives." She sighed. "It's a shame that I don't have more grandchildren."

Her breath caught and her mood lightened considerably when Luther gave her one of his rare smiles. "Well, as a matter of fact…"

* * * * *

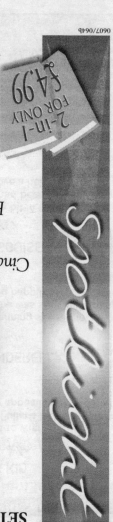

FREE!

2 Books
and a surprise gift!

We would like to take this opportunity to thank you for reading this Mills & Boon® book by offering you the chance to take TWO more specially selected titles from the Desire™ series absolutely FREE! We're also making this offer to introduce you to the benefits of the Mills & Boon® Reader Service™—

- ★ FREE home delivery
- ★ FREE gifts and competitions
- ★ FREE monthly Newsletter
- ★ Exclusive Reader Service offers
- ★ Books available before they're in the shops

Accepting these FREE books and gift places you under no obligation to buy, you may cancel at any time, even after receiving your free shipment. Simply complete your details below and return the entire page to the address below. You don't even need a stamp!

YES! Please send me 2 free Desire books and a surprise gift. I understand that unless you hear from me, I will receive 3 superb new titles every month for just £4.99 each, postage and packing free. I am under no obligation to purchase any books and may cancel my subscription at any time. The free books and gift will be mine to keep in any case.

D7ZEF

Ms/Mrs/Miss/Mr ....Initials....................................

BLOCK CAPITALS PLEASE

Surname ....

Address...

....

....Postcode ....

Send this whole page to:
UK: FREEPOST CN81, Croydon, CR9 3WZ

MILLS & BOON
Special Edition

On sale 15th June 2007

EXPECTING HIS BROTHER'S BABY
by Karen Rose Smith

Brock Warner returned to find the family ranch falling to pieces and his pregnant, widowed sister-in-law, Kylie, in hospital. She needed help; could he keep his feelings for her in check?

CATTLEMAN'S BRIDE-TO-BE
by Lois Faye Dyer

For four years a secret had kept Nikki Petersen and bad-boy Cully Bowdrie apart. But when she needed his help to save a child's life, they gave in to their primitive hunger for each other...

FOR HIS SON'S SAKE
by Ellen Tanner Marsh

Single dad Ross Calder's young son was hostile and unresponsive, except with Kenzie Daniels. The child was smitten...would the father follow suit?